Simon LeVay is British by birth and educated at
Dulwich College and Cambridge. Since then his
distinguished career in neurobiology has been spent
in the United States where he has held senior posts at
Harvard Medical School, the Salk Institute for
Biological Studies and the University of California.
In 1992 he co-founded the Institute of Lesbian and
Gay Education. His publication in 1991 of ground-
breaking research on the differences in brain structure
between gay and straight men sparked an international
controversy. Albrick's Gold is his first novel. He
lives in West Hollywood, California.

Other Books by Simon LeVay

The Sexual Brain, MIT Press, 1993
City of Friends: A Portrait of the Gay and Lesbian Community in America (with Elisabeth Nonas), MIT Press, 1995.
Queer Science: The Use and Abuse of Research into Homosexuality, MIT Press, 1996.

Albrick's Gold

Simon LeVay

HEADLINE
FEATURE

First published in Great Britain in 1997
by HEADLINE BOOK PUBLISHING

First published in paperback in 1998
by HEADLINE BOOK PUBLISHING

A HEADLINE FEATURE paperback

10 9 8 7 6 5 4 3 2 1

ISBN 0 7472 5854 6

Typeset by CBS, Felixstowe, Suffolk

Printed and bound in Great Britain by
Mackays of Chatham plc, Chatham, Kent

HEADLINE BOOK PUBLISHING
A division of Hodder Headline PLC
338 Euston Road
London NW1 3BH

for Mike Patel

PREFACE

This book is the brainchild of two people: myself and my friend from way back, Laurie Saunders. Together, over one crazy long weekend, we hammered out the outline of the plot. Since then Laurie has critiqued, encouraged, and even written a few pages herself. Without her, this book would never have happened. Laurie – thanks!

Like any work of fiction, *Albrick's Gold* is a blend of truth and lies. Except for Roger Cavendish, who obviously bears some relationship to me, the characters are made up – assembled from fragments of people I have known. None are intended to be accurate portrayals of real individuals. Of the places described in the book, Levitican University, the National Institute of Reproductive Health, and the East Cabrillo morgue are completely imaginary. West Hollywood is real, of course – and long may it flourish – but even here I have made some changes, for example, to the internal layout of the Pacific Design Center.

As for the science, much of it is based on actual research, although it has been distorted to suit the needs of the plot. For readers who wish to sort out the scientific truth from the fiction, I recommend my book *Queer Science: The Use and Abuse of Research into*

Homosexuality. In the present work, I have taken liberties with the physics of microwaves. Also, to speed up the action, I have made nerve cells develop in cell culture much faster than they really do. And the stereotaxic coordinates of the hypothalamus have been changed – to protect the innocent.

CHAPTER ONE

'You're hurting me!'

'Hurting you? C'mon babe, don't tell me . . . don't tell me you don't love it. I know when I'm giving . . . satisfaction!'

'John! I'm serious! You *are* hurting me. Go slower. And let my nipple alone, will you? You're biting it off, for God's sake!'

'It's pain, baby, pain. The agony . . . the ecstasy . . . what's the diff?'

'John, I'm *not joking*! Stop this or I'll scream! I'll wake . . . ow! . . . . I'll wake the whole dorm!'

'Yeah? And you'll get . . . you'll get expelled too, you know that, honey.'

'Let go of me! Take it out, will you! Let go of my arms! God damn it, John, I wish you were gay again!'

'Don't you *ever say that*!'

'I'll say it if I want . . . it's true. I wish you were gay again. You were a human being then. Now get the hell off of me!'

'Gay? Don't you *ever* speak that word again, *bitch*!'

'Get off of me, fag-boy! . . . ow, my God, you're going to kill me, you're breaking my neck!'

'*No one* calls me a fag! You hear me? *No one*!'

'My neck! Help . . .'

3

'Shut the fuck up! Now try screaming!'
'Mmm! . . . mmm! . . .'
'Now are you going to call me that?'
'Mmm! . . .'
'No?'
'Mmm . . . mmm . . .'
'Yes?'
'Mmm . . .'
'Okay, bitch . . . then take . . . *this*!'

CHAPTER TWO

Dr Mary Braddock stared into the gathering dark outside her bedroom window, fanning out her options like a poker hand as the last light fell across the contours of the Virginia countryside. 'Jesus!' she laughed, 'On the job nine months and I've got "Tailhook Meets Anita Hill" right on my lap.'

Since the day last August when she had left medical research to become Director of Extramural Programs at the National Institute of Reproductive Health, Mary Braddock's career had been on a gilded trajectory, guided by hard work and exquisite timing. She had spent ten years in the laboratory, begging for adequate funding for breast cancer research, as the disease grew into an epidemic. Then, one after another, famous women told about their battles with the disease, and finally the funds began to flow. Mary brought her research and that of her colleagues out of the shadows. She had shifted to administration to make certain that the newly released funds went into meaningful research. At the Institute, she had been able to piece together an enormous grant out of a variety of unlikely sources, in the middle of massive budgetary cutbacks. And just as everything was falling into place, this loose cannon from the Navy was threatening to set everything back to the Stone Age.

'Fire the bastard!' A voice behind her seemed to have read her thoughts. Mary laughed a second time, shaking her short auburn curls in mock exasperation as she accepted the drink that her husband wiggled at her inquiringly from the doorway.

'Marcus, I don't think you quite . . .'

'You have complaints from three staff members and a solid record of warnings and reprimands against him. Send the guy back to that Bible-thumping night school he came from, and hire somebody who can keep his dick in his pants.'

'Ah . . . the direct military approach.' Mary dropped her earrings on the dresser and moved toward the gray and mauve bathroom with its Japanese soaking tub. She bent toward the water, letting the steam envelop her face and shoulders. 'We administration types use different maneuvers than what you find in the Pentagon, honey. Unfortunately, it's probably the women who filed the harassment charges who will be sent packing. And Lieutenant Paul Aconda will probably continue jumping my staff until he's too old to remember how.'

Mary stepped into the water, feeling the tension at the base of her neck melt into the fragrant wood. She lay completely still, listening to the faint hiss of the steam escaping from the slats of the tub. Closing her eyes, she began to examine the problem of Paul Aconda with her mental microscope, twisting and shifting the lens to bring the solution into focus. Nothing.

'Here's the situation, General.' Her husband appeared in the doorway once again, this time carrying a book and peering at her over the top of his glasses.

'Aconda is the liaison from the Office of Naval Research. He's supervising that damn research program at Levitican University.'

Marcus laughed. 'Research at Levitican? Let me guess. They're digging for Adam and Eve in the La Brea tar pits.'

'I wish it were that respectable.' Mary jerked around suddenly to look at her husband, sending a small tsunami over the edge of the tub and onto the tiled steps below. 'Herr Professor Doktor Albrick takes brain cells from fetal monkeys and transplants them into the brains of adult monkeys . . . into the hypothalamus. He claims he gets changes in sex behavior . . . in sexual orientation, in fact.'

'Dr Frankenstein, I presume.' He was talking to his wife's knees, which rose out of the water as the top of her head sank briefly beneath it. Suddenly Mary stood up, pulled a towel around her waist, and stepped onto the floor.

'Ha, ha! . . . I'm not defending it, but it does have some interest as basic science. You remember Roger Cavendish's work on the hypothalamus and sexual orientation . . . the gay brain stuff? If Albrick can change a monkey's sexual behavior by adding cells to its hypothalamus, as he's claiming, that would mean that Cavendish is on the right track. It would mean maybe the hypothalamus really does decide whether you're gay or straight.'

Marcus cleared his throat, carefully closed his book, and repeated, 'Fire . . . the . . . bastard.'

'I can't. The Navy wants to fund Albrick. It's a deal . . . we let the Navy launder their money through us, and we get the okay on the breast cancer program.'

'Launder . . . is that what it amounts to?'

'Launder, you bet. "Research program to study the biological basis of sexual orientation." Ha! The Navy knows they'd never get *that* through. But from us, the warmhearted, politically correct National Institute of Reproductive Health . . . noooo problem. And what's it worth to us? It's worth exactly forty-three million dollars, which is what we're getting for the breast cancer program. We can't risk losing that, and besides,' – Mary paused to increase the dramatic impact of her announcement – 'if I can keep this stuff with Aconda out of the *Post* for a few more days, *you* may soon have a friend in the White House.'

'You're not serious? You got the job?'

'I got positive signals.'

Marcus put down his book and executed a solemn salute. 'Hail to my wife, the secretary.'

'That's *Sec*retary . . . capital S. As in Secretary for Health and Human Services.'

Marcus thought a moment. 'This Aconda fellow . . . tell him, if he so much as looks at another woman at NIRM, I'll lob a smart bomb across the Potomac, aimed for his hypothalamus.'

'Well, dear, I don't think you need go that far.'

CHAPTER THREE

'Next slide, please.'
The screen was lit with a swirling mass of blue dots – a seascape, perhaps, as it might have been painted by Georges Seurat. In places the dots clustered into darker masses; elsewhere they faded into foamy whiteness.

'Now here's the heart of the matter. These are microscopic views of the hypothalamus. On the left is the hypothalamus of a heterosexual man, and here on the right is the same region in a gay man. Each of these dots is a single nerve cell. This group of cells, near the midline,' – the sparkling red beam of a laser pointer homed in on an indistinct agglomeration of dots – 'this cluster is named the third interstitial nucleus. As you can see, it is considerably larger in the straight man than in the gay man. Now these are just two particular cases, of course. Let's take a look at the numerical data from all the subjects. Next slide, please.' The blue dots were replaced by a set of graphs and tables. 'These graphs show the volume of the interstitial nuclei for all the men and women in the different groups. You can see that there's a fair amount of overlap between the different groups, here . . . and here . . . but the average volume is over twice as large in the straight men as in the gay men. Now of course we have to consider various possible explanations for the difference . . .'

Roger Cavendish, Ph.D., associate professor at the Herrick Institute of Brain Sciences in Philadelphia, was on autopilot. He had given this lecture twenty-seven times before. Since announcing his discovery of the 'gay brain' six months previously, Roger had been in the center of a non-stop media whirl. It was his fifteen minutes of fame. Donahue, Oprah, Shirley – they lined up to get him on their shows. Endless invitations from colleges around the country and abroad. He'd turned most of them down. But this one was too intriguing to refuse, and too much money. Levitican University was well known as the richest, the most conservative, and the most homophobic of all the Fundamentalist schools. Why, they were rumored to have made a five-million-dollar 'donation' to the College Accreditation Board, and a month later the three words '. . . or sexual orientation . . .' had been quietly deleted from the Board's Equal Access to Education statement. Levitican didn't want anyone telling them to admit gay students. And yet they had invited him, an openly gay man, to give a lecture, and paid him ten thousand dollars for the fifty-minute gig.

It must have been Albrick's doing, Roger thought. His host, Guy Albrick, sat to his right, listening intently. He was turned somewhat toward Roger, so that he presented his right side to the audience. Roger wondered whether that was deliberate – whether he was keeping the left side of his face, which bore a large birthmark, away from the audience's gaze. It was a vascular malformation, benign but unsightly, that covered most of his left cheek and forehead with a pebbly purple encrustation.

Roger had known of Albrick's work for years, but when he received the invitation from Levitican he checked Albrick's listings in ScienceLine. As he scrolled through screen after screen of papers and abstracts and research summaries, Roger realized the magnitude of this man's achievement. For years Albrick had pursued an obsessive idea: that brain cells from fetuses could be transplanted into the brains of adults. The scientific community ignored him at best, ridiculed him at worst. Then, ten years ago, he had his first success. He used mice from a mutant strain which had a genetic tendency to obesity, thanks to a defect in the ventrolateral nucleus of the hypothalamus, the brain region which regulates body weight. Without treatment, these mice ate non-stop. By four weeks of age they were swollen like balloons, and by two months they had died of coronary thrombosis, stroke, or diabetes. But Albrick transplanted nerve cells from normal mouse fetuses into the hypothalamus of these waddling monsters. The transplanted cells survived and began to take over the function of the defective cells in the host animals' brains. Within a week the mice began to lose weight; within two weeks they were back to normal weight. In some cases, indeed, the transplant was too much of a good thing: Those unfortunate mice stopped eating completely and died of starvation.

Roger remembered the hoopla that followed. Albrick had trumpeted his technique as a revolutionary treatment for obesity. He was soon besieged by three- and four-hundred-pound men and women desperate to shed their crippling burden of fat. But the National

Institute of Health never gave permission for the transplant technique to be used in humans. It was considered too dangerous a procedure even to try, when the same goal could be achieved, in principle at least, with a strict diet. Meanwhile, though, other researchers applied Albrick's techniques to different conditions. Soon, neurosurgeons were trying to cure Parkinson's disease by injecting fetal brain cells into the brains of patients with the disease. Some of the patients were said to have recovered dramatically, losing their tremor and their rigidity, getting out of their wheelchairs and walking normally for the first time in years. There was talk of injecting light-sensitive cells into the retinas of the blind, motor neurons into the spinal cords of paraplegics, and who knows what else.

But Albrick was off on another track. And, Roger suspected, he needed Roger's expertise, Roger's knowledge of the anterior hypothalamus, where sexual functions are regulated, to achieve his goal.

'We know that the brain differentiates as male or female before birth,' Roger continued. 'This process of sexual differentiation takes place under the influence of sex hormones, chiefly testosterone.' His attention drifted off again. As he continued with his all-too-familiar speech, he gazed around the hall where he was speaking. Intersecting, upward-sweeping, concrete arches were separated by wood paneling. The side walls bore large oil paintings of biblical scenes, illuminated by spotlights concealed in the roof. In one scene, the Israelites crossed the Red Sea safely while thousands of Egyptians drowned behind them, their chariots dashed to pieces by the raging waters. In another, seven priests blew on seven ram's horn trumpets, and the walls of Jericho came tumbling down. Many of the defenders of the city, who had been stationed on the ramparts, were falling to their deaths. Along the back wall was inscribed in gilt letters: 'YE SHALL DO MY JUDGMENTS AND KEEP MY ORDINANCES, TO WALK THEREIN: I AM THE LORD THY GOD.' The whole architectural impression was a blend of Cathedral Gothic and Air Terminal Modern.

The students were attentive, clean-cut, and mostly white. Not one of them was wearing a T-shirt, let alone a T-shirt with a slogan on it. And Albrick was wearing a suit and tie. Roger felt distinctly under-dressed in his jeans and open-neck shirt.

Roger wondered whether Albrick was a Creationist. He knew that scientists sometimes were able to compartmentalize their minds to a remarkable degree. With one hemisphere they could believe something with blind faith, while with the other, they knew it was contradicted by all the evidence.

'Of course, my findings are open to many interpretations,' Roger continued. 'We don't yet know what is cause and what is effect. And the brain systems involved in the regulation of sexuality are so complex, we may expect that changes in any small part will affect many . . .'

Suddenly, Roger became conscious of a disturbance in the hall. Two women, who seemed to have appeared out of nowhere, marched down the steps toward the dais. One tall, one short, they were dressed in doublets and baggy pantaloons, striped vertically in pink and purple. They wore pink fools' caps, purple knee-stockings, and pointed shoes with little bells that jangled as they walked. The women were playing on recorders . . . it seemed to be some kind of medieval dance music. Behind them strode a thin, dark-complexioned youth, dressed in the same outlandish garb. He was beating a ragged tattoo on a snare drum that hung from his waist. Every now and then he spun a drumstick into the air and grabbed it again without missing a beat.

Caught in mid-sentence, Roger watched in amazement as the three troubadours reached the space in front of the podium, moved to the side of the hall, and turned to face the audience. The audience seemed baffled. Some laughed, some whistled, but most gazed in silence. As the music continued, two more figures, both men dressed in tights like ballet dancers, bounded out of the audience and took up position at stage center. They faced each other, a foot or so apart, and began, without touching each other's bodies, to act out a scene of passionate lovemaking. The audience responded with a chorus of catcalls. Someone threw a book but it missed the two actors. Roger turned to his host. He was shocked to see Albrick's face – it was grimacing, bulging with rage; he seemed on the verge of apoplexy. He rose half out of his chair and gripped the desk in front of him as if his life depended on it. He shouted: 'Go back to West Hollywood, you scum!' An usher at the back of the hall spoke urgently into a portable phone.

Now another man, who was wearing a white lab coat, came out of the audience and began trying to pull one of the pair of 'lovers' apart from the other. At first Roger thought he was trying to break up the show, and so did the audience – they cheered him on. But things

14

got stranger. As he managed to drag one protesting lover to the side of the stage, right in front of where Albrick was sitting, he produced from nowhere a kind of metal frame which he placed over the gay man's head, and he attached two wires to it. To the accompaniment of a long drumroll, the 'doctor' pulled an invisible lever. The victim jerked spasmodically. Then, the 'treatment' over, he walked with a mechanical, menacing stride over to his former lover, who had been lamenting silently at stage center. Wires still trailing from his head, he aimed a swift blow at his unsuspecting victim. The blow struck only air, but his lover staggered backwards as if mortally wounded, and with an exaggerated gesture of agony, collapsed on the floor. Having dispatched his one-time lover, the 'cured' gay man turned to the women musicians, threatening them with lascivious gestures. They fled from spot to spot around the stage, still playing their recorders, and always followed by their brain-altered admirer. Several members of the audience had come up and were trying to get the actors to desist from their performance by shouting or pulling at them, and more and more books and other objects were being thrown by students who were still sitting in their seats.

At this moment the double doors at both sides of the hall burst open, and a group of soldiers in uniform – fifteen or twenty of them – ran in. 'The cadets!' yelled a voice at the back of the hall. They were swinging white truncheons. Within seconds they made their way to the front of the stage. First they lashed out at the musicians. The recorders and drumsticks were sent flying in fragments across the hall. One of the cadets grabbed the drum and, after a brief tug-of-war, snatched it away from its owner and stomped on it. Deprived of their instruments, the musicians began chanting two words over and over. 'Act Out! Act Out! Act Out!' The cadets pushed the musicians aside and advanced on the actors. One of them seized the 'cured' gay man and threw him violently to the floor. His lover, rising to his defense, also went down under a flurry of blows. The taller of the two musicians tried to stab a cadet with the broken stump of her instrument. Another cadet grabbed at her long brown hair, but it was a wig: It came away in his hands, revealing the actress as a crew-cut bleached blonde with assorted hardware dangling from her multiply pierced ears. 'Act Out!' she shouted, followed by a scream as the cadet struck her across the face with his truncheon.

The students in the audience were in a turmoil. Many of them ran forward and joined the fracas, some helping the cadets, some trying to restrain them. Another group of students had begun to sing a hymn. Roger heard the chanting from the back of the hall: 'Onward, Christian soldiers, onward as to war!' Albrick was watching in apparent excitement as the cadets and the mime troupe engaged in hand-to-hand combat. The actor who had played the doctor seized the metal frame that he had used on his gay 'patient' and smashed it down on the head of the nearest cadet, who fell backwards, taking a couple of students down with him. Then the actor grabbed a chair and used it to fend off three more cadets who had come at him from behind. The blonde actress, still fending off blows with her arms, took a pair of handcuffs from her pocket and locked herself to a low railing that ran along the front of the stage. Blood was running down her face, but she kept up her cry: 'Act

Out! Act Out!' The other two musicians had also joined the fray: The second recorder player was whirling a microphone around her by its long cable, threatening to concuss anyone who came within its radius, while the drummer was having his head beaten repeatedly against a pillar.

Roger felt an irresistible impulse to wade into the battle on behalf of the actors, who were rapidly being cut to pieces. But an arm grabbed him as he lunged forward. 'Dr Cavendish, come with me!' said an urgent voice. A pale, black-haired young man yanked him backward, just as a fire extinguisher came flying through the air in front of him and exploded against the wall. 'Let's get out, sir, before you get yourself killed,' he shouted. The young man pulled the half-resisting lecturer through a door and down a short, dark corridor. He pushed open a fire door, and they emerged into the evening twilight.

CHAPTER FOUR

Roger sat down heavily on the grass behind a retaining wall, out of sight of the lecture hall. 'The cadets,' he choked, 'they were killing those poor guys.'

'I don't think so,' said the young man, looking away awkwardly. 'I don't think they mean for anyone to really get hurt.'

'Then they're better actors than the actors,' Roger snapped. Seeing his companion wince, he relented slightly. 'Look,' he said, rubbing his eyes and blinking into the sunlight, 'maybe that's just what you call academic freedom out here. But it's the worst violence *I've* ever been responsible for. And I'm not sure what to do next.' He got up and slowly began to walk back toward the doorway they had just exited.

'Dr Cavendish, please don't go back there right now. I'm sure it'll be okay. Maybe you could finish your lecture tomorrow in Dr Albrick's class.' As he spoke, two campus police cars swerved around the corner behind them and screeched to a halt. Eight or ten officers jumped out and ran into the lecture hall.

Roger hesitated. He wanted to know what was going on in the hall, but common sense, and his companion's insistence, told him to stay outside. After a few moments the police officers re-emerged, dragging the six actors with them, and threw them into the cars. 'Act Out! Act Out!' they were still shouting, as the cars sped away. Then the audience filed silently out of the hall and headed in various directions across the perfectly mown lawns. Albrick and the cadets were nowhere to be seen.

'Well, it looks like that decision has been made for me,' Roger laughed uneasily.

'There isn't anything you could have done. It was a horror show, that's for sure. We can call Professor Albrick later and see if he wants to reschedule the rest of your talk. Let me walk you back to the guest house . . . is that where you're staying, sir?'

'Yes . . . I guess so.' Roger let himself be persuaded. The two men walked along the esplanade, settling into a different mood. The air was mild, and a light breeze brought wisps of sea fog across the campus. Hibiscuses, oleanders, and trumpet vines softened the severe angles and forbidding facades of the neo-Gothic campus architecture. After Philadelphia, where a late-spring snowstorm had mired the streets in slush, Southern California seemed to fulfill all its seductive promise of blameless and unending pleasure. Roger's tension and anger began to drain away.

His companion restarted the conversation. 'My name's Jeff, sir . . . Jeff Galitzin.'

'Galitzin? So you're a Russian prince?'

'Hah! My great-grandfather was. Me, I'm from Downey. I'm in computer sciences. None of us ever went back.'

'Maybe now you could, now the Communists are gone? Reclaim your palaces, your serfs, dash across the taiga on a white stallion, wolves baying at your heels.'

Jeff wilted a little at the teasing. His pale, almost translucent, skin, the dark curls framing his delicate features, gave his face an angelic appearance that contradicted his tall, muscular body. Roger felt something stirring in him that had been buried for nearly two years.

'I was really interested in your lecture, sir,' Jeff went on. 'I wish I could have heard the rest of it.'

'Well, if you have any particular questions . . .' Roger said, trying to brush the sticky foam from the fire extinguisher off his shirt.

'Your research . . . I was curious whether you think it will make it easier for . . . for gay men to . . . to change . . . I mean if they really wanted to?' Jeff blushed slightly as he spoke.

'Do you want to change?' Roger asked.

The slight blush deepened. Jeff didn't speak for a moment.

'I didn't mean to pry into your—' Roger began.

'That's okay,' Jeff replied. 'I *am* gay, but I do want to change, yes.'

'May I ask why? I mean, these days, it's positively cool to be gay. There are people out there who would give their eye teeth to be gay; they'd pay for therapy to make them gay, it's so hip. Unfortunately it can't be done . . . neither one way nor the other.'

Jeff looked to see if Roger was teasing him. 'I'm a Levitican. I was brought up a Levitican. No, not the Galitzins . . . my mother, she was from Wyoming.' Roger searched through his scant knowledge of the history of Fundamentalist sects. Did the Leviticans come from Wyoming, or did they end up there? He had a momentary vision of Moses appearing, white-robed, tablets in hand, in a street in Teaneck, New Jersey, and commanding a throng of shoppers to head for the Bighorn Mountains. He smiled slightly.

'I'm a Levitican,' Jeff repeated, 'and homosexuality is a sin, it's . . .' He hesitated.

'An abomination?' Roger volunteered cheerfully.

'You make it sound ridiculous.'

'It *is* ridiculous.'

'Not to me.'

'Do you have a boyfriend?'

'Of course not. I'm a virgin.' Jeff blushed again. 'We have to take a vow of chastity here. No sex, not even straight sex, unless you're married.'

'And do your friends stick to it?'

'Probably not, some of them. But a lot of them get married. Half the students are married.'

'But if your friends have sex, why shouldn't you?'

'It's not what my friends do or don't do. It's the Law.'

'Well, that's settled then.'

Jeff sensed the irony in Roger's voice, and there was a silence. Then he said: 'Do *you* have a boyfriend?'

The sudden move of the conversation to his own private life startled Roger. 'I did . . . he died,' he said rather curtly.

'I'm sorry.'

'Thanks.'

There was another silence. Roger moved the topic back to Jeff. 'There's no hope of changing anyway, so why set your hopes on it?'

'Actually, there are people who have changed . . . students here.'

'You know any?'

'Yes, a friend of mine . . . John Hammond . . . but . . .'

'Tell me about him.'

'He was . . . like me. We talked about it a lot. He went to Dr Forrester, the therapist, and he had a course of treatment. You know, if you tell them you're . . . gay, or worried you might be . . . you have to have treatment, or else they kick you out of the school . . .'

'Better to get kicked out. There are other schools, you know. U.C. Irvine is just down the—'

'Not if you're a Levitican. This is the only school that counts for anything. Most of the kids here, their parents would never pay for them to go anywhere else. And besides, if they have these . . . these feelings . . . they really want to get rid of them. I mean, I'm sure there are happy homosexuals. Like you, I really admire you for it and all, for you it's fine . . .'

'Thanks,' Roger laughed.

'I mean everyone has to live by their own principles, I agree with that. What's right for one person may not be right for another. For us, it's not right.'

'So what kind of treatment did John get . . . electroshock?'

'No, they used to do that,' Jeff said earnestly. 'It worked, apparently.'

'That I don't believe.'

'Well, anyway, they had to stop, a few years ago, after a couple of guys sued them.'

'So what do they do now?'

'Psychotherapy . . . they call it reconstructive therapy.'

'What's that?'

'It's talk. She – Dr Forrester – she takes you back to your childhood, to re-live your relationships with your parents, to set them right or whatever. And she uses visualization . . . you imagine gay sex and then make it really unattractive. I've been having treatment with her for a few weeks.'

'It sounds stupid and self-destructive. And that therapist . . . she's probably some kind of repressed fag-hag . . . you know, wants to have sex with gay guys but doesn't know it, and this is her way of doing it.'

Jeff looked confused. 'I don't think so. Anyway, I'm optimistic about it. And later they do some blood tests and measure brain waves and stuff . . . Professor Albrick helps with that.'

'Albrick? How do you know?'

'John told me. He went through the whole program.'

'And what happened?'

'He became straight.'

'He became straight? Just like that?'

'Gradually . . . over several weeks.'

'I don't believe it.'

'He did. I know it. He couldn't have faked it . . . I would have known. Before the therapy he was totally gay. Sharon Stone didn't turn him on. Michelle Pfeiffer didn't turn him on. Geena Davis didn't turn him on. And then, gradually, they did. It was as simple as that. He was really happy – happy that he fit in with everyone else and knew who he was, and that it was the right thing. It made me want to feel the same way.'

'And guys?'

'It went away. He just stopped being attracted to them.'

'Did he change in other ways?'

'A little bit, maybe. Talked louder, drove faster, more macho. Anyway, he got a girlfriend.'

'They had sex?'

'Yes, they had sex, definitely. A lot of sex. For him, it was like a drug, or a game he'd just learned.'

'What about his vow of chastity?'

'Well, it was wrong, yes, but he really had the urge, he was unstoppable. And besides, I think Dr Forrester encouraged it on the quiet . . . she wanted him to put it into practice, kind of validate it, prove to himself that it was for real. And they were planning to marry.'

'*Were* planning?'

'There was an accident. She . . . she died.'

'Died? How?'

'They were making love . . . I don't know exactly . . . she fell or something . . . her neck was broken.'

'You're kidding. Did he kill her?'

'No, no . . . it was an accident, I'm positive. He told me it was an accident, and I believe him.'

'There must have been an investigation.'

'Oh yes, it's still going on. What happened was, the police arrested him, and he was in jail for a couple of nights. But Levitican really went to bat for him. They undertook to hold him at the infirmary, while the psychologists were doing their evaluation, so the judge allowed him out on bail. So he sits there in the infirmary with ROTC to guard him round the clock.'

'So is he going to be tried for murder?'

'Manslaughter, I think. The prosecutors already agreed to go down that far. I mean, there was no way they could have made a case that he planned to kill her.'

'Maybe they could if he was actually still in conflict about his sexual orientation.'

'He wasn't. He really changed . . . he has no interest in guys anymore.'

'So what does he say . . . were they trying something really kinky when it happened? Like doing it while they were swinging upside-down from a chandelier?'

'Please, Professor Cavendish—' Jeff flushed with annoyance.

'I'm sorry,' Roger said hurriedly, laying an apologetic hand on Jeff's shoulder. 'That was uncalled-for. What I meant was, how can he explain something like that happening? Unless there was drink or drugs involved or something like that?'

'There was no drink or drugs. His story changes quite a bit. It's not that he's lying or anything. It's just that his mood is really unstable. Sometimes he seems incredibly penitent, almost like he wants to be punished, other times he talks so callously about it. From one visit to the next, I never know how he's going to be. One time he got really angry with me, started shouting and cursing me out, calling me a fag and everything. He knows I'm going for the treatment, but still he talked to me, I don't know, as if he wanted to kill me. Then later he was all apologetic. He seems like he can't control his feelings. So once he says to me, "She got what she deserved, the bitch" – totally out of nowhere. Then he started crying and begging her forgiveness, and he went on and on about how guilty he feels, even though it was an accident.'

'You'd better hope he doesn't come out with that in court . . . about her getting what she deserved.'

'I know. They're working on him, of course, to get him in shape for the trial.'

'What a horrible business.'

The conversation lapsed for a minute. They were making their way around a formal pool that reflected the campanile of the college chapel on the farther side. Koi carp swam lazily in and out of a clump of lotus plants, whose exotic blossoms reared gaudily out of the water, seeming too sensual for this center of puritanical morality. At the edge of the pool stood a statue: A bronze husband and wife, in fifties garb and hairstyle, strode purposefully toward the water. Between them, holding one hand of each, skipped their young bronze daughter. Only their immobility saved the three from drowning. As he scanned the group, looking in vain for any sign of parody or camp in its design, Roger felt a twinge of anger. They were bronze zombies, he thought, role models for the thousands of real-life zombies that inhabited this campus, studying so earnestly, too earnestly; preparing themselves to lead their exemplary dull lives, preparing to fight the good fight against the forces of darkness, namely himself, Roger Cavendish, and every other human being who deviated one iota from their prescribed rules of life or love. This is their power, he thought, indoctrination of youth. But two can play at that game.

A bell began tolling from the campanile. Groups of students converged on the chapel. They entered by ivy-masked doors and disappeared inside. The sound of organ music drifted across the plaza.

'It seems so strange,' Roger said, 'a religious school having ROTC. What is this, the Church Militant?'

'They're famous, the ROTC here,' Jeff replied, glad of the change of subject.

'Famous? For what?'

'For what becomes of them. They do incredibly well in the Forces. Tons of generals and admirals and whatever. Two of the Joint Chiefs of Staff were ROTC cadets at Levitican. Even the cadets who don't go into the Service seem to do really well. Senator Price was a cadet here.'

'A lot of universities don't even allow ROTC on campus, because they don't let gays and lesbians in.'

'That's not an issue here, as you can imagine. Leviticans have nothing against military service. But the gay activists give us hell about it from time to time. They raided the ROTC building once and destroyed all kinds of files.'

'Quite right too. Next time I'll join them.'

'Well, watch out for the campus police if you do. The security nowadays is phenomenal. And it's not just the gays. The Animal Rights people have been very active too. Actually, I'm a sympathizer. You know Professor Albrick does research on monkeys. Brain lesions and stuff like that. It's very sensitive.'

'I can imagine.'

'The voters of the city of Cabrillo almost passed a proposition to ban all animal research within city limits. I worked for that. It would have finished Professor Albrick off, of course. I mean, I have nothing against him at all . . . his science is great, by all accounts . . . but I don't think that it justifies maltreating animals, however good it is. Anyway, the National Institute of Health sent its director to argue against the proposition.'

'Yes, I remember hearing something about it. The NIH thought that if Cabrillo did this, other cities would follow suit. Not just Berkeley and West Hollywood, but places like Cambridge or maybe even Bethesda. It would have been a catastrophe. So they made a big deal out of it – I think even Senator Price put his oar in, didn't he?'

'Yeah, he gave a speech. He gave them this BS about the research being important for the national defense or whatever. What a load of garbage. But it worked – the proposition lost.'

They had reached the front of a building whose sign proclaimed Joshua Hall. 'This is my dorm,' Jeff said. 'I'll let you through here, and then the guest house is out the back.' He led Roger down a corridor lined with doors. For a student dorm, there was a surprising lack of graffiti or pin-ups or weird slogans. Photographs of Albert Einstein were nowhere to be seen. Jeff stopped at one of the doors. 'This is my room,' he said. 'The guest house is through the glass doors on the right.' Jeff hesitated. 'I'd . . . it would be really . . .' He blushed again. 'There are some more things I'd like to ask you . . . I mean, if you had time.'

'Maybe tomorrow, before I visit Albrick's lab. I'd certainly like another chance to talk you out of that therapy.'

'No way!' said Jeff with a laugh. 'But it would be great to—' Jeff's voice halted abruptly. He had been reading a note that had been taped to his door. He seemed to rock on his feet, and Roger reached out to steady him. 'What's the matter?' he asked.

'Oh my God . . .'

'What is it?'

'John is . . . he's dead. He killed himself.'

CHAPTER FIVE

'I wish you would at least consider it, Mary. The Navy is most anxious to see this proceed.'

Paul Aconda and Mary Braddock were walking through the laboratory of reproductive anatomy at NIRH. The laboratory was lined with shelves carrying bottles of chemicals, all neatly labeled and arranged in alphabetical order . . . acacia powder, purified; alizarin crimson, certified stain; ammonium hydroxide, 50 percent aqueous solution . . . the series went right around the room. Each shelf had its anti-seismic lip, the one-inch strip of plastic that prevented the bottles from walking off the shelf during an earthquake. Not that an earthquake was expected in Bethesda any time soon. But Washington set the rules, and Washington had to live by them.

On the benches were arrayed the usual tools of histology: balances to weigh out the chemicals, mixers to dissolve them, centrifuges to spin them. Microtomes to cut tissue sections. Microscopes to examine them. Each item of equipment was bolted to the bench beneath it – another anti-seismic measure, but a useful one this time, as it also protected against theft. The balances in particular were sought after by every crack dealer in D.C.

The lab was spotless. Stirrers stirred without spilling a drop. Machines transferred batches of microscope slides cleanly from one staining solution to another. The one technician in the room, who was fiddling with a large piece of equipment by one wall, was wearing an immaculate white lab coat. The whole place looked exactly like a lab in the movies. Mary wasn't the boss here – she ran the outside research programs – but she approved of the scene. The in-house research might not be as brilliant as what went on elsewhere; in fact Mary knew it was dull and unimaginative. But the Bethesda labs made an excellent impression on high-level visitors from downtown.

'Absolutely not!' she retorted. 'Albrick's been approved for monkeys only, and that's the way it's going to stay. There is absolutely no justification for going to humans. Changing people's sexual orientation is not the goal of this project.'

'It's a possible application.'

'Our guidelines would rule it out completely.'

'I think we might be justified in following the Navy's guidelines in this case.'

'If the Navy wants to start carving up homosexuals, let them do it themselves. NIRH will never be part of it. What on earth's this?' Mary was glad to interrupt the tense conversation by engaging the technician in small talk.

Al smiled. 'The world's biggest microtome, Dr Braddock. And the world's biggest microtome blade.' He stood next to what looked like a large top-loading freezer. The inside was lined with cooling coils that were thick with frost, and it contained a long platform, big enough for a person to lie down on. The platform could be moved up and down with a motorized rack-and-pinion mechanism. A heavy steel carriage straddled the platform. It sat on polished, lubricated rails that ran the length of the machine, and had its own motor to propel it forward and back. Clamps on the underside of the carriage held a massive blade, three feet long at least. The blade had been swiveled to one side of the microtome, and the long cutting edge sparkled in the ruby light of a laser beam that was trained on it. The technician was checking the edge, millimeter by millimeter, through a mobile operating microscope.

Mary had always had a phobia of sharp objects. As the technician showed them the blade, she tensed up, trying to conceal her irrational fear. 'My God, you could slice a person up in this, Al.'

'That's exactly what we're going to do. A pregnant woman, to be exact.'

'Oh, yes, now I remember . . . the Digital Body project.'

'Digital Body?' asked Aconda.

'It's to provide a database for interpreting CAT scans and MRI scans,' Mary explained. 'They already did it with one man and one woman. Froze the body and sliced the whole thing into one-millimeter-thick sections. The sections are photographed and digitized, so the computer has a complete three-dimensional image of the body. That was over at the Cancer Institute. Now NIRH is going one better – we're going to do it on thirty-six pregnant women: one for each week of pregnancy.'

'You have volunteers already?'

'Very funny. They're accident victims, mostly. Traffic

accidents, falls. As long as the abdomen is okay they're fine. The heads are often in bad shape. We have seven lined up already in the deep-freeze. After the sections are photographed, they'll be buried or cremated, whatever the relatives ask for.'

'I love it!' said Aconda. 'A quick trip through the egg-slicer, then burial with honors.'

'Dr Braddock, I'm off to lunch,' said the technician. 'Stay away from the blade, if you please. It took our shop three weeks to grind that edge – it's perfect.'

'Sure will, Al,' said Mary, trying to sound relaxed.

'Mary,' began Aconda as soon as the technician was out the door, 'I must ask you once more to consider the importance of moving on with Albrick's work.'

'No, no, no!' said Mary, 'Please don't ask me again. We'll never fund it. In fact, there's talk of pulling all our money out of Levitican University.'

'The whole program? You're joking! For what reason?'

'Because of the school's reputation.'

'Reputation for what? Their religion?'

'For what some of the ROTC graduates have been doing.'

Aconda scowled. 'Like me, you mean?'

'We've dealt with your case, Paul, let's not talk any more about that. Much worse things. Rape, sexual assault, battery – there've been at least twenty cases in the last six months. What is this, a school for sex maniacs?'

'That's ridiculous. That's completely ridiculous. First, there are thousands of Levitican ROTC graduates around the country, maybe tens of thousands. It's a huge program. A few incidents . . . Why does that make the whole school to blame? For what their graduates did after they left the place?'

'And just yesterday a bunch of the cadets beat up some gay guys right on the campus, and almost raped two lesbians.'

'Perverts have no business being on that campus. They must have been asking for trouble.'

Mary took a deep breath. 'The point is, Paul, Levitican is getting a very questionable reputation, and NIRH is thinking seriously about dropping the program.'

Aconda flushed and clenched his teeth. 'That would be very unwise. Senator Price would *not* be happy.'

'Price doesn't know what's going on with you people . . . yet.'

'Don't threaten me, Mary.'

'Let me remind you, Paul . . . *I* am Director of Extramural Programs here. The final decision is mine and mine alone.'

'The Navy has a say too. You're interfering with my mission from the Naval—'

'Mission?' Mary looked at him with a puzzled scowl, then gave a tense laugh. 'There's no point in discussing this further.'

She turned to walk out, but Aconda caught her by the arm. 'Listen to me, bitch, do I have to make you cooperate?'

'Let go of me – you're crazy!' Mary shouted. 'Help! Help!' She realized how foolish she had been to let herself be alone with this man. She struggled desperately to get loose from his grip.

'I'll let go of you when I'm done with you,' Aconda snarled, and he started tearing at her clothes. She tried to fend him off, while continuing to scream for help, but Aconda pushed her against a bench, pinioning her hands to her sides.

Mary knew that her life depended on getting this maniac off her. Using the bench as support, she got her foot up to Aconda's hip and kicked with all her might.

Aconda spun away from her and collided front-on with the microtome blade. He slid along the length of the blade. For an instant Mary thought: *Thank God, his clothes are saving him.* Then he spun off the end of the blade, turning again to face Mary. His entire abdomen had been sliced open. Coils of bowel were already sliding out and falling down his legs, and the severed intestinal arteries were jetting pulses of blood over Mary's clothes and the wall of the lab. The odor of feces filled the air. Aconda's face was frozen in horror. He tried to steady himself by grabbing for the end of the microtome blade with his left hand, and four of his fingers were sliced off. He staggered backwards, his guts trailing along the floor. Then he fell heavily, striking his head on a bench as he fell.

Mary stared in speechless terror; she had even stopped screaming. Aconda was not quite dead. His guts continued their peristaltic contractions, extruding their blood-streaked contents onto the linoleum. For a moment he seemed to regain some kind of consciousness. He stretched out his mutilated hand toward Mary, and worked his jaws, as if trying to speak. Watching his lips, Mary read, or thought she read, the words: 'We'll get you!'

CHAPTER SIX

Santa Monica, Beverly Hills, West Hollywood, Hollywood, Los Angeles: All lay spread out beneath them in the gathering darkness, mile upon mile of shimmering lights, cut by the winding freeways with their ceaseless twin streams of white and red. To the west, the fading sunset over the ocean silhouetted the low hogsback ridge of Catalina Island. To the east, the peaks of the San Gabriels still caught the last and pinkest rays of the sun. On Mount Wilson, six thousand feet above the city, TV transmitters winked their lights hypnotically as they beamed game shows and docudramas to three million Angelenos.

'The Cities of the Plain,' mused Jasper Frinton.

His dinner guests looked puzzled. 'The Who of What?' one of them asked.

'The Cities of the Plain . . . Sodom and Gomorrah. When will it begin raining fire and brimstone, do you think?'

'*Not* tonight I hope, honey,' said a corpulent gentleman in a silk suit, as he peered with mock anxiety at the darkening sky. 'That brimstone, it's the devil to get off moiré silk. And do you *know* what my cleaner charges to do this suit? I might as well give it to some poor homeless person and buy myself a new one.'

'Please do, Ted,' said a dapper man in his forties. 'Come to my store and I'll set you up in something just a tad more *au courant*.'

'Well, what are the smart young queens wearing these days? I visit the Boulevard so rarely . . .'

'The smart *young* queens are wearing leather and scrotum rings, but for yourself, Ted, I would recommend something a little . . . a little more funereal.'

'Why, thank you, Tony, I shall remember you in my will . . . the second-best Rolls-Royce, perhaps.'

Frinton laughed. 'Tony's happy with his Maserati, Ted. He was never one for ostentation.' A door opened silently, and a waiter pushed in a trolley. The trolley carried a selection of desserts that the dinner guests surveyed with approval.

The chairs they sat in, like burnished thrones, glowed in the flame of seven-branched candelabra that stood on the table, their wrought-iron stems resembling fruited vines. From one of them a golden Cupid peeped out, while, on the other, a Cupid hid his eyes behind his wing. In the fireplace, huge driftwood logs, laced with copper, burned green and orange. Their odor mingled with perfumes rising from unstoppered vials of ivory and colored glass that lay in satin cases on the antique mantelpiece. Between them a dolphin, carved from jade, swam sadly in the flickering light. Along the walls, twelve plaster columns, painted to resemble marble, rose to the roof. There, by the illusionist's art, a second tier of columns, of paint only, seemed to carry the dark coffered ceiling to a giddy height. Between the columns, on one side of the room, French doors stood open to a balcony, where real vines framed the luminous cityscape. On the other side of the room, the walls between the pillars were painted with scenes of classical mythology: Narcissus gazing at his reflection in a pool, the Judgment of Paris, the abduction of Ganymede. The style was French. In front of the walls, filling most of the space around the dining table, stood plinths and inlaid cabinets. They carried busts of marble (or were they plaster, too?), glass flowers, and other priceless bric-a-brac. Through this maze the waiter moved cautiously with his edible cargo.

'Your home has been fully homosexualized, as we say in the realty business,' said a tall, rather gaunt man who was helping himself to a slice of raspberry-chocolate Black Forest cake.

'Thank you, George,' said Frinton with a smile. 'Yes, it has taken long enough, in all conscience. But I wanted the total effect, the *ensemble*. One cannot hurry that. Have you noticed that screen – my latest acquisition, and my last, I think, for this room at least.' Frinton pointed to a painted Japanese screen at one end of the room. It depicted two figures: a scowling, armed man and a bearded youth. 'A samurai warrior and his *wakashu*, his squire, his apprentice . . .'

'His boy-toy,' added Tony, and the diners laughed. 'Why, Jasper, have you been to the Orient since we last saw you?'

'To the Orient, to buy that? No, not quite that far. Just to the Pacific Design Center . . . all of half a mile from here.' He pointed through the window to two enormous glass buildings that dominated the West Hollywood cityscape beneath them.

'The Design Center?' asked Ted. 'Do you know, I've never been inside that place?'

'Oh my goodness, and you call yourself gay? Please,

go there immediately . . . spend a day there, a week, absorb it, soak it up, become it. First, the architecture. It's the most stunning pair of buildings in California. Walk around inside. The blue glass, the green glass, the spaces, the shapes, the angles. And then the stuff in it . . .'

'The stuff?'

'Everything you can imagine to beautify your home, to homosexualize it. Carpets from Isfahan and Shiraz, Ming vases, Belgian porcelain, Louis Quatorze furniture, bronze horses from Malta, terra-cotta figurines from Peru, drums from Bali, Impressionists, Expressionists, everything. It's like a museum, the Metropolitan, or the Louvre, except the stuff is better, and everything's for sale.'

'I shall hurry down, checkbook in hand,' said Ted. 'My garage could use a set of moose antlers.'

'There you go, Ted. And we were all wondering how long it would take you to figure that out.'

'Jasper, any good fish stories?' broke in another man, who looked every inch the banker he was.

'*Please*, Luke,' said Jasper, 'they are not *fish*. I'm the gynaecologist to the stars. I work only with the finest, most expensive vaginas. Have some cognac.'

'Fish to me,' said Luke, holding out his glass. 'Never liked them. I don't know how you can spend your whole day with your arms up pussy.'

'You've obviously never been near one,' said Jasper. 'Women's genitalia are beautiful, flowerlike, contemplative. Like women themselves. I may be gay, but I still think women's bodies are more beautiful than men's.'

'You pervert!'

'And Hollywood vaginas are squeaky clean. Or if not, then it's for some interesting medical reason.'

'Oh, please,' broke in Ted, 'you're putting me off this delicious *crème brûlée*.'

'Speaking of the fair sex, I believe that's Marta.' Jasper pointed through the window to a beaten-up Volkswagen bus that was laboring up the steep climb from Sunset Boulevard. At every hairpin bend, it seemed about to expire, and its grinding engine could be heard while it was still half a mile from the house. In anticipation of her arrival, the men seemed to undergo a subtle transformation, raising themselves into more formal attitudes in their chairs and abandoning the camp humor that had dominated the dinner. With two or three final explosions, the van came to a halt outside the residence.

'Now don't start in on her the minute she comes in the door, Luke,' said Jasper. 'Give her a chance to tell her side of the story. After all, we weren't there.'

Luke was silent, but gave the company a look of exasperation.

'Marta, you look terrible,' said Jasper as he opened the door for her. Entering the room, Marta bumped clumsily into a statuette of the goddess Diana, made entirely of cowrie shells, that stood on a high plinth by the entrance. Had not the chef steadied it in time, its fall would have set off a chain-reaction of destruction among the crowded *objets d'art*. Hardly daring to move further, she stood there frozen, breathing heavily, as if she had pushed rather than driven her ailing vehicle up the hill. She sported a black eye, bandages on her left wrist, and rows of stitches in her scalp that her crew cut did little to hide. Two pretty dimpled boys, painted

41

on the wall behind her, seemed to be cooling her with painted fans, but she only perspired the more. Then she grinned, wiped her hands on her overalls, and sank into a chair next to Ted.

'It looks worse than it is,' she said. 'It's really only the wrist that hurts. I'm never going to try that handcuff trick again.' Without waiting for it to be offered, she reached for the cheese board and cut herself a hunk of Edam.

'I hope you won't try any of that again,' said Jasper. 'We're very concerned about you, and the others, too.'

Luke snorted with ill-concealed impatience. Turning to look at him, Marta said carefully, 'They're fine. Cindy and Jimmy were kept overnight for observation, but they're okay.'

'Marta,' said Jasper quickly, 'it's not just your health, though heaven knows that's important enough.'

'It's what, then, Jasper – spit it out.'

'It's what happened, the violence, everything.'

'The violence? We didn't do *any* violence to anyone. *They* did the violence. Those cadets . . . they're a bunch of zombies. I couldn't believe it. And then *we* get arrested! It's crazy.'

'Well, what we're concerned about is that, in the future . . .' Frinton hesitated.

'In the future, what? Get a permit to perform? Wait till we're invited to step forward? We didn't break any laws, not one!'

'Marta, we support you, you know that. Not just with money. We really want to see Act Out! achieve something. You *are* achieving something. But this is too much. It's too dangerous.'

'For who?'

'For you, and the others.'

'And for you too, right?'

Jasper was silent for a moment, and Ted broke in.

'Marta, we're a bunch of closet queens, you know that. We really want to help, within certain boundaries. And we *do* help. If you don't think so . . .'

'I know you do, of course – we couldn't . . .'

'If you don't think so, try the County Hospital next time. And try the Public Defender, Marta . . . you'd all still be in jail. But when you get into scenes like that, it attracts the wrong kind of attention. Listen, a reporter from the *LA Times* asked Blaustein who was paying his bills. A bunch of queer kids represented by a Beverly Hills lawyer . . . it does rather stick out. We can do without that, Marta.'

Marta stared for a moment at one of the tribal masks that adorned an end wall of the dining room.

'You really don't need to hide, you know,' she said.

'How dare you, Marta?' Luke broke in angrily. 'I'm on the board of the Los Angeles AIDS Foundation, and the Bankers for Human Rights . . . is that hiding?'

'The Mayor's on LAAF too, does that make him gay? And the Bankers for Human Rights . . . *whose* human rights? Political prisoners in Chile? I don't think so. The very *name* is in the closet. Call it Fags with Moneybags and *then* I'd—'

'Marta, please,' said Frinton hurriedly. He relieved Luke of the antique crystal brandy snifter that he was threatening to smash down onto the table. 'Marta, this is pointless. You have your style, we have ours. But we have the same goal, that's why we're working together, that's why we're supporting you. All we're saying is, keep it within reasonable limits; we don't want anything that could provoke violence – that's dangerous for you and it will hurt the movement.'

'Well, I get the message. We'll be good girls and boys in the future. But it doesn't sit well with me: getting flak for what those creeps did to us.'

'Marta's kind of right,' said Ted. 'Those Levitican cadets are really incredible, they're animals.'

'I'm not saying you're to blame, Marta,' said Frinton. 'But the plan was to focus attention on Cavendish, wasn't it? To bring up the social implications of his work. I wish you had focused on that. The ROTC thing is another issue. But we may have other ways of dealing with that.'

'Like how?'

'The National Institute of Reproductive Health is funding Albrick's research. I'm on the Institute's advisory council. Mary Braddock – one of the big muck-a-mucks there – she and I go way back.'

'So what are you thinking of?'

'Maybe if I explain to Mary what's going on, she can threaten to cut the funding if they don't kick the ROTC out of Levitican.'

'You think they love Albrick more than they love their ROTC? I doubt it.'

'He's a big name. He's their claim to fame when it comes to science.'

'They could support him without the Feds,' said Luke, who had recovered his calm and his brandy glass. 'That grant is peanuts to Levitican, let me assure you.'

'The grant is peanuts, but they need the prestige of Federal support, and they need the Federal okay for the animal work, for any human work they might do in the future, for the isotopes, for everything. You just

44

can't run something like that privately anymore. Anyway, ROTC is becoming an embarrassment to them.'

'Well, Jasper,' said Ted, 'if you can swing that, my hat will be off to you. Get ROTC out of Levitican and there'll be dancing in the streets of West Hollywood.' Ted turned his gaze to the little gay city that lay spread out below them.

'I'm going to try. I'll be seeing Mary tomorrow . . . a Council meeting. I'll pitch it to her as best I can. NIRH is supposed to be the socially responsible institute in Bethesda. And Marta, we may need your help. We need more dirt on the ROTC.'

'Well, they just beat up a bunch of innocent queers, isn't that dirt enough?'

'Beating up queers? You must be joking. I mean stuff that people don't like.'

'Okay, well, let me know. To hear is to obey. I could use a rematch with those punks anyway . . . just kidding, just kidding!'

CHAPTER SEVEN

The office of the medical examiner of Orange County, Dr Jean-Michel Leblanc, was in East Cabrillo, only a mile and a half from the campus of Levitican University, but in a far less desirable neighborhood. One approached it, not by a gracious palm-lined driveway, but by a mean service road that ran alongside the interstate. The county morgue – for that is what it was more commonly called – was a single-story cinder-block building, accented by two or three dusty oleander bushes. It lacked charm. It lacked any remarkable characteristics. It was not even especially ugly. One might drive by it twice a day for twenty years and never develop any consciousness of its existence.

Dr Leblanc liked it that way. He had no wish to draw attention to the building, to what went on inside it, or to himself. Not that he was ashamed of his trade. On the contrary, he knew that he was performing an invaluable service to the people of the county. But flamboyant? Media-hungry? No, he left that to his colleagues up the freeway, with their Beverly Hills murders, their Hollywood overdoses. In his younger days, Dr Leblanc might have been at ease in those circles. But he had ended up, by some combination of indolence and bad luck, in East Cabrillo, and he had learned to adhere to that community's way of life, and its way of death.

This particular morning was a busy one for him. The suicide at Levitican had brought a string of visitors. The grief-stricken parents, of course, begging for him not to do an autopsy. As if he had any choice in the matter. He had taken them to identify the body. He was glad that was over. Then the police, the DA's office, school officials. Then the autopsy itself, which he left to one of his assistants. Absolutely nothing to find, of course. And now Dr Forrester, of all people. They talked in Dr Leblanc's office. Piped-in chamber music softened the office's otherwise austere atmosphere.

'Dr Forrester, you ask me things about which I know nothing,' Leblanc was saying. He spoke English with the correctness of a foreigner. 'How he died . . . that is simple. He exsanguinated from a razor cut to the radial artery at his left wrist. More than that I cannot say. A suicide, almost certainly. But why he did it . . . that is outside the sphere of my professional competence. That is your role, perhaps. The business with his girlfriend . . . that would be a factor, might I not imagine?'

'It'd make sense.' Dr Susan Forrester, a dark-haired woman with a permanently disheveled appearance, struggled to articulate her questions. She wasn't even clear in her own mind about why she had come, what she was looking for. But she and John Hammond had spent many long hours together, digging into his psyche, turning it over, planting new seeds and nurturing them. The news of his suicide had disturbed her deeply. She wanted to know what had gone wrong. And she needed to feel that she had reached closure at his death.

'But are you sure,' she tried again, 'that there was no physical reason – a brain tumor or a drug problem – that could have made him do it?'

'No, no, I am sure. He was an entirely healthy young man, insofar as it was possible for me to ascertain. Naturally, we will be making some histological preparations. And the toxicology. They may change the picture, but I have to doubt it. How could he have been using drugs? Was he not under supervision at the college infirmary? No, this was simply the suicide of a man who was crushed by the weight of an intolerable burden. Did you not suspect that he was at risk for suicide?'

Forrester stiffened at the abrupt question, almost an accusation of negligence. 'No, no. There was no reason for me to believe so, from the conversations we had. And besides, I was not responsible for his supervision. I merely examined him once or twice, at the request of his lawyer. He was not under my care. Certainly not.'

'I never meant to suggest that you were in any way deficient in your duty, Dr Forrester. On the contrary. On the contrary.'

A buzzer sounded on Leblanc's desk. He pressed a button, and a voice sounded: 'Roger Cavendish is here, Dr Leblanc.'

Forrester stiffened. 'I must be off,' she said, standing up and reaching for her bag. 'I'm late already . . . let me know if you find – I don't know – a reason I can believe in.'

'Oh, nothing will show up, let me assure you. I have a much more interesting case . . .'

'Yes, yes,' she said, bolting for the door. 'But I have to go . . .'

Leblanc rose also and opened the door for her. As they said good-bye, Roger and Jeff approached them along the corridor.

'Jeff, what on earth are you doing here?' Forrester asked in a strained voice. Then she turned to Roger. 'I'm Susan Forrester. Why have you brought Jeff here?'

'I'm Roger Cavendish, good to meet you,' Roger answered. 'Jeff tells me he is having treatment with you. I was trying to talk him out of it, I have to confess.'

'I'm sure you meant well,' Forrester said, 'but such interventions can cause setbacks. The healing process is very sensitive . . . a private matter between therapist and client. Jeffrey, what are you doing here, don't you have classes?'

'I wanted to say good-bye to John, Dr Forrester,' Jeff said.

'I don't think this is the best place for that. Isn't there a funeral service?'

'John's parents are taking him back to Crescent City.'

'Well, I'm sure there'll be an occasion. Besides, we have a session, don't we? Let me give you a ride back to campus.'

'I can bring him back in thirty minutes,' said Roger, 'I think this is important to him.'

'I'm sure casual visitors aren't allowed into the morgue, are they, Dr Leblanc? Jeffrey, let's see if we can't make some progress today. You've been exposed to some negative influences; we must work on resolving that.'

Reluctantly, Jeff agreed to go with Dr Forrester. Roger watched Jeff leave. He was surprised at how annoyed he felt at Dr Forrester. He felt like a teenager cut in on at a dance.

'Please, come into my office, Dr Cavendish,' said Leblanc, leading his visitor to a chair. 'I am most interested to meet you. Your work has fascinated me. Do you know Dr Forrester?'

Roger was far away, imagining a different outcome to the conversation that had just ended. With difficulty, he extracted himself from the fantasy and refocused on the pathologist's jowly face. Leblanc looked like a European aristocrat who had come on hard times. He would have seemed more at home in a casino at Monte Carlo than in this *faux* adobe blockhouse. 'It's very kind of you to take the time,' Roger said. 'You must have had a busy morning.'

'It is always busy here. Nights, weekends, holidays . . . the Grim Reaper takes no vacation.'

Uncomfortable with this line of thought, Roger brightly remarked, 'I like your choice in music. Brahms, isn't it?'

'You like Brahms? Ha, that is the title of a film, is it not . . . *Aimez-vous Brahms?*'

'Some Brahms. The chamber music. This is one of the clarinet sonatas, isn't it? But it is being played on a violin—'

'Viola, viola. Brahms himself transcribed it. I prefer it . . . I play viola myself.'

'Really? An unusual choice of instrument.'

'I love it. The warmth of a cello, the agility of a violin . . .'

'Do you play publicly?'

'For friends. An occasional recital. We have a quartet. A little Schumann, a little Brahms. When I was younger I was a professional.'

'A professional viola player and a medical examiner.

That's a remarkable combination.'

'It was before I went to medical school. I played for three years in L'Orchestre de la Suisse Romande.'

'The Suisse Romande? I'm impressed. Under Bloch?'

'Lejeune. That dates me, does it not?'

'Under Lejeune! I have a recording of his . . . Schubert's Unfinished.'

'Yes, I am there.'

'Ha! I must listen again. It's been a while.'

'I hope that you do not hear me. We are supposed to sing with one voice. That was my problem . . . too much of an individualist for the orchestra, but not talented enough for the solo circuit. And Lejeune was a tyrant. So I said *adieu* and went to medical school at Basel.'

'An interesting life story.'

'There is more . . . not quite so auspicious. But tell me what brings you here.'

'You know about my work on the hypothalamus. As I mentioned on the phone, I'm still gathering samples. I would be most interested to obtain the hypothalamus from John Hammond.'

'From Hammond? But he wasn't homosexual, surely?'

'Well, it's not clear. He had been originally, but apparently he went through a course of treatment here, with Dr Forrester, and it's said he became heterosexual. Whether he truly became straight I don't know, but he certainly was functional enough to have a girlfriend, and to be very sexually active with her, Jeff tells me. Jeff and John were good friends.'

'That is most surprising. Why did Dr Forrester say nothing of this to me? We were just speaking about him.'

'I don't know. But you can imagine my interest in his hypothalamus.'

'You mean, whether it grew bigger?'

'Yes. Not the whole hypothalamus, just the third interstitial nucleus. I mean, we know that we don't get any new neurons when we're adults, but conceivably there might be hypertrophy of the neurons that were there already, or something of the sort.'

'And if the nucleus didn't become larger?'

'Well, perhaps it would be some indication that John's sexual orientation had not really changed. There would be a number of possible interpretations.'

'I understand what you are saying. It is a little irregular, but if you undertake to maintain complete confidentiality . . .'

'I do. It will be written up in such a way as to make it impossible to guess the source of the material.'

'It certainly would be interesting. Well, why not? The brain has been sliced already, I think it is still lying out there.'

'You don't harden it in formalin?'

'Not in a case like this. We don't have the luxury of taking that much time. We need to get the results quickly. So we slice it as best we can . . . it's a little messy. Why don't we do it right now?' Leblanc rose and showed Roger out into the corridor. 'Please,' he said, taking a not-entirely-clean white coat off a peg and handing it to Roger. He led Roger down the corridor to the lobby, where they entered an elevator.

'They say Schubert was a homosexual,' said Leblanc, as the elevator descended to the basement.

'Yes, I've heard that, too,' said Roger. 'And one can hear it in his songs, I think.'

'In his songs? *Die Schöne Müllerin?* The poor boy was in love with the miller's daughter, not with his son!' Leblanc began to sing quietly in a pleasant baritone: '*Ach, Tränen machen nicht maiengrün, machen tote Liebe nicht wieder blühn . . .*'

'He didn't write the words. The music . . . it's hard to explain . . . a certain sensibility, a certain tone.'

'You think that homosexuality and artistic expression are connected?'

'Perhaps . . . a certain kind of expression.'

'It's possible. But what does the hypothalamus have to do with art?'

'Nothing, I imagine. The hypothalamus is tiny, after all. Just looking after your sex life is a big enough job for it. Art? Music? Maybe somewhere in your frontal lobe. But every part of the brain is connected with every other part, directly or indirectly. They may be interdependent systems . . .'

The elevator doors opened, and they stood in another corridor, facing stainless-steel doors. The smell of formalin was overpowering, but behind that smell was another, of decaying flesh, quite unlike the smells Roger had encountered at the medical school morgues he had been to before. He felt slightly queasy as Leblanc pushed open the doors, still humming Schubert under his breath.

The room was large, probably as large as the entire upper floor. Twenty or so steel tables were arranged in two rows. Each table was incised with diagonal gutters to catch any fluids that ran off during the dissection; these were collected in dirty plastic buckets that stood under each table. Some of the tables were bare. Some had sheets draped over what must have been bodies.

At four or five tables, pathologists were bent over their work. There was a subdued murmur, as the pathologists dictated their findings into microphones that hung from the ceiling. 'Liver, 1400 grams, unremarkable,' drawled a bored voice from one table, followed by a slap as the organ was taken out of a scale and plopped down onto the cold metal surface. 'Incomplete avulsion of the right arm at the shoulder, with cut/crush injuries of upper arm suggestive of entrapment in machinery,' rattled off a pathologist at another table. Above the voices continued the clarinet sonatas in their rendition for viola. The entire building was wired for classical music.

As they walked past one table, Roger noticed a shapeless evil-colored object lying on it, about the size of a sack of potatoes. Focusing more closely, he realized with a shock that it was a headless, limbless, torso. It was rotted away on one side, and it was crusted with some kind of greenish vegetation. A pathologist was digging away inside the thorax with a large metal spoon. 'A child found that in the Ortega aqueduct,' Leblanc said. 'In the county's drinking water, can you believe it? Anything on the cause of death, Mike?'

'Not yet,' answered the pathologist, 'but let me show you what we found in here.' He reached down into the bucket under the table, and pulled out what Roger at first took for a snake. 'A two-foot conger eel . . . its sucker was attached to this fellow's heart.' The eel was still sluggishly moving. Roger felt glad that Jeff had not accompanied them into the morgue.

A little further down the room they passed another table where a pathologist was working. The body here was complete, but mangled almost beyond recognition.

The head and trunk were crushed, and the right arm and right leg were in several pieces. From the body's size, Roger guessed that it was a child of ten or so. 'Road-kill,' said Leblanc. 'An undocumented alien. She was crossing the freeway. An eighteen-wheeler and at least twenty automobiles went over her before they succeeded to stop the traffic. *¡No cruces las autopistas!* Her mother's over there.' Roger hurriedly adjusted his features into an expression of pained sympathy before looking in the direction Leblanc indicated, but all there was to be seen was another body, this time under a sheet.

On the next table lay the body of a young black man. He was holding his right hand, palm outward, up against the front of his face, as if warding off a blow. Roger saw that the center of the palm was transfixed by some kind of metal spike. 'A crossbow bolt,' said Leblanc. 'Fired from about twenty paces. The point went through his hand, through his left eye, and now it's located somewhere in his cerebellum. It may be difficult to believe, but he survived for twenty minutes. He told the police the name of his murderer. Something to do with drugs, of course.'

It certainly wasn't a medical-school morgue. No boring cancers or heart attacks here. And no bright-faced medical students to hang on the pathologist's words of wisdom. Here were the end products of random accidents and senseless violence. Roger could almost hear the police sirens. He was relieved when they reached the table where John Hammond's body lay. Just a normal cadaver. Almost too normal, actually; too muscular and healthy-looking to be lying dead on a slab. Except, that is, for the Y-shaped incision running the length of the thorax and abdomen, revealing a bloody cavity from which the viscera had been removed. The pathologist had completed his examination. The pathologist's assistant, the *diener* as he was called, was sewing up the incision with large, uneven stitches, just as if he were trussing an oversized Thanksgiving turkey.

Roger turned his attention to John's head. The scalp and the upper part of the face had been dissected free and rolled down to the level of the mouth, exposing muscle and bone. The eyes remained in their sockets: They looked enormous without their lids, as they stared emptily in different directions. The upper half of the skull had been removed with a single horizontal saw cut, and the brain had been taken out. Finishing with the thorax, the diener now began repairing the head. He picked up the sawed-off skull-cap and put it back snugly in its place. As he did so, Roger noticed a small round translucent patch in the skull, close to the midline at the top of the head. The skull was thinner there, so that the light shone through.

He was about to ask Leblanc about it when the latter said, 'So here's your brain,' and pointed to a smaller steel table off to one side. For a moment Roger's attention remained fixed on John's head, as the diener skillfully rolled back the face and scalp, restoring John's features to their proper arrangement. He was certainly good-looking, even in death. Roger thought of the T-shirt slogan that guys wore in the gay ghettoes; 2QT2BSTR8 . . . too cute to be straight. The diener began sewing the scalp back together. John was beginning to look like someone who had been through major surgery but still had a chance of recovery. It was more unsettling than when he was clearly a corpse.

'Your brain, sir,' repeated Leblanc. Roger finally shifted his attention to the side table. The brain had been cut into slices about half an inch thick, and the slices were arranged in serial order on the tray. 'Let me get you a scalpel and a specimen jar. Ten percent formalin, phosphate-buffered?'

'Yes, that's fine, thanks,' said Roger, and Leblanc went off to the other side of the room. Roger bent over the slices, working his way through the brain from the back forwards. Here he was in familiar territory. The *colliculi* – the 'little hills'. The *arbor vitae* – the 'tree of life' – with its hundreds of *folia* or leaves. Olives (*olivae*) and almonds (*amygdalae*) flanked a central watercourse (*aqueductus*). The *pons* – the 'bridge' – half-hidden by dangling fronds or *fimbria*, led to the *insula* or island. The ancient anatomists seemed to have imagined the brain as a miniature garden, such as one might see on a Chinese vase. Maybe it was because they knew so little about its real function, because they knew nothing of action potentials and synapses and receptors, that they could see those similarities. Yes, there was something botanical about it, he thought, with its graceful order, its sweeping curves and buds and branches. All that was missing was a bamboo garden house and a pair of doves fluttering in the sky. It suddenly occurred to Roger – perhaps Leblanc's artistic sensibility had momentarily rubbed off on him – that this object, the brain, which had been his focus of study for so many years, which he had sliced and diced and impaled with electrodes and ground up for its precious transmitters, that this object was an inner landscape as worthy of admiration for its beauty as any created by nature or laid out by humans. More beautiful, certainly, than anything else in this chamber of horrors.

Remembering his goal, he moved forward through the slices, methodically checking the various tracts and nuclei. They all looked very normal and healthy. Epithalamus, thalamus, subthalamus, hypo . . . He stopped in surprise and looked again. Where the hypothalamus should have been there was a gap. A block of tissue had been neatly excised from the slice with a sharp blade. Evidently it had been removed by an expert, since the cut followed precisely the boundaries of the hypothalamus, curving around the under surface of the anterior commissure and the inner edge of the lenticular fasciculus. There was no hypothalamus to harvest.

Leblanc returned carrying a small screw-cap jar, a scalpel and a pair of disposable latex gloves. Roger pointed at the slices.

'The hypothalamus is missing,' he said.

'Missing? Oh, Albrick must have been here before us. Did you notice that modulation?' Leblanc waved in the general direction of the loudspeakers that hung from the ceiling. 'C-sharp minor to E-flat major! Brahms was quite the radical in his old age.'

'Albrick?' asked Roger sharply, ignoring Leblanc's musicological aside. 'Does he get brain specimens here?'

'Yes, occasionally,' said Leblanc. 'He has a human tissue approval for that. But I wasn't expecting him today. I'm sorry, I think he was the early bird. Perhaps it's possible that you could coordinate your work with him?'

'I hope so. That's strange. I thought Albrick only worked with primates?'

'I have no idea. I don't know much about his work, even though he's the star at Levitican.' Leblanc took off his gloves and white coat, and helped Roger to do the same. The diener was moving John's body from the dissecting table to a gurney. As Leblanc walked his visitor back to the elevator, he added: 'If you will be here on the twentieth, I would be delighted if you would come to Samuel Hall on the campus. We will be running through a Schubert piece – *Death and the Maiden*. You can point out the homosexual aspects.'

Roger smiled grimly. 'I'm sure they're there,' he said. 'Thank you, but I will be back in Philadelphia by then.'

CHAPTER EIGHT

'So, does all this ring any bells with you?'

Jeff pondered the scenario Dr Forrester had been laying out. 'Well, possibly. It seems a bit far-fetched, though. My mother wasn't really like that, I don't think. A bit rigid perhaps, but still, basically she was a really loving mom. She still—'

'Jeff . . . that's the whole point. Loving, yes. But there's love, and then there's love. There are different kinds of love, some healthy, some not so healthy, especially between a mother and her son.'

'Well—'

'Your mother . . . didn't you tell me last week, she used to say "Jeff, grow up, will you!" or "Jeff, stop acting like a kid!" when she was annoyed with you?'

'Well, you asked me if she ever said anything like that, and yes, I guess she did sometimes. So did my Dad. Is there anything unusual about that?'

'It all depends. You remembered her saying this to you when you were four years old. When you really *were* a kid . . . when it was appropriate to act like a kid, right?'

'Right—'

'And from some of the dreams you've told me about, I'd guess she was saying it even earlier.'

'So?'

'Jeff, saying "So?" like that . . . tell me about your feelings, when you say that . . . "So?"'

Jeff blushed. 'A bit skeptical, I guess.'

'And a bit hostile? As if this is an area you'd prefer we didn't get into?'

'Well, no, more like—'

'Because this is crucial, as I'm sure you can imagine, and the resistance you're experiencing is very natural. But we have to get through that if we're to make progress.'

Jeff tried to be more submissive. 'Well, yes, sure, she did say that kind of thing.'

'Why do you think she said that kind of thing . . . "Grow up, Jeff!"'

'I was probably acting like a ba—' Jeff sensed some negative vibrations, and hesitated. He tried to co-operate. 'Because she knew I was too young . . . to satisfy her?'

'And why were you too young to satisfy her?'

Jeff forced himself to say it. 'Because . . . because of just having a kid's . . . anatomy?'

'And if you grew up?'

'I could—' Jeff swallowed his inhibitions, secretly begged his mother's forgiveness, and blurted out, 'I could do it with her.'

'Indeed.'

'I—'

'It's eleven-thirty, Jeff, we'd better get on with the visualization. But think about what we've been talking about, will you please. It'll become more real to you. Now run and put on your thingy.' Dr Forrester turned to make some notes at her desk.

This was the part Jeff hated most of all. Just the word 'thingy' sent waves of humiliation and embarrassment down his spine. Sometimes, as he picked up the tubing and set off down the corridor, he almost decided that it was better to stay the way he was than to endure this. But he had committed himself. The therapy had worked for John, and the therapy was going to work for him, too.

It was a single-user toilet, at least, so Jeff could lock the door and do the necessary without fear of being disturbed. Even so, he felt sure someone was watching him, maybe through a hidden security camera. He dropped his pants, pulled his underpants down to his knees, and rolled up his shirt, giving himself an unobstructed field of action. Jeff was a well-endowed young man, but as always on these occasions his penis had all but disappeared. It had shriveled up and retreated into his abdomen, like a field mouse waiting out a storm. Jeff grabbed what was visible of it with the fingers of his left hand, tugged mightily, and then tried to get the balloon end of the tube over it. It was hard to accomplish without either catching his fingers in the balloon or letting the little critter slip back into its hideaway. After a few tries he got a reasonable fit. Thank goodness Dr Forrester no longer demanded to check his handiwork, he thought. He put his clothes back in order, tucking the free end of the tubing inside his fly. Then he double-checked his appearance, opened the door, and went back to Forrester's consulting room.

'Have you been doing the visualizations regularly?' Dr Forrester asked.

'Every day,' Jeff said. He slipped the free end of the tubing through a hole in the lining of his left-hand pants pocket. He had made the hole specifically for this purpose, in order to avoid having to undo his fly again in Dr Forrester's presence. In one moment of black humor he had fantasized writing a research paper about his invention. '*A Simple Modification of the Penile Plethysmographic Technique to Permit Maintenance of Decorum During Connection to the Monitor,' by Jeffrey N. Galitzin, BA, BS*. He led the tubing out of the pocket and reached over to a machine sitting on a trolley next to his couch. He pushed the end of the tubing over a miniature spigot that stuck out between two dials, and flicked a couple of switches. He felt a sudden slight pressure as the balloon filled with air. Then he calibrated the left-hand dial at zero and twenty pascals, and the right-hand dial at zero and fifty cubic centimetres. If he looked carefully at the needles he could see a slight oscillation: his pulse, as recorded at his penis. He was becoming an expert plethysmographic technician.

'That's good,' Dr Forrester was saying. 'But it's these sessions that are key. If you do it right when you're hooked up to the monitor, then you will do it right by yourself, too.' She settled herself back in her chair. 'Well, let's get started,' she said. 'We're a little late.'

Jeff closed his eyes. 'I'm in my room, working at my computer,' he began. 'It's late, and I've already taken a shower and I'm wearing my robe. My silk robe. I'm feeling kind of toasty inside of it . . . you know, pleasantly warm. Like, when I stroke my hand up and down on my skin it feels really clean, really good. I have some cologne on. Like, down there. And while I'm working away . . . it must be well after midnight . . . there's a knock on the door. I go and open it. It's this guy . . . I haven't seen him before . . . really attractive. Older than me . . . he's wearing a suit. Kind of urbane, I guess you'd say. He looks at me, asks whether he can come in, and I say, "Sure." I realize as he comes in that . . . that I forgot to tie my robe, it's kind of open, and, well—'

'Go on, go on,' said Dr Forrester.

'I have a hard-on the size of a station wagon.'

According to the monitor, Jeff did not yet have an erection of any size, but he plugged gamely on. 'He comes in. I've tied my robe again, but well, it's kind of obvious. He says "I've been wanting to meet you for a long time, Jeff." We're standing there, really close, and he grabs my arms and pulls me toward him until we're touching. He's looking deep into my eyes, saying "Jeff, Jeff!" in this really rich voice. I don't know who he is, but he seems like the man I always wanted to meet. We're pressed against each other, and I can feel him against my . . . against my dick, and he puts his lips against mine and gives me this gentle, gentle, kiss, just a light touch, while he's looking into my eyes and holding my shoulders . . . sliding his hands up and down gently, through the silk. And then he eases back a little and with one swift movement, he rips the robe right off of me, and I'm standing there butt-naked and, well, throbbing away—'

The needles finally eased off their pegs and began a hesitant climb toward the first gradation on the dials. Jeff started to feel a little more comfortable with his task. When he first began these sessions, he had had a real problem thinking what to say. Being sexually inexperienced, he didn't have much idea what went on between men. But he solved the problem one morning by going out and buying some porno. He avoided the strip in East Cabrillo and instead drove all the way up to Costa Mesa. He found a store that seemed to be empty. After some hesitation, he slunk in and started studiously browsing through the girlie magazines. He picked up five of them, and, on his way to the counter, surreptitiously snagged a copy of *Badboy* from the gay section. 'We have booths if you're interested,' said the greasy check-out clerk as he ran Jeff's purchases through the scanner. Then he added, 'I could close the store for a few minutes.' Jeff paid his money and ran. On the way home he dumped the girlie mags in a trash barrel and hid *Badboy* inside his jacket. It had solved his problems all right, although sometimes he wondered if his recitations came across as a little too literary.

'Go on, Jeff,' prompted Dr Forrester drowsily.

'He takes off his jacket and tie, and there's a tuft of hair poking out of his shirt that really turns me on. Then he takes hold of me again, more roughly this time. He plants his mouth against mine, and his big muscular tongue comes plunging into my mouth. I can feel his clothes against my skin, all up and down my body, and I can tell he has a massive hard-on. His hands are grasping my back, and one of them goes down to my butt and starts squeezing it.'

'Good, Jeff, good, keep going.'

'With his other hand he pulls out his dick and starts rubbing it against mine. Then he runs his hand down my chest, and he says, "Smooth ripped body, I knew that's how you'd be, Jeff," and he starts massaging my chest, and then he puts his mouth over my right nipple and starts biting and sucking, and I'm gasping, I feel so excited. I let my hands go down to his dick, it's a horse-dick and there's already something dribbling out of it. I feel his big hands on my shoulders, pushing me

down, and now I'm on my knees looking at this
monster boner, and he grasps me with both hands
around the back of my head and brings me down on
him. "Eat it, Jeff," he's saying, "Oh yeah!" He's driving
it into my mouth and I'm gagging it's so big—'

'Yes, good, good,' said Dr Forrester. The needles
were well on their way to the second gradation.

'He's thrusting it in and out and each time he goes
in he goes in to the max and my mouth is up against
his pubic hair and his balls and I can smell his man-
smell. He goes halfway down my throat every time and
I want to gag but I'm in heaven, just having the feel of
him in my mouth. I want him to come in my mouth
and fill me with that silky-slick hot liquid, but he
doesn't, he pulls out. I'm begging him to go on, but he
lifts me up again onto my feet and then he gets his arm
under my crotch and lifts me right off the floor. He
carries me that way over to my desk and then he turns
me around and bends me over the desk. I'm holding
on to my computer as he leans over me and bites my
neck, savagely. I know he's going to mark me but I don't
care, I'm in ecstasy as he spreads my buttcheeks, and
his finger is playing around my butthole—'

'Oh, yes, that's good,' said Dr Forrester, and she
squirmed in her chair. The needles reached the third
gradation. 'Go on, Jeff, more.'

'His finger is playing around my butthole, stretching
it, going in a bit. Then he smears something cold and
slick there, and I feel his dick up against me, just resting
there, and I'm begging him, begging him to fuck me,
and for the longest time he doesn't and I'm just in
torture. Finally he slides it in, ever so gently, but it hurts
for a second. He's holding a bottle of poppers under

my nose . . . I inhale deeply and my mind seems to disintegrate, it just blows away in fragments. All I'm left with is the consciousness of him inside of me, pumping away, and I'm in every heaven that ever was. He's going right down till I think he's going to rip my guts out, and he's slapping my butt and pounding away. I have to hang on to the desk, and finally he comes inside of me. I feel the jets of hot come filling me up as he groans "Jeff, Jeff!" and finally he slacks off, and pulls out his dick—'

'Jeff, Jeff, that's good,' Dr Forrester said, panting breathlessly. 'Keep going.'

'Now I'm really hot, and I grab him and pull down his pants, and now it's *his* turn to bend over the desk as I grab my dick and shove it roughly into him. He shouts out, "Go slow!" but I drive it down, he's begging me to go slow but I'm outta control, I just want to pound and pound and pound, all the way till my balls are crushed against his butt, and I'm shouting, "Roger, I'm gonna fuck you till I come." He's trying to get loose but I'm holding him tight and going in and in . . .'

'Oh, give it to me, Jeff, give it to me,' Dr Forrester was moaning, but Jeff didn't hear her.

'I'm pounding away, I'm so excited I'm almost knocking Roger and the desk through the wall. My whole body is on fire. I'm getting ready to shoot my load . . .'

'Give it to me, Jeff . . .'

'I'm gonna come! I'm gonna come!'

Dr Forrester opened her eyes in panic and looked at the monitor. The needles were up at the ninth gradation and pulsating madly.

'*Negative!*' she shrieked. '*Jeff, go negative!*'

This was the hardest part of all, the part where

Badboy offered little guidance. 'I'm just about to come,' Jeff cried out, 'but something's happening . . .'

'Quick, Jeff, more negative!'

'Something's coming down his gut, all liquidy and lumpy, and now it's running past my dick and spilling out his butt-hole. It's diarrhea . . . the worst diarrhea, green and stinking. I pull out, and as I do the diarrhea explodes out of him, covering my dick and my groin and running down my legs. I even get some in my face and my eyes, and the taste and smell are making me sick . . . there are worms in it, I get one in my mouth, and I try to spit it out and I throw up, my vomit goes everywhere, all over his back, and down his legs where it mixes with the diarrhea . . .'

'Good, keep going, quickly . . .' The needles were rapidly sinking back toward zero.

'And it's not a guy at all, it's a wrinkled old hag, with bedsores all over her. And she's scratching at me with her long sharp nails. And the whole school is watching . . . they're mocking me. I try to run but I'm slipping in the pools of diarrhea and vomit. I'm falling face down in it. I'm choking on the stuff and retching again and again . . .'

'Okay, Jeff, that's enough,' said Dr Forrester. Jeff opened his eyes and thankfully said good-bye to his fantasies. The needles were back firmly against their pegs. The session seemed to have exhausted Dr Forrester more than it had Jeff, and she lay back to recover her breath. Jeff noticed a damp patch in her slacks, and he smelled an odor that he did not find attractive.

'That was very good,' Dr Forrester assured him, recovering her professional demeanor. 'The timing was excellent. Get as high as you can, then make the down phase immediate and rapid. We are going for *extinction*, Jeff. Total wipe-out. You must get as much negative reinforcement as you can into the first thirty seconds after the high point. You did well. Okay?'

'Yeah, I guess.'

'You really did. Try to do it the same way when you're by yourself. Just make sure all the imagery on the up phase is with guys, then wipe it out.'

'Okay, I'll try.'

'But I'm concerned about you and Cavendish.'

Jeff got defensive. 'Cavendish? There's nothing between us. I've only met him twice. We just talked about stuff.'

'You're not attracted to him?'

'No . . . well, I don't think so, not more than—'

'Then why were you using him in the visualization?'

'What? I wasn't using him. It was just some guy I didn't know.'

'Jeff, you were saying "Roger, Roger!"'

Jeff blushed deeply. 'I was? I . . . I was out of my mind. It must have been the poppers.' He tried to make light of the matter, but Dr Forrester was not smiling.

'If you want to get better, you have to stay away from him, because he stands for everything you don't want to be. Don't let him ruin everything, now that your treatment is going so well.'

'I'll try.'

'Good. You are on track, Jeff. In a couple of weeks I'll be wanting you to get your blood tests with Professor Albrick. Now, it's past noon. Let's get disconnected.'

Jeff unplugged himself from the machine and padded off towards the men's room.

CHAPTER NINE

As Roger took the elevator down to the basement of the Neuroscience Building, he felt a twinge of anxiety, not unlike what he had felt that morning on his way down to the morgue. But this time it wasn't the prospect of seeing gruesome bodies that disturbed him. It was the prospect of spending an hour with Guy Albrick.

Roger had met Albrick several times over the past few years, but never in a one-on-one situation. They'd shaken hands at scientific meetings, maybe shared a few thoughts about a presentation or a poster, before one of them was buttonholed by a job-hunting graduate student. And they'd been on a grant committee together once, for the Belthoff Foundation, handing out money for research on spinal injuries. Nora Belthoff had come by to give them a talk about her son, his accident, how she had collapsed, turned to drink, the abyss, then the glimmer of light, the purpose, the cause. Roger had half expected her to wheel her son in, too, but she didn't, thank God. Not that he would have minded meeting David – he was a real live wire, to judge from the TV interviews. He deserved a medal just for getting out from under that engulfing mother. But Nora was winding up to a peroration that, with David there, would have gone beyond tacky.

'There *is* a cure, gentlemen,' she said. Roger noticed for the first time that the committee was all male. 'There *is* a cure! In those papers . . . search for it, search for it. It's waiting to be released, like Michelangelo's *David* from that block of marble. And if it's not there, then it's in your minds . . . open them, brainstorm, talk freely, take as long as you like, be creative, don't be ashamed of seeing what was there all along . . . the negative space, the paradigm shift! This house is yours, for as long as it takes. I thank you, David thanks you, the world thanks you.' Roger thought glumly of the last shuttle back to Philadelphia and the fourteen applications that had to be reviewed before they could call it a day.

'We will do everything humanly—' the chairman had begun to reply, when Albrick roared, 'Schwann cells! Stimulate the Schwann cells!' Everyone cringed, but Albrick launched into a long harangue about extracting Schwann cells from peripheral nerves, culturing them, and injecting them into the damaged section of cord. They would build the bridge, he said, and the nerve fibers would cross that bridge. Nora Belthoff thought his idea was inspired, and no one disagreed, not out loud anyway. And as it so happened, Albrick had a postdoc who was eager to embark on exactly that project. 'Call him right now,' said Nora, 'tell him to do his first experiment tomorrow. Hurry! We don't believe in red tape here.' She had all but volunteered David as the first guinea pig.

Exiting the elevator, Roger walked down a short corridor lined with posters detailing various aspects of Albrick's research. One of them described the spinal cord work. Albrick (or his postdoc) had indeed succeeded in culturing Schwann cells, and had used various molecular tricks to change their surface characteristics so that nerve fibers in the spinal cord would adhere to them better. The poster showed microscopic photographs of a rat's spinal cord that had been cut clean across; after the operation, the altered Schwann cells had been placed in the gap. One photograph showed tendrils of nerve fibers feeling their way from one Schwann cell to the next; some of them had made it right across the gap and were touching the nerve cells on the other side. Yes, it had been a brilliant idea, Roger had to admit, worth the Belthoffs opening their coffers for it. But nothing came of it. The fibers crossed the gap, but once on the other side they did nothing; they just sat there and refused to go any further. They wouldn't even form synaptic connections locally in the spinal cord, let alone continue on up to the brain. They tried everything . . . a lot of people tried . . . but nothing worked, so Albrick never got to use the treatment in human patients, and David Belthoff and thousands like him were still lying there, motionless, as if encased in marble.

Roger passed through a security door that had been propped open, and then faced a choice of two more doors, one labeled Authorized Personnel Only, the other, Laboratory of Molecular Neurology – Guy Albrick, M.D. Ph.D., director. He went through the latter and found himself in the front office of Albrick's empire. A receptionist and two postdocs were working away at terminals, probably revising manuscripts for publication. All three gave him looks of polite recognition, touched with pained sympathy. Roger wasn't sure whether that was on account of the debacle at his lecture two days ago, or because he was homosexual and therefore suffering from a serious congenital disease. The receptionist said, 'Dr Cavendish, welcome, I'll tell Professor Albrick that you're here,' and he scuttled off.

The front office opened directly into the main laboratory, a low-ceilinged, cavernous space that, with its lack of windows and its bare, poured-concrete walls, seemed almost to have been hewn out of the bedrock. It was a hive of activity. Men and women were working at the benches, casting gels, slicing rat brains, staining tissue sections, loading centrifuges, and entering data at computer terminals. Others were going to and fro between the main lab and various side rooms that Roger could recognize as cold-rooms, darkrooms, tissue-culture facilities, and offices. Some of them carried rubber buckets full of smoking dry ice, or trays loaded with beakers containing colored solutions. One woman was pushing a cartload of squeaking rats, still in their air-freight boxes. She had to navigate around two men who were squinting intently at a fresh X-ray film that one of them was holding up to the ceiling lights – it was still wet, and the rinse water was dripping down his arm and onto the linoleum. At least three different radio stations were pumping out a blend of classical, soft rock and country-western music. It seemed like a disorganized scene, but no doubt it was all orchestrated by Albrick, who eventually came out of a side office, greeted Roger, and grasped his hand firmly enough to make him wince.

'We owe you our deepest apology,' Albrick began.
'For . . .?'

'For that disgraceful, that *despicable* scene on Tuesday.'

'Well, it was hardly your fault.'

'Our security is still too lax. Those perv——, those *demonstrators* should never have been allowed onto the campus. We have their photos, their names, all of them, they should have been stopped at the main gate and sent packing. And they're off scot-free, the charges were dropped that same evening, thanks to that bleeding heart Judge Exner. We'll have that man's scalp at the next election; we'll have him recalled, he doesn't belong in Orange County. Anyway, we have rescheduled your talk for Wednesday the seventeenth, if that—'

'Well, unfortunately, I have to—'

'It will be a separate event, financially, from the first, on the same terms, of course.'

Roger hurriedly changed his tack. 'Let me check with my staff back in Philadelphia; I may be able to get some help with my teaching duties.' The prospect of staying on at Levitican a few more days suddenly seemed more attractive. And in his free time, he could wage war with Dr Forrester for the soul of Jeff Galitzin.

'Please do,' said Albrick. 'Please do. But come into the library, we can talk better, it's too noisy here. And my office is too small.' He led Cavendish into a side room lined with racks of scientific journals, some in bound volumes, some as loose single issues. The room was lit only by a few reading lights. It was quieter, but it felt even more oppressively subterranean than the main lab.

'Surely you could have had a lab above ground, couldn't you?' Roger asked.

'Of course, of course, they wanted to give me the

top level . . . the top two levels. But underground is better. The floor is rock solid . . . we mount our intracellular set-ups directly on it. Same with the ultramicrotomes. We can cut at twenty-five nanometers without even turning on the isolators. Upstairs, the floor shakes with every guy who walks down the corridor, even the electrode-puller needs an anti-vibration table. The temperature and humidity are more stable down here too; that really helps with the cell culture. And the darkrooms are dark, really *dark*. Since we moved here, the background on our auto-radiographs has gone way down. At Purdue, so much light leaked into the darkroom, we had to use the slowest films, and even then they got fogged. We spent all our time trying to find the light leaks. Sunshine . . . who needs it? You're from the East Coast, but here it's cheap, it's on tap, you can go upstairs any time, any day, and get an eyeful. But darkness, that is priceless! Have you been on Palomar, by the telescope, at night? It is so dark, so profoundly dark, you can see to the edge of the universe. And in the valley, every town dims its lights for the telescopes. Once I visited the Leadville mines, in Colorado, where they used to get uranium ore. They turned out the lights, and after twenty minutes you could see the radiation coming out of the rocks. They found the ore by eyesight . . . in total darkness.'

'Interesting,' said Roger, a little nonplussed by Albrick's train of thought. After a brief pause to allow for the change of topic, he asked, 'How is your work on the hypothalamus going?'

'Excellent, excellent,' said Albrick hurriedly, as if being brought back to reality. 'Let me say first, we have replicated your findings; there is no doubt about it. I will show you our data.'

'That's good to hear,' Roger said, with a glow of pleasure. 'I was beginning to wonder if anyone would replicate it. Are you going to publish?'

'Yes, naturally . . . in due course. I was confident that you would be right. You had to be right. Homosexuality is caused by a disturbance in the sexual differentiation of the central nervous system, there is no doubt about that.'

'Well, I wouldn't call it a disturbance,' Roger put in tentatively. 'More like a variation, perhaps.' But he was too pleased at Albrick's news to make a big political-correctness issue out of his terminology.

'Disturbance, variation, whatever,' went on Albrick breezily. 'But it's a change in molecular development, in the centers that regulate sexuality, there is no doubt about that, in my mind.'

'Very likely. I didn't know you were doing human work, though.'

'We're not, except for this one project.'

'And where do you get your material?'

'From Miami, mostly. I have a good relationship with Mike Marshall, the pathologist at Dade County General. But we have even more interesting results with our monkeys.'

'I'd heard you were doing some transplant experiments.'

'Yes, indeed,' said Albrick. 'I believe we have very strong evidence that the anterior hypothalamus – the INAH3 – controls sexual orientation, just as you have postulated.'

'Well, I don't think I have gone that far. Some

involvement, yes. But surely there must be extended circuits involved, not just INAH3.'

'Take a look at this, then you won't be quite so hesitant.' Albrick walked over to a side table, on which sat a TV and VCR. He pushed Play. The first item on the tape was a title that read Sequence 1: Control. 'This is a normal male rhesus monkey, sub-adult,' Albrick said, 'just to show you how we do the testing.' A medium-sized rhesus monkey was crouching in a cage. He had two buttons in front of him, and he was busily pressing the right-hand button. A few feet away were another two cages, each of which also contained a monkey. The cages were mounted on rails, and one of the cages was moving jerkily forward, toward the monkey with the buttons. 'The monkey in that cage is a mid-cycle female,' Albrick said. 'Every time the test monkey presses the right-hand button, it brings her cage forward one centimeter.'

'And the other is a male?'

'Yes, wired up the same. But he hardly ever presses that button, not when he's sexually aroused, anyway. See, he has an erection already. All the normal monkeys learn to do this very quickly. From the rate at which he presses the two buttons, we can derive a precise measure of his sexual orientation. This guy is a Kinsey zero-point-three: completely heterosexual, or nearly so. The few times he presses the other button, he's probably just wanting to have a fight or get groomed or something.'

'Have you done any recordings?'

By way of answering, Albrick turned up the sound on the tape, and Roger became aware of an irregular crackling sound, which he recognized as the electrical activity of a nerve cell, amplified and converted from electricity into sound. Albrick went on: 'We record the activity of neurons in the hypothalamus with a McNaughton-type electrode array implanted under the scalp. You can see the bump . . . wait till he turns a bit . . . there. We can usually pick up ten to fifteen units simultaneously. The data are transmitted by ten megahertz telemetry and stored on optical disc. Later, we sort out the spikes with a waveform analyzer.'

Roger was impressed. 'This cell sounds like it's picking up,' he said.

'Yes, for most neurons in the anterior hypothalamus, the impulse rate goes up continuously as the female's cage is brought closer. As if the cells' activity somehow represents the animal's level of sexual arousal. When the cages come together . . . watch . . .' The two cages docked like space capsules, and the male monkey stopped pressing the button and started shaking the cage door. 'This part is low-tech,' said Albrick with a grin. On the videotape, a white-sleeved arm reached into the picture and raised the two cage doors. The male bounded into the female's cage, and the activity of the nerve cell being recorded increased dramatically – the sporadic single impulses were replaced by a constant barrage of firing. The female was happy to accommodate the male's interest, and they were soon copulating. It took only a few seconds of thrusting before the male threw back its head, bared its teeth, and gave out a kind of choking groan. At the same moment, the activity of the nerve cell peaked in a frenzy, then dropped away and was completely silent. The male monkey looked around vacantly, while the female seemed ready for more. Despairing of her partner, she began showing her rump to the male in the third cage, who up to now had been only an interested onlooker. He was turned on by the sight, but at that moment the tape segment ended, and a new title appeared: Sequence 2: Prenatal Demasculinization. Again, a male monkey sat in a cage with two buttons, but he was pressing the left-hand rather than the right-hand button, and the cage with the male was approaching, while the female sat forlornly in her stationary cage.

'This fellow's mother had a testosterone blockade from day 105 to day 120 of pregnancy,' Albrick said. 'Flutamide and an aromatase inhibitor, delivered by mini-pump. Basically it's the same as if we'd castrated the fetus for those seven days, then given him his testes back.'

'So that's the sensitive period in rhesus?'

'Yes, it's actually probably only four or five days, days 110 to 115 especially, but there's some variation from fetus to fetus, so we bracket the time a little, just to be sure.'

'Do you get any anatomical changes . . . in the genitalia, for example?'

'No, no, it's too short a period. There may be some temporary slowing in the growth of the penis, we haven't checked, but by the time he's born it's caught up again. Certainly no hypospadias or undescended testicles or anything like that.'

'That's interesting.'

'Interesting because of the human analogy?'

'Yes, I suppose that's what I meant.'

'Actually, I meant to ask you, is there any increase in microphallus or hypospadias in gay men, in your experience?'

Roger thought: *'In my experience?' Is he saying 'You must have spent years in the bathhouses . . . how often do you see a stunted penis?'* He answered, 'I've never read anything to suggest that, no.'

'Well, then, our results are consistent with that, since we can get a complete dissociation of bodily and mental development, just by timing the treatment appropriately. It's quite unlike the situation in rats.'

'Were you recording from this monkey?' Roger asked.

'No, we've tried it, but we never pick up anything in the anterior hypothalamus in these guys. It's shut down completely, as far as we can tell.'

'But he's clearly aroused . . . he has an erection, and it looks like he wants to have sex with the male.' The cage containing the male was getting steadily closer.

'Yes, that's the paradox. There has to be another center driving this monkey's behavior, a "male-seeking center" if you like, but we don't know where it is. That's where we need your help. But first, let's finish the story with this little fellow.' As the two cages came together, the clip ended, and another title came up, that read Sequence 3: Restitution of Function.

'Don't you let the two males get together?' Roger asked, with a trace of disappointment in his voice.

'No, the studs always attack the demasculinized monkeys as soon as they solicit for sex, and they're too valuable for us to let them get injured. They don't even defend themselves properly. I'm pretty sure the amygdala is demasculinized too . . . their aggressiveness is way down. So we just measure the button presses during approach. This guy was a Kinsey 4.8 – mostly homosexual but some heterosexual interest

– usually when he was totally frustrated. After a couple of sessions of hauling in the studs, eventually he'd break down and go for the female. An orgasm is an orgasm, I guess, even when it's with the wrong sex.'

'*Was* a 4.8?' Roger was beginning to get the picture.

'*Was*, yes.' Albrick smiled. 'Watch. This is the same monkey.' The scene switched to an operating room. The monkey was anesthetized on the table, its scalp was cut open and drawn back, and a needle-like device was being lowered into its brain through a small hole in the skull. Several white figures clustered around the operating table, but their faces were out of view.

Albrick and Roger were suddenly distracted from the videotape by Albrick's receptionist, who had come quietly into the library. 'Dr Albrick, there is a group of students here, from Many Sparrows.'

'God dammit, can't you keep them out of the place? What the hell do they want this time?' Albrick's birthmark seemed to turn a deeper shade of purple.

'They want to see round the vivarium. Shall I call security?'

'This is too much. We're not running a petting zoo. Get rid of them. No, hold on, I'll speak to them. Tell them to wait. In the front office . . . not a step further or it'll be a chamber hearing and expulsion for the lot of them.'

The receptionist left. 'What's Many Sparrows?' Roger asked.

'The student animal rights group.' Albrick was visibly upset. 'Jesus said: "A man is worth many sparrows" . . . Luke-something-something. It's so ironic . . . he meant how much more a man is worth than a sparrow, but they twisted it . . . took the sparrows' side, for heaven's sake. I'll deal with them in a minute. Watch the tape,' he almost barked.

'What are you injecting?'

'It's a suspension of dissociated fetal cells from the basal forebrain, modified to express testosterone receptors constitutively. About ten thousand cells on each side, along with a cocktail of growth factors. We get about twenty percent survival, so we end up with about four thousand grafted cells altogether.'

'And where do you inject?'

'Right into where INAH3 should be . . . the stereotaxic coordinates are from your paper, corrected for rhesus monkeys of course.'

'That's a small target, for so far down in the brain.'

'We record on the way down. There are landmarks . . . the ventricles, the anterior commissure. The optic tract if we go too far down. Sometimes we have to make two or three penetrations to find the right spot.'

On the tape, the needle had already been withdrawn, and Albrick was sewing up the monkey's scalp. Then the scene ended and was replaced by Sequence 4: 7 Days Post-Op. The monkey was back in its cage with the two buttons. The scalp sutures were still in place, but otherwise the monkey looked none the worse for the surgery. It pressed the left-hand button most of the time, bringing the male toward it, but occasionally gazed at the female and tentatively pressed the right-hand button a few times.

'A week is the earliest we see anything,' Albrick said. 'Let's go on.' He fast-forwarded through sequences 5, 6, and 7, then hit Play gain. Now the monkey was hitting the right-hand button most of the time.

'My God,' said Roger. 'It works. My God.'

'It works,' said Albrick. 'He's a Kinsey 2.5 at this point, but going lower every day. That's on the basis of button-pushing. He's not so good on the follow-through yet . . . watch.' As the cages came together and the white-sleeved arm opened the cage doors, the male cautiously entered the female's cage. He sniffed and touched the various objects in the cage, and nervously circled the female without touching her. He had a full erection, though. The female became impatient, and after a minute or so she took matters into her own hands. She grabbed the male's right thigh and pulled him toward her, turning her rump to him as she did so. The male finally cottoned on; he mounted her and began thrusting. Soon he reached orgasm, dismounted, and gazed slack-jawed off into space.

Roger smiled, but his mind was in turmoil. Albrick's experiment proved that sexual orientation was controlled by the hypothalamus – in monkeys anyway. It was incredible. It was far more clear-cut and simple than he had ever imagined. No other part of the brain seemed to be involved. It was a neural switch, like those dip-switches they used to have at the back of computers. You set it when you bought the machine, it decided how the machine worked, and you forgot about it. But later you could always open the back of the machine and flip that switch, and that's what Albrick had done. And by flipping that switch, Albrick had swept away the dusty superstitions, the Freudian theories, social constructionism, everything, forever. It was that simple. It was an extraordinary thrill, suddenly to see so clearly, what his own research had hinted at, now laid out incontrovertibly for all to see,

whenever Albrick chose to publish it. Sure, it was
monkeys, not men, but it must be the same, Roger
thought, it must be . . . and the anxiety that had been
gathering at the back of his mind settled over his
consciousness like a black cloud, masking the pure joy
of realization that had so briefly seized him.

Albrick seemed to read Roger's thoughts. 'We have
not done anything like this in humans, of course,' he
said.

'Do you plan to?'

'Not unless there is a demand for it.'

'Which means yes.'

Albrick stared at Roger with narrowed eyes. 'So you
think most gay men would rather be heterosexual?'

'No, of course not.' Roger was angry at himself for
letting Albrick put him on the defensive. 'Most gay men
are happy to be gay. But there will always be some who
aren't . . . teenagers mostly, or young adults, students
at schools like this one, cut off from the modern world,
who never hear anything but evil spoken against them
. . . "abomination before the Lord," "crime against
Nature," all that crap. All they need is a little love, a
little reassurance, someone they trust saying, "You're
okay." Brain surgery? *That* would be a crime against
Nature . . . against *their* nature. You can't do it! That's
not why I did my research.'

Albrick hastened to calm Roger's feelings. 'It's very
hypothetical that we would ever initiate anything like
that. There would have to be a broad public debate on
the issue. And besides, brain surgery isn't necessary.
Behavior modification works fine.'

'You mean what Dr Forrester does?'

'That's right. She uses covert sensitization, combined

with traditional analysis. And counseling, prayer, and so forth.'

'You know as well as I do that none of that stuff works.'

'That's what I thought, but she has had remarkable successes.'

'You mean like with John Hammond?'

'Hammond? The one who killed himself the other day? I don't know what was going on with him. Guilt, I assume, for his girlfriend's death. But he changed his sexual orientation, that's for sure.'

'Dr Forrester told me that you take part in her program.'

'We have nothing to do with the therapy. But we do monitor her subjects from a physiological point of view. We do LH tests during the period the kids are becoming heterosexual. Inject estrogen and measure the luteinizing hormone response, to see if there are neuroendocrinological changes, from a female to a male response pattern.'

'And are there?'

'Not that we've seen so far. And we do an EEG – electroencephalography – to measure unconscious cortical responses to erotic stimuli, male and female. Haven't seen much there either. But the subjective change is real, I assure you.'

'You have Hammond's hypothalamus?'

Albrick froze. After a pause, he went on smoothly, 'You must have met our musical friend, Dr Leblanc.'

'Yes, I was hoping to get Hammond's hypothalamus myself, but you got there first.'

Albrick was treading cautiously. 'Well, maybe we can work something out,' he said. 'But if you'll excuse me for a minute or two, I have to deal with those animal lovers. Let me get James to show you around the laboratory.'

Albrick shepherded Roger into the main lab and introduced him to a burly man who was adding some drops to a large flask of liquid. A white magnetic stir-bar whirred around at the bottom of the flask, sucking the frothy surface of the liquid into a rotating vortex. James kept his eyes fixed to a pH meter next to the flask. 'I'd be delighted . . . one moment,' he said and kept on adding drops until the pH reached 7.4. 'Okay, sorry,' he said finally, turning off the stirrer, and sealing the top of the flask with paraffin film. 'I didn't want to mess up a whole batch of culture medium. Our cells are very sensitive.'

While Albrick went off to deal with the visitors, James began the tour of the lab, introducing Roger to some of the postdocs and technicians along the way. Eventually they came to a door leading off the main lab. 'This is my empire,' James said. He gave Roger a lab coat and mask to wear, and he put on a mask himself. Through glass panels in the door, Roger could see a hazy but intense blue glow. As they entered the room, James threw a couple of switches, and the blue light was replaced with regular fluorescents. 'The ultraviolet is to keep the yeast and bacteria down. It's our own private ozone hole. If you want an instant tan, I can leave them on.'

'Thanks but no thanks,' said Roger. 'So this is where you do the cell culture?'

'This is it. Take a look.' He opened the door of one of the cabinets; it contained several metal racks, and on each rack a number of large plastic test tubes, sealed with orange caps, were lying on their sides. Some kind of mechanism was keeping the tubes rotating gently, so that the cloudy fluid within them was kept in constant motion.

'What kind of cells are they exactly?' Roger asked.

'Basal forebrain . . . fetal . . . three to four months' gestation or thereabouts.'

'So around the sensitive period?'

'Sensitive period? I've no idea.'

'Albrick said the sensitive period was around one hundred and ten days.'

'In rhesus. No one knows when it is in humans.'

'Humans? This is *human*?'

'Sure, yeah, sorry, should have made that clear. Since the fetal tissue ban was lifted, we've been using tissue from elective abortions.'

'But, I mean, you're transplanting it into monkeys, aren't you?'

James gave Roger a reassuring smile, though only the creased eyes were visible above the mask. 'Absolutely . . . rhesus macaques. But you can imagine the expense of getting fetal macaque tissue? A timed-pregnant rhesus from Yerkes costs four thousand dollars . . . just for one! And that would be enough for three tubes, with luck. Look at this room, we have two hundred tubes rolling right now.'

'They're not rejected?'

'No, and that's for two reasons. First, the brain is an immunologically privileged site: graft rejection is much slower because of the blood-brain barrier. But also, the neurons lose a lot of their species-specific surface antigens while they're in culture, so they don't provoke so strong a reaction anyway.'

'And what does the college think about it? I mean, using material from abortions?'

'They turn a blind eye. None of us are Leviticans, so I guess they don't extend their moral code to us.'

'Albrick isn't Levitican?'

'No, I mean sometimes you'd think he was, he sees eye-to-eye with them on so many things, like about . . . your people. But he's not religious, actually. Certainly he isn't concerned about using fetal tissue or anything like that. Hey, it's feeding time.' A technician had come into the room, carrying a flask and some pipettes. She collected some culture tubes from one of the incubators, sat down at a chemical hood, and lit a Bunsen burner. 'Janet,' James said to her, 'Would you let Dr Cavendish watch what you're doing? The feeding frenzy of the neurocytes!'

Janet laughed. 'Sure. I open a tube, so. Then I add four drops . . . one . . . two . . . three . . . four. Then I flame the mouth of the tube, so, just to keep everything sterile, and then I put the cap back on. Done. Next please.'

'I didn't see much of anything,' said Roger, who had been watching the contents of the tube intently.

'You kind of have to use your imagination,' said James. 'It's all microscopic, of course. But it's a life-and-death struggle in there. Pseudopodia tearing at each other, fighting for the choicest morsels of neurokinin and NGF. Sometimes I can hear the screams as they rip each other's nuclei out.'

'Well, how exciting. But tell me, are these cells dividing?'

'No, they're beyond that . . . they're post-mitotic. They're ready to settle down and form connections.

Which makes problems for us, because we have to put the gene for the testosterone receptor into them. If they were replicating their DNA it would be a lot easier.'

'They must have the gene already, though, don't they? I thought all cells had a complete set of genes in their nuclei?'

'Yes, of course, but we put in a new one, one that's permanently switched on. Also, we've linked it to a portion of the rhodopsin gene . . . the exons that code for the membrane-spanning domain. That way, the receptor incorporates into the external membrane of the cell, instead of floating around in the nucleus. For some reason, that greatly improves the likelihood that the cells connect into the right circuits, once they've been transplanted. We suspect that the testosterone receptor is a cell-recognition molecule as well as a hormone receptor.'

'Really? So how do you get the gene in? With a viral vector?'

'No, physical methods. It's a little technique we've dreamed up. We'll be publishing it soon, but right now it's kind of confidential. Anyway, let me go see if Dr Albrick is finished with those students. I'll just be a moment.' James left the room, and Roger made himself useful carrying the roller tubes to and fro for the technician. After a brief interval, James returned with Albrick, but they paused at the door of the culture room, as if to complete a conversation out of Roger's hearing. Roger nevertheless overheard a few phrases: 'Why not let them . . . nothing to see . . . they're all healthy . . .' James was saying.

'That's exactly why not, you idiot!' muttered Albrick forcefully.

At that moment another technician came up, carrying a tray. 'Are these the ones you wanted, Dr Albrick?'

'Yes, thanks. Dr Cavendish, let's take a look at these . . . they're the sections from John Hammond's hypothalamus. Processed already.'

Roger followed Albrick to a table against one wall of the main lab, where a microscope and a digitizing tablet were set up. 'Fifty-micron frozen sections, stained with thionine,' Albrick said, as he picked up one of the slides and put it onto the microscope stage. 'That's the method you use too, isn't it?' Albrick was not an especially proficient microscopist: He seemed uncertain about which objective lens to use and moved the condenser up and down erratically. Finally, after scanning a number of slides, he said, 'This is INAH3, isn't it? About a millimeter lateral to the ventricle, just dorsal to the anterior tip of the paraventricular nucleus.' He yielded his seat to Roger.

'Yes, that's it,' Roger said. 'Is this the section through the biggest extent of the cell group?'

'I believe so.'

'Well, it's very small, just a few cells. Typical for a gay man.'

'So no change as a result of the therapy, then, you think?' asked Albrick.

'Therapy? I don't call it therapy, more like psycho-torture. But no, there obviously hasn't been any change. Which confirms that it doesn't work.'

'It does work,' said Albrick. 'I'm sure about that. But not at the hypothalamic level, evidently. The wires remain crossed there, so to speak. But the cerebral cortex is where the plasticity is, in adults. The therapy

must cause a compensatory crossing of wires there, too
. . . a re-crossing, so to speak, so that battery and spark
plugs are connected with the right polarity again, but
through the wrong cables.'

Roger didn't think much of the automotive
metaphor, or of Albrick's whole train of thought. He
scanned the sections again, moving from slide to slide.
Something puzzled him, but he wasn't sure what.
Eventually he gave up the search and pushed the slide
tray away from him. 'What was it you wanted my
advice for, anyway?' he asked.

Albrick pulled up a chair. 'The other half of the story
. . . the female half. INAH3, it's for male sexuality, that's
why it's so small in homosexual men. But there has to
be another cell group, another center, for female
sexuality . . . for attraction to males.'

'Well, the ventromedial complex is the best
candidate. You know the lesion studies.'

'Yes, the ventromedial complex for sure. But that's
a big area. There's regions there that have nothing to
do with sex. The weight-regulating center, for example
. . . that's in the ventromedial complex. That's where I
did the transplants in the obese mice.'

'I know what you mean,' said Roger. 'My bet is that
there's a small sub-region somewhere in the
ventromedial complex . . . the female equivalent of
INAH3, so to speak. I wanted to look at this issue, but
you can't get autopsy specimens from lesbians. Not
even from known heterosexual women. Their sexual
orientation is never recorded in their charts . . . not
that I've ever seen, anyway.'

'Well, I may be able to help you there. We have
obtained some suitable specimens.'

'Really? How so?'

'Through the military. We have good connections here. There have been a number of service women who've died in accidents, and a couple in the Gulf War.'

'Lesbians?'

'Some of them. Of course they are closeted, so long as they're alive. But when they die it becomes obvious, you know, if they were coupled. The commanding officers make very close inquiries. I know of at least one occasion when the CO gave the flag to the woman's lover, at the funeral. She was reprimanded . . . should have been court-martialed . . . probably a damned lesbian herself.' Albrick was about to launch into some anti-gay rhetoric, but thought better of it. 'Anyway, I have quite a number of specimens already, both lesbian and heterosexual. I was hoping to persuade you to study them. Of course, if it comes to publication, you would have to be circumspect about where they came from.'

Albrick had pushed Roger's buttons again. The prospect of completing the missing half of his research project was extremely tempting. But he was also frightened. It looked like Albrick was well on his way to developing an effective means to convert gay men to heterosexuality, thanks to Roger's own discovery. That would be battle enough, to stop that being used . . . if it were even possible to stop it at this point. Did he really want to expose lesbians to the same thing? Torn by conflicting desires, Roger merely said, 'I'll need to sleep on that one.'

'Of course,' said Albrick. 'Let's talk about it again tomorrow.'

CHAPTER TEN

Jasper Frinton did not sleep well on planes. He had an irrational fear that, if he nodded off, the aircraft would veer off course and crash. By the time he arrived in Washington, he was tired and irritated. His mood did not improve when he found that, inexplicably, there was no car waiting for him at the airport. It was a cold, rainy morning. Cursing the federal government in general and the National Institute of Reproductive Health in particular, he took a taxi over to Bethesda. When they arrived, the taxi was not able to drop him off under the Institute's sheltering marquee, because that space was occupied by several TV news vans, a police car, and a van marked U.S. Navy. With more imprecations, Frinton leaped out into a large puddle of water and ran for the entrance. He marched down the hall and pushed open an office door. A receptionist looked up. 'Dr Frinton? Oh my gosh, I'm so sorry! The Council meeting has been canceled.'

The gynaecologist to the stars was preparing to launch into a tantrum worthy of one of his patients, when the receptionist added, 'On account of the accident, sir.' Within a few moments, he was informed of the events of the previous day – news that most of Washington had received with its breakfast cereal. Mary was in a state of shock, he was told, and was recuperating at home. After a phone call, Frinton was off on another taxi ride, this time out into the rain-sodden countryside.

Marcus opened the door. 'Hello, Jasper,' he said. 'Good of you to come by. A bad business.'

Mary was sitting by the fire. She was dressed, but a score of details shouted 'invalid'. The blanket Marcus had put over her knees, the slippers, the little table with a bunch of flowers and a mug half-full of cocoa, and above all, her hollow-eyed gaze. She had had a worse night than Frinton, that much was obvious. The Ativan had only put her nightmares into slow-motion. Frinton signed to her not to get up, and gave her a warm hug. Marcus, meanwhile, went off to find a vase for the lilac blossoms Frinton had bought along the way.

'Don't talk about it, unless you want to,' Frinton said. 'Let's talk about something else. Your trip to Greece . . . I've been waiting to hear about it.'

Mary smiled and reached for a photo album, but after a few minutes of white-sailed windmills and tumbled-down temples, Mary put down the book. 'It's no good, Jas. It's there all the time. It's easier to talk about it.'

'Well, then, tell me this. Do you feel, in any way, in your heart of hearts, responsible for what happened?'

'No . . . well, maybe in some crazy neurotic way . . .'

'It *would* be crazy and neurotic, wouldn't it, to think that?'

'Yes, but—'

'Do the police or anyone consider you responsible?'

'No. I mean, they grilled me for hours yesterday. It felt like I was being accused. But no, they've assured me that, on the basis of what I told them, I'm unlikely to face any charges. I'll have to testify at the inquest, of course, and there's who knows how many committees of inquiry being set up. I'm sure the Navy will give me a hard time. And media interviews, and who knows what. I think my days will be full of it, for the foreseeable future. And my nights, too.'

'That's just it, Mary, the nights. You must be able to come home and cast this thing off. Your conscience is clear, you must keep that always in your mind. Horror fades, but guilt does not fade . . . whether deserved or undeserved. It doesn't fade, it festers. You understand that, don't you? You are *not* guilty . . . don't even for one fleeting second play with the idea that you are.'

Marcus came back into the room. He had trimmed the lilac sprigs to a precise length and arranged them in stultifying order in their vase. 'May I, Marcus?' said Frinton, and he fussed the blossoms around a bit. 'There are some areas where we have the edge.'

'That's fine, that's fine,' the general replied. 'Never could understand the principles of flower arrangement anyway. The one course I flunked at West Point,' he added with a wink.

'So who does the flower arrangements in the Army, anyway? I mean, you must have flowers sometimes, don't you? For funerals and such?'

'Who does the flowers? The homosexuals do the flowers, of course.'

'The homosexuals . . . in the Army? How do you know who they are?'

'The homosexuals? *Everyone* knows who they are, and no one cares . . . except for a few damn troublemakers. This whole thing is so absurd . . . so damned absurd. If it weren't for the politicians, homosexuals would get on just *fine* in the Army, just fine. It makes me mad.'

Frinton thought back to his medical school days at Cornell. Mary had developed more than a minor crush on him. And to fend her off a bit, he came out to her . . . one of the first colleagues he ever told. On the rebound, it seemed, she went for Marcus. Totally unsuitable, Frinton had thought, wondering what she could see in that insensitive military man. But he had eventually come to realize that she had chosen well. Marcus, he said patronizingly to himself, had a heart of gold.

'Dear, did you tell Jasper about Aconda's record?' Marcus asked. He moved the flowers over to a side table, and added, 'Anyway, I'll be in the den if you need anything. Sylvia's putting some lunch together.' He left the room.

'Yes, his record . . . He had been reprimanded for sexual harassment, several times. I would have fired him . . . Marcus really wanted me to . . . but there were political issues. He was liaison officer for a joint Navy-NIRH program at Levitican University, and—'

'Levitican? I can't believe it!' said Frinton. 'Or rather, I certainly *can* believe it.'

'You know something about the place?'

'Do I indeed. That's part of the reason I came over. I brought some stuff to show you about Levitican . . . about their ROTC program. This . . . what was his name?'

'Aconda.'

'This Aconda . . . was he a graduate of the Levitican ROTC program, by any chance?'

'Yes, he was. And I know what you're going to tell me.'

The phone rang. Mary picked up the cordless handset that was sitting on the little table. 'It's for you, Jas,' she said.

'Oh, sorry, yes. I gave my service your number, hope you don't mind. Excuse me a second.' Frinton took the phone. 'Sure, yes, put her through . . . Honey, how nice to . . . uh-huh? . . . uh-huh? . . . They want to *film* in there? . . . Darling, I wouldn't recomm— it wasn't cosmetic, that was your face, remember? It was to save your life . . . well, don't they have cunt doubles? . . . sorry sorry sorry! . . . Well, not this afternoon . . . Because I happen to be in Washington . . . it turns out the First Lady is a hermaphrodite, but *please* darling on your life don't tell anyone . . . Okay, tomorrow morning, ten o'clock . . . bye, love.' Frinton put down the phone with a sigh. 'She *loves* me to be vulgar with her. Her one remaining turn-on.'

'Who?'

'That I can't tell you, I'm afraid. But watch out for an action thriller where piranhas go for the heroine's cervix. The aging heroine's cervix.'

Mary smiled wanly. 'You're too much, Jas.'

'But anyway, let me tell you about Levitican and their ROTC. Maybe you don't realize the scale of this thing. Aconda was not an isolated case.'

'That's what I said to him . . . and that's when he went berserk. Apparently, he had a lot of loyalty to that program, even though they turn out some real crazies.'

'Here . . . take a look.' Frinton handed over a folder of newspaper clippings and e-mail printouts. Mary looked at the first page:

PENDLETON MARINES CHARGED
IN GANG RAPE

Oceanside – The names of seven Camp Pendleton marine officers who allegedly raped three women in an Oceanside bar late Wednesday night were released today. According to a statement issued jointly by the North County district attorney's office and by the office of the commandant at Camp Pendleton, the officers faced charges that include rape, attempted rape, sodomy, aggravated assault, and resisting arrest.

The incident occurred around midnight in the pool room of the Great White Cafe on Hill Street. According to witnesses, the three women had been drinking with the marines. The marines asked one of the women to perform a striptease. When she refused, the marines forcibly undressed her and . . .

Frinton pointed at the names of the officers. 'Of these seven, six had graduated from the Levitican ROTC program.' He pulled out another file. 'This is a printout of all the ROTC graduates from 1990 on. Three of the men are here, two here, and one here. Go on.'

Mary turned another page, and read:

WIFE-BEATER ACQUITTED

Paso Robles – A realtor who admitted striking his wife with a cast-iron skillet, fracturing her skull and blinding her in one eye, was acquitted of aggravated assault by an all-male jury in San Luis

Obispo County Court Friday. John Rooney, 32, claimed that his wife Mary, 27, violated his constitutional rights by refusing to have sex with him . . .

'Here's Rooney . . . '94. Go on.'

EAST SIDE BATHHOUSE TORCHED –
THREE HELD

The Spartan Club, a bathhouse on East 53rd Street patronized by gay men, was destroyed by fire in the early hours of Monday morning. Three men have been charged with setting the fire, in which four patrons of the bathhouse were injured, one seriously. The case is being treated as a hate-crime . . .

'Two of these three men graduated in '94 . . . here they are. And the third, Grisham, we believe he was a drop-out from the program.'

Mary skimmed through the clippings. *Lesbian activist shot execution-style . . . Arizona National Guard officers held in KFC rape . . . Sexual harassment cases in Air Force are increasing, says report . . . Sentences decried in Tallahassee gay-bashing . . .* They went on and on. 'This is incredible,' Mary said. 'But how did you figure out that all these guys were from the Levitican ROTC?'

'It wasn't me who did it, it was the hate-crimes project at the Coalition for Gay and Lesbian Rights. They did an extraordinary job. After they got indications that something was going on from some of the news reports, they got hold of the list of graduates and did a systematic search. They checked police and court records all over the country, as well as the news databases. Here's what they came up with.' Frinton produced a set of graphs. 'Before twelve months ago, Levitican ROTC graduates were completely unremarkable. The incidents started around May of last year and have been increasing steadily since then . . . look at the curve. And what's really interesting is the breakdown by year of graduation, here. Of the classes of three years ago and earlier, less than five percent have been involved in any incidents of this type. That's no different from the rates at other schools . . . the Coalition did some comparisons. Of the cadets who graduated two years ago, nine percent have been involved in something or other, and of those who graduated last year, seventeen percent have been involved. And that's a minimum, of course . . . just the ones the Coalition has been able to track down. That's an incredible rate of increase, especially when you consider that last year's graduates have had half the time to do something, compared with the graduates from the previous year.'

'So it's just the ROTC graduates?'

'Pretty much. The Coalition looked at a sample of the regular Levitican graduates and didn't see anything. There was one suggestive case this March though. A student still at Levitican killed his girlfriend . . . while they were making love. Name of Hammond. He claimed that it was an accident. But he committed suicide, just the day before yesterday. I can't help wondering whether it was part of the same thing.'

'So what's going on, do you think?'

'Well obviously, the ROTC is indoctrinating their cadets into a pattern of violent hatred directed against women and gays. It must be part of the program.'

'Have you tried to contact the school about it?'

'Well, not me personally. But the local chapter of the Coalition certainly has. They've contacted the president's office and some of the trustees and various other people there, but they've been totally stonewalled. Of course, gay groups have been after the ROTC for years because of their discriminatory policies. So it's not like the Coalition expected a sympathetic hearing. We've also tried informal persuasion of various kinds, without success so far. This is where you come in.'

'Where I come in? Uh-huh, Jas. I don't come in.'

'Mary—'

'Jas, I know what you're going to say. Cut the Albrick grant, or threaten to, right?'

'It would help put pressure on them.'

'Jas, you must realize how impossible that is. First, that would be seen as personal retaliation for what happened to me. Second, it would be playing politics with the science . . .'

'Albrick's grant has been pure politics from the word go. You would be cleansing the Institute, if you got rid of him, you know that. And you'd have at least one supporter on the Council.'

'We made the decision to support his research. I wish we hadn't, but we had good reason to, you know that. Now you're saying dump it, for a reason that's unconnected with Albrick or Albrick's research.'

'Albrick is the big wheel of the ROTC program.'

'He is?'

'He certainly is. It's his hobby. His passionate hobby.

103

He spends all his free time with those cadets. He has some weird position with them . . . honorary commandant or something.'

'I didn't know that.'

'He's a freak, Mary. He has no private life. He's unmarried. No girlfriend. No boyfriend. Tells everyone he had an unhappy love affair in his youth. Wouldn't surprise me, with that thing on his face. Decided to dedicate himself to humanity. Oh, please! So he works all the time. For lunch he brings Army-issue ready-to-eat meals. And on weekends he careens around Orange County in a Bradley fighting vehicle.'

'Jesus.'

'And he's homophobic as hell.'

'Well, that much I assumed.'

'And probably a woman-hater too. I just hope to hell he isn't gay.'

'Well, if he's homophobic he's not likely—'

'I sure hope not. Because I've had it up to here with those types. I mean *I'm* closeted, I admit it. I happen to enjoy my lifestyle, and I'm not going to put that at risk. But I do *everything* for our community . . . it's my life. But Albrick, who knows? Listen, this whole thing with the ROTC graduates started after he arrived in town . . . a year and a half after he arrived. He's the one, Mary. It's him who's doing it, it's got to be. He's turned ROTC into a kind of cult . . . really, exactly like a cult . . . and he's their charismatic leader. He's poisoning their minds with his sexism and his homophobia. He's probably wrapping it up in some God and Country bullshit. And they're falling for it. They're falling for it, and they're going out and killing people . . . people like you. You've got to dump him.'

'Jas, there's nothing I would like better than have the earth swallow him up. But the point is, the only way I could cut that program would be if there's scientific misconduct. And there's no hint of that. Not one hint. He's exemplary. You must understand what you're asking me to do. You want me to cut his research support, for a reason that has absolutely nothing to do with his research. That's illegal, Jas. And after what happened yesterday, everyone would take it as a personal thing . . . a blatant abuse of my powers. Think what Senator Price would make of it. This connection between Albrick and what's going on, you may be right about it, but still, it's just your guesswork. He may not be doing any of that. And didn't you just tell me that there's a case where the guy wasn't even *in* the ROTC? How was Albrick involved in that? It's just Levitican, Jas. It's a totally retrogressive, sexist, homophobic school. Albrick fits in perfectly, I'm sure that's why he moved there. But that doesn't mean he's responsible for all this stuff. You want to punish the school by pulling whatever levers you can, and I'm one of them. It's not fair, Jas.'

'Mary—'

'Jas, there are other avenues you can pursue, surely. Public relations . . . Levitican must be sensitive to that. Can't your Coalition put pressure on them that way? Publicize these statistics?'

'They're in a different world, Mary. A world in which anything coming from the Coalition is automatically a lie. They mention us in their prayers . . . a special request for us to be condemned to hellfire. And God will be only too happy to oblige, I'm sure . . . *their* God.'

'But their supporters, their donors?'

'They're all in the same world. The Family Values Task Force has its headquarters a block from the campus . . . two of the elders are on their board. The Law of Jesus Foundation gives them nearly a million dollars a year. And Leviticans all over the country, of course, they pour money into the place. It goes on and on. They are completely embedded in a self-sustaining, isolated world . . . a world we can't reach. And you, Mary Braddock, have given them the U.S. Government's seal of approval.'

'Jas . . .' Mary's eyes were brimming.

'I'm sorry, Mary. I'm getting carried away. I came here to comfort you, not to harass you. Forgive me.'

'Jas . . . it's too much, it's all too much.' Mary let out a wail, and the tears came flooding down her face like the rain on the living-room window.

CHAPTER ELEVEN

'Jeff!'

Roger had been looking for Jeff for twenty-four hours. He'd not been in his dorm, nor had he called Roger at the guest house. And he'd failed to show up yesterday after Roger's meeting with Albrick, as they had planned. But as Roger was doing his daily workout in the school gymnasium, he saw Jeff come in with a group of friends and begin to work on the machines. Jeff seemed none too comfortable when Roger came up to them. Rather than introduce Roger to his friends, he led him a few steps away.

'I need to speak with you,' Roger said.

'I . . . I can't,' Jeff stammered, blushing deeply.

'Why on earth not? Are you embarrassed to be seen with me?'

'No, absolutely not. It's just—' He paused.

'Just what?' Roger asked impatiently.

'It doesn't seem . . . I don't know . . . helpful.'

'Is that what Dr Forrester told you?'

'No . . . yeah, maybe. But it makes sense. You know, this is nothing personal. I like you lot . . . really a lot, more than I should probably. But that's not the way I'm trying to go with my life. Do you know what I mean?'

'Jeff, I respect that. Your life is your own. But there

107

is something important I need to discuss with you. Can we just have five minutes, then that'll be it?'

Jeff didn't need a whole lot of persuasion. 'A few minutes, then, I guess,' he said, looking at his watch. 'Let's spell each other.' He said something to his friends, and then led Roger toward another part of the gymnasium, where fewer people were working out. As they walked across the room, Roger couldn't help admiring the glistening, near-naked bodies of the students, male and female, who were heaving and grunting within the black steel contraptions. They seemed to be struggling to escape from the machines, like Parthian warriors entangled in the siege engines of Caracalla. And behind them all, along the back wall of the gymnasium, ran the green and gilt words: WHATSOEVER HATH A BLEMISH, THAT SHALL YE NOT OFFER UNTO THE LORD.

'The ROTC cadets . . . do they work out here, too?' Roger asked.

'That's them over there. They've sort of command-eered the free-weight area. Everyone else uses the machines.'

Jeff began a set of chin-ups. 'That tall guy you came in with,' Roger said, 'he's one of the Many Sparrows, or whatever you call them, isn't he? I saw him at Albrick's lab yesterday.'

'Scott, yeah . . . I'm a member too . . . although I don't . . . I don't do a lot . . . let me finish first,' Jeff said as his breathing became labored.

He completed the set, and Roger did his. While they were gathering their breath, Roger said: 'I wanted to ask about your treatment with Dr Forrester. How far along are you?'

'Eight weeks.'

'I understand she uses covert sensitization . . . visualization and so forth.'

'That's right. It's pretty gross. Better than actually throwing up or getting electric shocks, though.'

'It doesn't work. There's all kinds of studies.'

'I'm hopeful. I'm going to give it a try.'

'Are you making any progress?'

'Dr Forrester thinks so. She says I'm moving into the neutral phase, which is a stage when you don't really know what you are anymore, before you start to become heterosexual. I'm going to get my blood tests with Professor Albrick in a few days' time.'

They went on to the butterfly press, where they each did two sets. Roger wiped his face with his towel. 'It's Albrick I wanted to talk to you about. You have to stay clear of him, there's something very sinister going on in his lab.'

'Sinister? Like what?'

'Brain grafts.'

'*Brain grafts?* You mean, monkeys with two brains?'

'No, injecting brain cells into people . . . into gay guys, guys like you.'

'To make us smarter? We're smart enough already . . . that's not our problem.'

'You don't *have* a problem, Jeff, you don't have a problem! There's nothing wrong with you. You don't need any treatment, not with Dr Forrester, not with Albrick, not with anyone. You're absolutely fine the way you are. Can't you see that?'

'If you're Levitican, it's not absolutely fine to be gay. Let's do the pull-down.'

After a couple of sets on the pull-down, Roger

continued the same line of conversation. 'Your mother is Levitican, right?'

'Right.'

'And your father?'

'He accepted Leviticus when he married my mother.'

'Is he devout?'

'No, not really, I think it was more to marry my mother. Leviticans only marry within the church.'

'What was he before?'

'Russian Orthodox, I suppose . . . my grandfather is, anyway. But my Dad isn't very religious.'

They moved on to leg curls. For a computer nerd, Roger thought, Jeff was very well built. During the breather that followed, Roger went on: 'Was your grandfather born in Russia?'

'Yes, but they left before he was a year old.'

'Do you know much about your great-grandparents . . . what kind of life they led?'

'Well, affluent, of course.'

'You know, your great-great-grandfather, he must have been – Prince Alexei Antonovich Galitzin – he was a great patron of the arts.'

'You studied Russian history?'

'No, but I'm interested in art and music and such. His name comes up. When he was young, Tchaikovsky used to play at their home . . . at the Galitzin Palace in St Petersburg. Tolstoy was there a lot, too . . . another aristocrat, you know. Rodin visited . . . the French sculptor.'

'I know who Rodin is, thank you. They had a Rodin . . . it was a study for one of the figures in the *Burghers of Calais*. It was destroyed in 1917, my granddad said.'

'Sergei Diaghilev, the . . . sorry, you knew that, too.

He was a close friend of Prince Alexei . . . he was his protégé before he became famous. And many of the leading dancers . . . Lifar, Fokine, Nijinsky, Massine, they were all there at one time or another. And writers . . . Rilke, Proust, such a snob as he was. Meeting Prince Galitzin . . . he dined out on it for months, I'm sure.' Roger paused a moment for effect, then added: 'Gay, all of them.'

'*Gay?* Hey, we're supposed to be working out. Let's do leg extensions.'

Before he was halfway through the set, Jeff stopped and said: 'How do you know they were gay?'

Roger rested his arm against the column of counterweights. 'Well, let's start with Tolstoy. I once had sex with a guy whose ex-boyfriend – I think his name was Ian – had been the live-in lover of an old man who used to import dates, the fruit, you know, from North Africa, and that guy, when he was much younger, had a brief affair with a soldier in the French Foreign Legion – he was an amputee but still serving somehow – and that soldier told *him* that once, when he was in the Crimea . . . not the Crimean War of course, this was much later . . . he was invited to a party with some aristocrats which turned into an orgy – he still had his leg at that time – and one of these aristocrats told him that his neighbor – another aristocrat but I don't know his name – told him that he had caught his father, the neighbor's father I mean, he had caught him in bed with a stable hand who had previously been the boyfriend of the Tolstoy's estate manager . . . after Tolstoy died. According to the stable hand, Tolstoy and the estate manager were lovers . . . and Tolstoy's wife thought so, too.'

'Thanks . . . I just calibrated my BS meter,' said Jeff with a smile. He went on with the set.

'Now with Rodin it's a little more complicated—'

'Look, Roger, I should get back to Scott and the others. But what were you saying about brain cells and Albrick?'

'Okay . . . this is no BS though.' He sat down on a bench, and Jeff sat down next to him. 'I'm pretty sure Albrick has been injecting brain cells into the hypothalami of gay students . . . to make them straight.'

'Volunteers, you mean?'

'No, not volunteers. Without their knowledge. I think he did it to John.'

'That's impossible . . . how could he possibly do that?'

'It seems really far-fetched, but I still think it must be what happened. I suspect so, anyway. John was a patient of Dr Forrester's, right?'

'Right. That's how he became straight.'

'Maybe, maybe not.'

'What do you mean? He *did* become straight.'

'He became straight . . . I don't doubt that anymore. But it wasn't Dr Forrester who changed him . . . it was Albrick, by grafting genetically-engineered cells into his brain. He made John's INAH3 larger.'

'That's ridiculous. John put everything into the therapy. He had complete faith in it, and it worked. He didn't need brain surgery.'

'Listen, when I went down to the autopsy room, after you left with Forrester, I saw something really strange.'

'Like what?'

'John's skull . . . there was a patch that was thinner, a really small patch, maybe a quarter of an inch across, right here,' Roger touched the top of Jeff's head lightly with one finger. 'It looked like a drill hole had been made, maybe a year ago, and then the bone had partially filled it in again. Did John ever have brain surgery?'

'Not that I know of. Not while he was at Levitican, I'm sure of that.'

'Did Forrester send him to Albrick for anything?'

'Yes, a blood test, and an EEG.'

'The EEG, what did he tell you about it?'

'Not much. He stayed overnight there. They gave him something that kind of knocked him out . . . a truth serum or something like that . . . and he didn't have much memory of it. And . . . oh . . .'

'Oh, what?'

'Well, come to think of it, there were some stitches in his scalp, I remember him showing me. Yes, right up here. He said something about the recordings had to be beneath the scalp, so they made a small incision, while he was under the drug I guess; he didn't remember that part at all.'

'And was it after that that he became straight?'

'It was a gradual thing. I think he had already reached the neutral stage before then. That's when Albrick does the tests.'

'But had he actually said he found women attractive, sexually, before that?'

'No, I don't think so. More that he was confused about his sexuality.'

'And afterwards? How long afterwards did he start being attracted to women?'

'Well, I remember at the end of the following week, on Friday night, when we went out, he made some comments . . . about girls we saw. But really it was more like two or three weeks before he had any kind of consistent feelings. And his feelings towards guys . . . he still had those, off and on, for about six months.'

'It figures. And there's another thing. Yesterday, when I visited Albrick, he showed me what he said were sections of John's brain . . . we looked at the hypothalamus.'

'What did you see?'

'Nothing interesting. It didn't look like it had had any treatment at all. But . . . it wasn't *John's brain*. I'm sure of that.'

'How could you tell? Doesn't one brain look like another?'

'Two things. First, the Permount . . . that's the stuff you use to stick the coverslip on with . . . it was rock hard. I tried to dig my fingernail into it, and I couldn't even make a mark. That means it had been drying for several days at least . . . but Albrick only got John's brain the day before yesterday. And the other thing: When I looked at the brain slices at the morgue, I saw he had removed the specimen by making a cut exactly along the underside of the anterior commissure . . . that's like a landmark you can see with your naked eye, just above the hypothalamus. None of the anterior commissure itself had been removed. But the sections on the slides he showed me included at least a millimeter of the anterior commissure, maybe more. It was a different guy's brain.'

'That's crazy. He must've just made a mistake. Or maybe it *was* John's brain, and you didn't look at quite the right level to see where the anterior whatever was cut. Whyever would he want to show you the wrong guy's brain?'

'He was in a spot. He hadn't known that I knew that he had taken John's hypothalamus. He didn't want to show it to me, because there's something incriminating there, so he showed me someone else's . . . someone who hadn't had a graft.'

'This is crazy. There's no way Professor Albrick would be secretly injecting stuff into guys' brains. If he really has a method that works, why doesn't he just tell everyone and offer it openly to people who want it?'

'Probably because the government wouldn't let him do it. He's pretty paranoid about that . . . he had some bad experiences a few years ago.'

'It just isn't true. It can't be. You're the paranoid one, Roger . . . Dr Cavendish.'

'Roger's fine. But paranoid I'm not. I'm worried about you, though, if you get into his clutches.'

'It just can't be true. And hey, what if the worst happened and he injected me . . . I'd still end up straight, which is the way I wanted to be. Want to be, I mean.'

'Look what happened to John. Yes, he ended up straight, and he also ended up dead, and his girlfriend too.'

'What's that got to do with Albrick?'

'Who knows? But it could be connected somehow.'

'It's just not true.' Jeff got up. 'I should be going.'

'I'm sure that there's something in those sections that he didn't want me to see,' said Roger, standing up, too. 'I've got to get a hold of them, somehow. Then I can prove it to you.'

Both men stared blankly off into space for a few moments. Then Jeff looked at Roger and said: 'Maybe I can get them.'

'How on earth?'

'Can I tell you something, and have you promise not to tell another soul?'

'I guess, yes, absolutely, if that's necessary. Why the conspiracy?'

Jeff looked around. There was no one very close by, but he didn't think it sufficiently private. 'Let's go to the changing room,' he said, and he led Roger down a few steps into an area of lockers and benches where several men were changing. The air was full of body odor and steam from the showers. They passed through the room and down a dark passageway that turned a corner and then led toward a deserted storage area.

Jeff stopped in the passageway. He stared at the ground and muttered beneath his breath: 'Many Sparrows are planning to break into Albrick's lab on Saturday night . . . into the animal quarters. They're going to photograph the monkeys, maybe liberate some of them. I could go with them.'

'What? This is so out of character. Liberating monkeys? I mean, isn't that forbidden in the Bible somewhere? I'm stunned.'

'Out of character? How well do you know me? I have principles, yes, which I try to follow. But sometimes to follow one principle, you have to sacrifice another. I'm serious about animals. And hopefully they'll just take some photographs and leave . . . document what he's doing to the monkeys, especially if they're sick or injured or whatever.' Jeff kept looking around nervously, in case a passerby came within earshot.

116

'While we're there, I could go to his office and find the right slides, and bring them out. You'd have to promise to return them to him afterwards. After you've seen that nothing's been done to John's brain.'

'Yes, okay. But how are you going to get in?'

'With a passcard.' Jeff looked around nervously again. The sound of bantering voices came from the locker room. 'When Scott and the others went up there yesterday, they took an energized card blank and did an echo read from the slot. I had a program with all possible codes running from my PC in Joshua Hall, patched over to Security through the system manufacturer in Massachusetts. I guess they like to keep tabs on their systems after they sell them. Anyway, when it hit a valid code, the card blank picked it up. I'm pretty sure it's Albrick's, because it seems to be the only universal master for that department.'

New facets of Jeff's personality seemed to be revealing themselves by the minute. 'I'm impressed,' said Roger. 'Jeff Galitzin, latter-day saint and hacker extraordinaire, soon to be doing time in Federal Pen.'

'Leviticans aren't Mormons, please.'

'No, and you're lucky about that, otherwise they'd be tying you down and electrocuting the homosexuality out of you.'

Suddenly, the sound of running feet and excited laughter came down the corridor. 'Ackroyd, you pervert!' someone shouted. 'We're after you!' A moment later four or five men, one of them naked, came hurtling down the corridor and collided with Jeff and Roger. Roger and two of the men went down in a tangled heap. Jeff helped Roger up. 'Are you okay?' he asked.

Ackroyd and his pursuers were laughing hysterically. 'Sorry, guys!' one of them said. 'Didn't realize this was the schmoozing area.' Then they dashed back into the locker room, still laughing like madmen.

'ROTC,' said Jeff, helping Roger to dust himself off. 'Anyway, I've got to go. I'll talk to you, though. I need to know how to recognize the slides and stuff.'

'Okay, I'll be around,' said Roger. 'It was good talking with you. And in the meantime, ask your granddad about old Alexei. You can tell a man by the company he keeps, you know.'

Jeff laughed, clutched Roger's arm, and hurried off.

CHAPTER TWELVE

Mary pored over the densely written application. She was starting to go dizzy with the effort of working through the tangled prose and the endless figures. Sometimes images of Aconda's death throes appeared like hallucinations on the pages in front of her, blocking out the words she was trying to read. She had to beat them out of her consciousness and start the paragraph over. *Immunoperoxidase . . . co-principal investigator . . . in situ hybridization . . . semilog scale . . . anteroventral periventricular nucleus . . .* the words began to take on the special craziness of anything that is concentrated on for too long. Albrick's lab was growing in her mind into a Bluebeard's castle: door after door opened on creaking hinges, revealing spectral visions of weird science. But the one room she was looking for remained locked.

The previous afternoon, after Frinton had left, Mary had thought long and hard about what to do. Eventually, she decided to do nothing. That, she reasoned, was both right and expedient. Right, because there was nothing about Albrick's science that warranted intervention. And expedient, because doing anything was bound to land her in hot water of some kind, and would certainly jeopardize her chances of a

Cabinet appointment. She promised herself that she would make it up to Frinton somehow. Who knows, maybe Albrick's next grant renewal would receive a priority score below the funding cutoff. She knew how to choose the reviewers to get the scores she wanted. Or maybe, just maybe, she would be out of NIRH by then . . . maybe she would be looking down on all this petty infighting from her office at the White House. And from there, she felt sure, she would be able to do so much for the gay community, Frinton would forget she had ever refused him anything. But this blessed resolution to her dilemma lasted only six hours, because that evening she received a call from Roger Cavendish that changed everything.

She knew Roger only slightly; they had met at a conference on sexual behavior the previous summer. Frinton had said some pretty negative things about his work, or rather about the potential fallout from his work. And that resonated with her own views on the subject. Sometimes these scientists had the best will in the world, but little sense of reality – of what depths the human race was capable of sinking to, once it was given the means. She remembered how joyful she had been when obstetric ultrasound came in. What an unmitigated blessing, she had thought, along with everyone else. And now, in India and China, it was open season on female fetuses. Aborted by the hundreds of thousands, girls were becoming a rarity. It was truly frightful. And the inventor had wrung his hands and tried to get the genie back into the bottle – fat chance! God, if people could do this against women, what wouldn't they be willing to do against gays?

But when Roger told her about his suspicions, she

really took notice. For he was suggesting that Albrick, in outright violation of the terms of his funding agreement, had secretly extended his work to humans. What Aconda had been demanding that she authorize, Albrick had done without authorization, or so Roger was saying. She found it difficult to believe that it was true. To conduct research on humans without first jumping through the thirteen prescribed hoops was to court an untimely end to one's career. Surely Albrick wasn't that stupid. But if it *was* true . . . well, it would both demand and justify everything that she was able to throw at him.

And that had brought her back to NIRH this morning. Disregarding the news crews, her solicitous staff, the cards, the overflowing voicemail, the screens of e-mail, and a mountain of flowers both real and digital, she demanded Albrick's files and started looking through them. But it was hard going. Most of the application dealt with matters well outside of her own area of expertise: It looked perfectly reasonable, but it was hard to be sure. She went on to the budget.

Under 'equipment' she noticed a listing for two stereotaxic headholders, at $8,500 each. They were Kopf model 4800D primate headholders. Why had Albrick wanted two of the same thing? Typical budget padding, maybe . . . perhaps he had only bought one, and had kept the rest of the money for a slush fund . . . everyone did it. She looked at the budget justification. 'Two stereotaxic assemblies are required,' she read, 'to enable both recording and lesion experiments to be carried out simultaneously.' That was certainly BS. There was only a single anesthesia machine listed, and only a single operating microscope, so how could they do two procedures at once? And the lab plans showed only one neurophysiology room. So it *was* some kind of skullduggery, either financial or scientific.

Mary called David Kopf Instruments in Tujunga. It took them a while to dig out their shipping records from nearly three years ago. They had been transferred to tape and dumped in some outhouse. But eventually the clerk called back. 'Okay, I have it now,' he said. 'To G. Albrick, Molecular Neurology, Levitican University, right?'

'Right.'

'I'm looking at just one 4800D shipped, ma'am.'

'Anything else?'

'Er, no, I don't . . . oh, hold on, yes, there's a 6800D.'

'6800D? What's that?'

'One moment, item description . . . 6800B, 6800C, 6800D . . . stereotaxic headholder assembly, human.'

'Human?'

'Yes, ma'am.'

'Thank you. Please fax us a copy of the invoices.'

'I'll be pleased to do that, ma'am.'

Mary buzzed her assistant. 'Robert,' she said, 'get me a ticket to Orange County Airport, will you, for Sunday afternoon. And a room at the Cabrillo Sea Lodge.'

CHAPTER THIRTEEN

A t 1:30 a.m. Jeff and the four animal rights activists
entered the basement of the Neuroscience
Building. Jeff left the others to investigate the vivarium,
while he headed for Albrick's lab. What if some night
owl was still working? He quietly cracked open the
door. To his relief it was dark inside; he edged himself
in and closed the door behind him. Red and green
indicator lights winked at him from cryostats, ovens,
and power supplies. There was a gentle murmur of air
being drawn into the chemical hoods. He waited in the
darkness till his eyes could better distinguish the layout
of the lab, then he moved cautiously along the
sidedoors until he found Albrick's office. It was open.
The office itself was a tiny space, barely a cubbyhole,
with no window. Scientists prided themselves on the
small size of their offices, he knew. To have a big office
was to be an over-the-hill administrator, a refugee from
science. Jeff turned on his flashlight. The wall on one
side, over Albrick's desk, held shelves of books and
journals: Journal of Neurochemistry, Journal of
Molecular Endocrinology, Journal of Stereotaxic
Neurosurgery. On the other side, barely an arm's reach
away, were stacks of black plastic slide boxes. Each box
had a colored label. On each label was a code: CGL 1,

CGL 2 up to CGL 74, then BRM 1, BRM 2, and so on. It seemed like the letters signified the name of a project, and the number was the number of a particular experiment. But which was John's hypothalamus? Jeff opened some boxes at random. They were all brain sections. There must be a file, a key.

Over in the corner was a filing cabinet. He rifled through the files. Grant applications, correspondence, off-prints. Reviews of manuscripts. As Jeff flipped through them, a name on a label caught his eye: *Cavendish*. He pulled out the file. There were two pieces of paper stapled together and a manuscript. The first sheet of paper was headed *Brain Monthly*, with an address in Boston. It ran:

Dear Dr Albrick,

We would be grateful for a review of the enclosed manuscript, 'Brain Structure and Sexual Orientation,' which has been submitted to *Brain Monthly* by Dr Roger Cavendish.

Would you please give us your opinion of the manuscript's scientific merit, its originality, and its suitability for publication in *Brain Monthly*? Your comments will be sent on to the author but your identity will be held in strictest confidence. Please destroy the manuscript after you have completed the review. Thank you for participating in the peer review process . . .

The other sheet was evidently a copy of Albrick's reply:

This manuscript by Cavendish is on an important, even sensational, topic, but his findings are not adequately supported by the experimental evidence. The numbers of subjects in each group are insufficient to allow for proper statistical analysis. Furthermore, Cavendish has failed to allow for the possibility of differential shrinkage of the tissue, or to consider the effects of . . .

The manuscript itself was heavily annotated, especially in the part that described the position of the cell groups in the hypothalamus.

So Albrick knew about Roger's work four years ago! And he got the paper rejected by *Brain Monthly*. Jeff returned the folder to the cabinet, making a mental note to tell Roger about it. But where were the experimental protocols? Time was passing, and the others might be finishing their work with the monkeys. Nervously Jeff scanned the room. A computer terminal sat in the middle of Albrick's desk. Of course! Now Jeff was in his element. He logged on.

> Name? Albrick
> Password?

What password would Albrick use . . . a guy who left his office door open, his filing cabinet unlocked? He tried 'Albrick.' It worked! *Would they were all so dumb,* he thought, as he raced through directories and files. 'Here . . . Protocol . . . CGL, BRM, HB . . . subfile . . . subjID# . . . 24, 25, 26 . . . br, pf, jh.' JH? John Hammond?! Jeff called up John's file. 'Electron microscopy . . . light microscopy . . .' *Boy, he's really interested in John's brain,* thought Jeff. Box HB 12. Jeff soon found the slide box and opened it on the desk. It contained about eighty slides. John's brain, realized Jeff, and he thought of his old friend camping it up at The Turncoat, and how disapproving he'd been. *What a nerd I was, what a stupid closeted self-loathing nerd.* But he had to hurry. Seven of the slides in the middle of the series had been marked with a red grease pencil. The cover glasses of these slides had been marked with a diamond scriber, as if to indicate a particular region of the tissue sections. He grabbed these slides and put them in his pocket. He replaced the slide box on the shelf and switched off the computer. Then he turned off his flashlight and made his way out of the lab.

When he got to the vivarium, everything was quiet. No one was to be seen. The monkeys were watching television, playing idly with their toys, or grooming themselves. When they saw Jeff they started chattering and shaking the bars of their cages. Jeff felt uncomfortable: He fantasized about them getting loose and attacking him. Even rhesus monkeys had formidable canine teeth. He noticed a wall cabinet marked Emergency Restraint. He wondered whether whatever was inside could save him from their attack.

Why hadn't the Many Sparrows done anything? They didn't seem to have freed any monkeys or created any mayhem, they'd just left. He looked at the monkeys more closely, gradually working his way down the row of cages. It was strange . . . not one of them had any scars or stitches or shaved areas on their heads. None of them looked as if they had had any experiments done on them at all. They were just healthy, pampered monkeys. The Libbers must have been disappointed: They'd been looking for monkeys with oozing wounds or with pieces of metal attached to their heads. None of that here. Maybe this was all a cover. Maybe Albrick wasn't doing any monkey operations anymore. He turned to leave, anxious to get out of the building. He felt suddenly ill at ease, like someone left behind by his friends while walking in the woods as darkness begins to fall.

Jeff reopened the door to the corridor and started to walk toward the elevators. At that same moment the elevator doors opened and three men rushed in. Jeff barely had time to recognize Dr Albrick among them. He dashed back into the vivarium, but the men were right after him. He rushed among the cages. Surely there must be another exit! The men burst in after him, setting the monkeys to hysterical screaming. There was no way out. Jeff squeezed himself desperately between two cages, grabbing the bars and pulling the cages into a protective wall in front of him. Two of the men, who were wearing some kind of uniform, pulled at the cages. The monkeys in the cages went wild. One of them sank his teeth into Jeff's fingers; he screamed and let go of the bars. The cages were torn aside and Jeff was grabbed by the security guards. As he struggled, he felt the crunch of glass in his pocket as the brain slides broke into fragments. Finally the guards each held him securely by an arm.

'Damn vandal, damn punk,' yelled Albrick. 'Soft-hearted moron! Here are the monkeys, still in their damned cages, and you'll be sitting behind bars soon too, and you think they'll thank you? Ha, she bit you! Good job, Flossie, good job! You wanted to stay and watch the soaps, right? You didn't want to go joy-riding with this sicko. Animal Lib? Ha! They're in a monkey hotel, luxury suites! But you'll be doing time, no toys for you, you vermin, you criminal, you low-life asswipe—'

'You're the criminal!' screamed Jeff, struggling again to free himself. 'You homophobic fascist bastard, I know what you're doing upstairs!'

'Oho! Oho-ho! A little queer animal lover! The monkeys' fairy friend come to the rescue!' The tangle of blood vessels in Albrick's birthmark were visibly pulsing.

'Yes, I'm queer, I'm a fairy, a fag! And I'm going to tell the world what you're up to. You're ruined, you're dead meat. I'm gay, and I'm staying that way, and you're—'

'Staying that way? We'll see about that, you faggot! James, ketamine! In the cabinet! Ten cc's!' While the guards tightened their grip, Albrick's assistant opened the cabinet and grabbed a syringe. He handed it to Albrick, who snapped the cover off the needle. In one swinging motion he plunged it through Jeff's jeans into the depths of his thigh muscles and ejected the entire contents of the syringe. The pain was searing.

'Aaah! Let me go! What in Chrissakes . . .?'

'Hold him tight! This'll take a minute or two.'

Jeff began to struggle again.

'That's it!' mocked Albrick. 'Get the circulation going, it'll work all the faster.'

'You operated on John Hammond! What did you do to his brain? You killed him, you killed his girlfriend!'

'John Hammond killed his girlfriend, and he killed himself. An unfortunate aberration. Sometimes one can have too much of a good thing. We will do much better . . . with you.'

'Don't you touch me, you freak!'

'Oh, she's so sensitive! Don't worry, sweetie, you're not my type. But we're going to make a man of you, aren't we?'

'We'll put some hair on his chest!' laughed his assistant.

'The girls are going to go crazy about you. You'll love it!' said Albrick.

Jeff tried to lash out with his leg, catching Albrick off-guard. 'Nazi pig!' he yelled.

'Quiet down, you dumb fruit,' said Albrick, wincing from the kick. 'Another ten cc!' He injected the second syringe even more violently than the first. The needle struck bone and Jeff felt the pain explode like a bright flash. But he was already beginning to feel distant and woozy. He felt like an observer of the scene, not a participant. 'Albrick . . . Roger . . .' he burbled. His jaw sagged, and he drooled saliva down his chin.

'Roger? Roger? So you and Cavendish . . .?' Albrick laughed. 'Ha! What a pretty couple! That's delightful. My congratulations! But I see a rocky road ahead, I'm afraid. Hey, he's going under, get him to the OR!'

'Aren't you going to do it by infusion?' asked James.

'No, the old way . . . we need quick results.'

Jeff was consumed by waves of nausea, but he couldn't throw up. The whole room seemed to be sliding diagonally upward and to the right, as his head sagged to the left. He felt intensely cold and started to shake. The guards half led him, half carried him, out of the vivarium. As they marched out, the monkeys started howling and banging their toys against the bars. It was like a scene on Death Row when a prisoner is taken off for execution.

The operating room was just a few steps down the

corridor. Guided by the guards, Jeff lurched through
the doorway. In the center of the room was a stainless
steel table covered by a thin mattress. Overhead was a
bank of lights and an operating microscope that hung
from an angled metal arm, as well as what looked like
an enlarged version of a dentist's drill. Mobile towers
of electronic equipment and an anesthesia machine
stood on one side of the table. Sinks and freezers and
autoclaves lined the walls of the room. Racks of sterile
instruments were on display in glass-fronted cabinets.
The men lifted Jeff onto the table and fastened his body
in place with restraint straps. He grimaced as the
operating lights were turned on, but the warmth they
radiated comforted him. He could follow what was
going on, but he felt unable to act. His hands and feet
were making continuous small writhing movements;
he felt the movements but seemed not to be responsible
for them or capable of stopping them. His mouth was
full of saliva that threatened to choke him; an assistant
hooked a suction line over his lower teeth, and the
saliva went gurgling off down the tubing.

'Set a cell suspension to thaw out,' said Albrick. An
assistant opened a freezer and pulled out a box labeled
'106-NB-TRab.' From the box he took out a small blue
plastic vial and placed it on the countertop. Meanwhile
Albrick was measuring Jeff's head with a caliper. *They're
going to operate on my brain*, thought Jeff. *That's so weird
. . . Why are they doing this? They want to stop this
seasickness, don't they? That's it* . . . He said aloud,
'Seasish,' but Albrick ignored him. He was entering
measurements into a computer. 'Brachycephalic,' he
said, 'the width-length ratio is 81 percent . . . let's see,
standard coordinates corrected by 2 percent in the

vertical and minus 4 percent in the lateral . . . that's . . .'
He entered some more numbers. 'That's anterior 14.7,
lateral 4.2, vertical 20.7. Now convert to polar
coordinates . . .' He pressed some more keys . . . '42.4
degrees lateral, 173.0 degrees anterior. The advance
should be 117.5 millimeters to the hypothalamus from
the brain surface.' Albrick seemed to be losing his anger
as he became absorbed in the technical details of the
procedure.

A stainless steel frame was placed around Jeff's
head. He felt as if he were trapped in a miniature jungle
gym. Metal rods were advanced into his ears until they
lodged snugly in the ear canals. The humming of the
equipment suddenly became fainter. 'Infraorbitals
please, James,' he heard Albrick say in a distant muffled
voice. He saw two levers descending toward his eyes.
Everything was so strange and shiny. *Surely this will
stop the seasickness*, he thought. The levers grasped the
bony ridges under his lower eyelids. Another two bars
were placed in his mouth and then gradually raised,
pushing up against his upper teeth so that his
cheekbones were jammed against the eye-bars. 'Is this
hurting?' he mumbled. 'I think it's hurting him . . . no,
that's me . . . he's the one that's seasick . . . couldn't
you stop the rolling?'

'Do you want the probe electrode, Dr Albrick?' asked
an assistant.

'No, let's go straight in with the micropipette; it's
two a.m. and I want to get some sleep tonight. We can
stimulate through the pipette leads. This way we can
do the whole thing on ketamine.'

Albrick and James went over to the sink to scrub
up, then an assistant helped them on with the gowns

and the gloves and masks. Jeff was dreamily gazing at the ceiling, at the warm lights that beamed down on him. He remembered sunbathing at Black's Beach with Jane, and all the body-builder types who strolled past them on their way to the gay end of the beach, in couples or alone. There he was, with Roger, arm-in-arm. Why doesn't the beach stop rocking? he wondered. Something wet and cold was being daubed on his scalp.

'Lidocaine, please,' said Albrick. A tiny pinprick, then another, way out of sight on the top of his head somewhere. 'Scalpel.' A dull pressure. 'Swab.' More dull pressure. 'Swab . . . retractors . . . cauterize that, will you, James.' A brief sizzle, and the faint aroma of a barbecue drifted into Jeff's consciousness.

'Drill, please,' said Albrick. The whine of the drill, and more pressure, and more barbecue odor as the drill bit raced through the skull. 'Scope, please.' Jeff saw the operating microscope being swung over on its long arm. 'Dura hooks, scalpel.' Another sharp pain, though ever so distant. 'Nice pink cortex,' Albrick muttered to himself, then out loud: 'How's it loading?'

'Smoothly,' said a voice from the side of the room. 'A good batch . . . Ellis swears by it . . . 25,000 cells per microliter and a receptor titer near 43K.'

'Okay, load 40 microliters and we'll inject 5. Put the pipette in the drive . . . careful . . . watch the leads . . . Okay, now tighten gently, don't break the glass, there you go, now the pressure lead . . . ready for a test eject? . . . nitrogen on . . . 10 pounds . . . nothing . . . 20 pounds . . . nothing . . . stop stop stop, it's ejecting, splendid, really smooth . . . okay, back it up into the guard tube, okay, so into the brain we go, tum-di-dum, not too fast and not too slow, tum-di-dum.' Albrick was in his element, enjoying the triumph of precision technology over that messy pit of subjectivity, the human mind. 'Just think, James, for every millimeter the guard tube advances, we're destroying a million neurons in the cerebral cortex. And what difference does that make to this fine young chap? None at all. He has far more cerebral cortex than he knows what to do with, don't you, my friend?' Jeff was vaguely conscious that he was being asked a question, but what was the question? He was floating now, no longer as seasick: the rocking had quieted down a little.

'Forty-three point two millimeters,' said James.

'Okay, the guard tube should be through the corpus callosum. Now advance the pipette.' The stepping motor began to emit a rapid clicking as it drove the glass pipette slowly out of the metal guard tube and deeper into the brain.

'Forty-four . . . forty-five . . . forty-six . . .'

'You know, that guy Cavendish, he's such a fool, such an innocent, you almost have to like him,' mused Albrick. 'He blithely came up with the means to eliminate his whole tribe, and he doesn't even know it. We really must invite him to try a graft or an infusion one day, he'd be ever so grateful, just like this pretty young man is going to be in a week or two.'

Jeff was trying to focus his mind on Albrick's voice. 'Cavendish . . . pretty young man . . . grateful . . .' *What is he talking about?* He listened to the clicking of the stepping motor.

'One hundred and fifteen . . . one hundred and sixteen . . . one hundred and seventeen . . . slow speed . . . point three . . . point four . . . point five . . . motor off. That should do it, Dr Albrick.'

'All right, let's see what we've got here. Try a stimulus, let's see, twenty Hertz, five microamps, ten seconds.'

'Stimulus on.'

Jeff was seized out of his floating state. A mindless anger, a rage enveloped him. 'Goddamn,' he tried to scream, 'you bastards, I'll kill you, I'll kill you . . . all of you.' He struggled to free his head from the stereotaxic apparatus. His eyes bulged, his tongue protruded and turned purple, and the clamps bit into his face and jaw. 'Wait till I get my hands on . . .'

'Off! Off!' yelled Albrick. The switch was turned, and Jeff's rage subsided as fast as it had appeared. He returned to his floating state, perhaps a little closer to reality than before.

'I hate it when we hit the amygdala,' said Albrick with a nervous laugh. 'At least that tells us where we are . . . too far lateral. Back the pipette up into the guard tube and move five millimeters medial.' The high-speed clicking started again.

'Shall I give him more ketamine?' asked one of the assistants. 'He's a little more responsive.'

'No, we'll be done soon, and I want him to be able to run home under his own steam. No sense wasting money on a taxi for the gúy.'

'Ready for the next penetration,' said James.

More clicking. The writhing motions of Jeff's hands and feet were calming down. He managed to say 'Where . . . monthy . . . ?' His hand hurt from the monkey's bite.

'One hundred seventeen point five.'

'Okay, same stimulus.'

'Stimulus on.'

Jagged lightning and shooting stars streaked across Jeff's field of view. He scrunched up his eyes to try to keep out the blazing scene, but it made no difference.

'What's happening?' demanded Albrick. 'Tell us what's happening.' He prodded Jeff in the side to try to bring him nearer to consciousness.

Jeff managed to get out one word: 'Fireworse.'

'Fireworks . . . that's the optic nerve. Okay, stimulus off. We're too far down. Back up three, no, three point five millimeters.'

Clicking again. 'One hundred seventeen . . . sixteen . . . fifteen . . . fourteen . . . we're there.'

'Stimulate again, same parameters.'

'Stimulus on.'

Jeff felt himself transported in a dreamy way to some rapturous scene of lovemaking. He was embracing a man . . . was it Roger, was it John? . . . they were both naked, and the man's hand roamed over his shoulder, his side . . . he smelled the odor of his lover's skin, and a warmth built in his loins, an excitement . . . 'Roger . . .' he murmured.

'Off! Off! Off!' said Albrick. 'That was quite a boner for a little fairy like you.' Jeff's vision faded, his excitement dulled. He began to become a little more alert. He struggled to speak. 'Let me . . . let me . . .'

'Okay folks, we are at ground zero,' said Albrick. 'Let's do it. Give me pressure.'

'Nitrogen line open. Valve at zero pounds.'

'Go to ten pounds.'

'Ten . . . no motion.'

'Fifteen.'

'Fifteen . . . no motion.'

'Twenty.'

'Twenty . . . still no motion.'

Jeff began to stir. He tried to move his right arm up to his face, but the straps held it down securely. He blinked and tried to move his head.

'He's moving . . . do you think he dislodged the pipette tip?'

'Go to thirty!'

'Thirty pounds . . . no motion . . . the pipette must be blocked . . . we should take it out and clear it.' Jeff again tried to squirm his head out of the stereotaxic apparatus. 'Let me go . . . let go . . .'

'Go to fifty!'

'Fifty? If the pipette unblocks he'll get a tankful of nitrogen into his brain.'

'Fifty pounds, dammit!' shouted Albrick. 'Hold him down.' The two assistants tried to prevent Jeff's struggling movements.

'Fifty . . . no motion . . . no motion . . . wait, she's moving . . . damn, damn . . .'

'What happened?'

'The whole lot went in.'

'Forty microliters? Well, that'll certainly do the job.'

'I'll say. If he has any brain left.'

'What's happening . . . let me go . . . let me go!'

'Shut up, faggot, this is for your own good! Turn the nitrogen off.'

'It *is* off.'

'Then back out.'

The clicking began again at high speed.

'The pipette's back in the guard tube,' said James.

'Okay, out with the guard tube, let's sew this guy up before he blows a gasket. Lie still, will you. He'll relax once we have him out of the ear-bars.'

Jeff's hands were struggling clumsily to reach the straps that restrained him. An assistant offered Albrick a needleholder and suture. 'Wait,' said Albrick. 'I have a better idea.'

'What's that?'

'He won't remember a thing of this . . . the ketamine will see to that.'

'So what? We've still got to sew him up.'

'No . . . let's make it an accident . . . a misadventure . . . a very stupid escapade this young man got into, with unfortunate consequences. They'll never see the burr-hole, it's hidden under the scalp muscle. Get him up and back to the vivarium.'

They loosened the straps and tried to get Jeff up off the table, but he was far too woozy to stand. So they carried his limp body out of the operating room and back to the vivarium. There they lay him in a dark corner, where he promptly went to sleep. Albrick found a spray can of paint that the animal-rights activists had left behind, and sprayed slogans across the walls: Animal Rights Now! Stop the Torture! Albrick – Nazi Butcher! He overturned several cages and a cabinet, so that water basins, feed pellets, and other paraphernalia rolled across the floor. Then he pulled the television set from its high platform and let it crash to the floor. The tube imploded. 'Never understood why they needed TV anyway,' he grunted. He maneuvered one of the fallen cages so that it lay near Jeff's head, and he worked one of its bars into the incision in his scalp, smearing the metal with half-dried blood. Then he opened all the monkeys' cage doors. Some of the animals stayed cowering in their cages, but other emerged to explore the room. Albrick led his anxious assistants out of the vivarium. As he left, he took a backward glance. Some of the monkeys were sniffing at others' rear ends. He laughed. 'Let the good times roll,' he said, and closed the door.

CHAPTER FOURTEEN

'**B**roken, I thought you had indicated . . . not pulverized!'

Like a crime boss inspecting the proceeds of a jewelry heist, Dr Leblanc looked dubiously at the dozens of fragments of glass that Roger had emptied onto a sheet of paper in front of him. He turned to Mary. 'Pathologists take apart, dissect, analyze. But putting together, repair, synthesis . . . for that you need a different specialist. Perhaps you know an enthusiast for jigsaw puzzles.' He gazed around his laboratory as if such a person might be hiding under a bench or behind a refrigerator.

'We don't really need to put them together though, do we?' Mary asked. 'Can't we just find the pieces that have INAH3 in them?'

'Possibly so. But that must be Dr Cavendish's task. When I studied neuroanatomy, they did not yet have a structure corresponding to that acronym. In fact, they did not have acronyms at all. It would have been – how shall I say – disrespectful, inelegant. One took the time to employ the full name, to deliver it eloquently, with fine diction, like a *recitatif*. And of course one always included the name of the gentleman who had discovered it. *Le faisceau de Vicq d'Azyr, les grandes cellules superficielles de Tartuferi, le ruban de Reil latéral, le ganglion géniculé du nerf intermédiaire de Wrisberg*. Ah, those were names . . . little poems . . . libretti. "INAH3?" What kind of a name is that?'

Roger was poking around among the fragments. 'It should be next to the third ventricle. Let's collect all the pieces that have ventricle in them . . . it's a clear space, like this one here.'

Leblanc knew what ventricles looked like, but he didn't feel compelled to join the hunt. Instead he sat back and appraised Mary's physiognomy, as she and Roger picked over the fragments. *A fine figure of a woman*, he thought appreciatively. *An excellent Salomé, if she could sing*. Out loud, he said: 'So your young friend . . . is he seriously injured?'

'No, no,' said Roger. 'In fact he's out of the infirmary already. He's resting in his dorm. He was pretty woozy at first, but he just needed a tetanus shot and some cuts cleaned up. He's in big trouble with the college, though. He has to go to a tribunal in a few days . . . what did he call it? . . . the Chamber of Elders. It's probably something like the Spanish Inquisition. very likely he will be expelled, maybe even excommunicated, if that's what the Leviticans call it. It's terrible . . . and it's my fault.'

'He seemed a presentable young man. Why did he get involved in an escapade like that?'

'His main purpose was to get these slides. But it seems he also took it into his head to liberate Albrick's monkeys. Only they didn't take kindly to being liberated. He doesn't remember exactly what happened, but he must have been concussed when one of the monkeys pulled a television set down on top of him. And that must have been when the slides broke. They were in his pocket.'

'Was he by himself?'

'Oh, yes . . . a solo effort,' Roger lied smoothly.

Mary, who was the only one continuing to sort out the fragments of the slides, held one up to Roger. 'This one has some kind of mark on the glass, maybe from a scriber.'

Roger squinted at the fragment, which was only about four millimeters across. 'Yes, it kind of looks like that. Could we put this under the 'scope? It may be that Albrick marked this area as being of special interest.'

The fragment was too small to rest on the microscope stage, so Leblanc took a couple of paper clips and jury-rigged a cradle to hold it. While he was fiddling with this, Mary looked idly around Leblanc's lab. It was a far cry from the spit-and-polish neatness of her Bethesda empire. On one bench, a butcher block and assorted scalpels and forceps were waiting to be cleaned of the dried blood and fragments of tissue with which they were encrusted. Glass specimen jars, sealed with rags and identified with long-since unreadable labels, contained unsavory-looking body parts; from one of the jars, drops of murky fluid fell from time to time onto a pile of unfinished autopsy reports. A yellowing wall chart displayed drawings of fetuses of various ages, while another contained photographs of a variety of knife wounds, along with the weapons that had caused them. As if the pictures were not graphic enough, it seemed that they had been spattered with real blood, for several dark red streaks ran along the front of the chart and continued down the wall beneath.

Some piano music was playing that Mary did not recognize.

Mary had received a lot of conflicting information since her arrival Sunday night. On Monday morning – was it just yesterday? – she had gone to visit Albrick, expecting to present the shipping records and see Albrick collapse in guilt and shame. Far from it. 'Oh, my goodness, I feel terrible to have caused you this concern,' he had said. 'I should have sent a revised budget . . . I have no excuse! We use the human headholder for the largest macaques . . . it gives us more room to place the electrode carriers.' And he had shown her a videotape of exactly that . . . a large rhesus monkey in the human-sized headholder, with all kinds of apparatus attached to the rails. Mary had felt unbelievably stupid. The smoking gun had turned into a piddling water pistol. Albrick smoothly led the conversation to other matters, showing her some recent results, asking her about funding prospects, and bemoaning the animal-rights break-in. And he tried to create the impression that he thought she was just dropping in on some West coast tour she was doing, not that she had crossed the country for this sole purpose. But Mary knew all about face-saving protocol, and she knew that Albrick had made a complete fool of her.

Yesterday evening, though, everything had changed again when she had dinner with Roger. He told her of the true reason behind Jeff's break-in and the fact that they had recovered the broken slides. Maybe there *was* something to Roger's suspicions after all. And they had agreed to go over to Leblanc's lab to check them out.

'Yes, I think this is INAH3, over to the left,' said

Roger. 'It's just above the tip of the paraventricular nucleus. It looks a little strange, though. What are all those small cells?'

Leblanc took another look. 'They are certainly unusual . . . a very undifferentiated appearance.' He switched to a higher-power objective lens. 'Most curious . . . are you sure that this specimen is from the young man we are talking about, John Hammond?'

'I believe so . . . Jeff knew which slides to take. But why?'

'Well, these cells . . . I would not expect to see them in an adult. Dr Braddock, you are a cancer expert, are you not? Perhaps you could give us your opinion.'

Mary squirmed onto the stool and peered at the specimen. 'They certainly look like malignant cells . . . the nuclei are very polymorphic. They've infiltrated most of the area on the left, and there are some over on the right too, a little more differentiated. There are a few mitotic figures . . . they're definitely dividing, though not at a high rate, I'd guess. But the type of cancer . . . I have no idea. It's not breast cancer, of course. That's the only kind I know much about, really. Do you think it's metastatic, or is it some kind of brain tumor?'

Leblanc took another look. 'If this wasn't an adult, I would swear that these are neuroblastoma cells. The appearance is absolutely characteristic.'

Roger looked quizzical. 'Neuroblastoma . . . that's a kind of brain cancer, isn't it?'

'A brain cancer, yes, but seen only in fetuses and young infants. It arises from neuroblasts, the primitive cells that give rise to neurons in the developing brain. After the formation of neurons is complete, at about two years of age, there are no neuroblasts remaining.

143

So it is impossible to develop a neuroblastoma, after that age . . . quite impossible. And yet the appearance is very suggestive. We should write this up for the *Journal of Neuropathology*. Or perhaps the *Zeitschrift für allgemeine Nervenheilkunde*. The editor is a good friend of mine . . . an excellent bassoonist.'

Roger stared at Mary. 'No wonder Albrick didn't want me to see this.'

'What do you mean? You think he induced this cancer somehow?'

'No . . . he injected it. These must be the cells they're culturing in those roller tubes. It's incredible, but it has to be what he's doing. He showed me the results in monkeys. He said they hadn't done any humans, but obviously he has done one at least . . . John Hammond. And probably more.'

'But why would cancer cells do anything? Wouldn't they just destroy that part of the brain? Why would they change someone's sexual orientation?'

'Well, he's altered the cells in some way so that they develop into neurons once they're in the brain. That may not be too hard. After all, neuroblasts normally develop into neurons. He must have incorporated some genetic switch into them so that they lose their invasive properties after a while and grow processes and form synapses and so on. He told me so many lies, I'm not sure what was true and what was false. He told me they were normal human brain cells, from aborted fetuses, modified with a gene for a testosterone receptor that was permanently switched on. The part about them being normal cells was obviously a lie, but maybe the other part is true . . . maybe having that receptor causes the cells to lose their cancerous properties once they're in brain tissue and exposed to testosterone.'

'And how do you imagine that he could have got these cells into John Hammond's brain?' asked Leblanc.

'He injected them stereotaxically, while John was under anesthesia. John thought he was having some sort of brain recording done . . . to check the changes that were happening as he became heterosexual. He was being treated by Sue Forrester, you remember. Probably Forrester has no idea what Albrick's doing . . . she thinks it's *she* who's making these guys straight, by her covert sensitization mumbo-jumbo. She's Albrick's cover. And Jeff was going to be Albrick's next victim.'

'Well, if he's expelled, he'll have saved himself from that fate, at least,' said Mary.

'He injected the cells?' asked Leblanc. 'So he must have made a burr-hole through the skull somewhere . . .'

'There *was* a burr-hole, at the vertex, just to the right of the sagittal suture. I saw it at the autopsy.' Leblanc looked somewhat embarrassed, presumably by his own failure to spot the hole. Roger hurriedly added: 'It was partially healed over, but there was still a translucent spot . . . you could see it from certain angles.'

Mary was seized with an idea. 'Do you think this could explain what happened to John . . . the murder, I mean? Could it have made him prone to violence?'

'I suppose it could. There's clearly some spread of the cells out of INAH3. If they reached the amygdala they might have increased his aggressiveness. Especially with the testosterone receptors permanently switched on. Jeff said something about that . . . he said John had become more aggressive generally during the same period that he became heterosexual.'

Mary turned to Leblanc. 'May I use your phone?' she asked. 'I have a horrible thought.'

Leblanc pointed out the telephone, which lay half-concealed under a large book entitled *Handbook of General Toxicology – Volume 15: Industrial Alkaloids.* While she was making the call, Roger and Leblanc examined other pieces of the broken slides. It was clear that the neuroblastoma cells were concentrated in INAH3 on the right side of the hypothalamus, but some of the cells seemed to have migrated out to other locations, including the amygdala. In addition, Leblanc pointed out a faint vertical line in the brain tissue above the hypothalamus. 'Reactive astrocytes,' said Leblanc. 'In a straight line like that . . . that must be the damage caused by the track of a needle . . . the needle Professor Albrick used to inject the neuroblastoma cells. By the appearance of the cells – the lack of microglia especially – I would say that the injection must have been made several months before Mr Hammond's death . . . several months at least.'

'That figures,' said Roger. 'His conversion therapy was last year.'

Mary came back from the phone. 'I put a call in to Bob Stephens, the pathologist at Bethesda General. He did the autopsy on Paul Aconda . . . the guy who attacked me. They should have done the brain histology by now. He'll call back.'

Leblanc looked quizzical. 'You imagine that he also was injected with these cells?'

'Wouldn't that make sense? He was at Levitican.'

'But was he homosexual?'

'I have no idea. But he certainly became pathologically aggressive.'

'Hold on,' said Roger. 'Aconda was in the ROTC here, right?'

'Right. That's just the point. There's an epidemic of this kind of thing.'

'But you're not going to tell me that every one of the ROTC graduates who's been involved in these incidents was a gay guy who Albrick injected, like John Hammond?'

'That's what I'm thinking.'

'I don't believe it. *Hundreds* of brain operations . . . and no one knew about it? Besides, how many gay guys could they have had . . . we're only about five percent of the population, at most. And surely most of the gay students have sense enough to keep it a secret.'

The phone rang. It was Stephens. Leblanc switched on the speakerphone.

'Bob?' Mary began. 'Thanks for calling back. I wanted to ask about the autopsy on Aconda. Did you get the brain slides back already?'

'It's funny you called. I got them yesterday, and there's something really remarkable.'

'Neuroblastoma?'

'How the *hell* did you know?'

'We have a similar case here. On the right side, in the anterior hypothalamus?'

'They're all over. Hypothalamus, amygdala, nucleus of the stria terminalis, nucleus accumbens. Even a few cells in the cortex . . . especially the hippocampus. Both sides.'

Roger broke in. 'Roger Cavendish here. Don't you have a main focus in anterior hypothalamus on one side . . . left or right?'

'No, it's pretty diffuse. The highest concentration is

in those regions I mentioned. But there are cells elsewhere, too. We even saw them in the spinal cord, way down in the sacral segments.'

'Is there a burr-hole in his skull? We think the cells were injected.'

'Injected? What on earth do you mean? No, there's no burr-hole.'

'Are you sure? Maybe partially healed over?'

'Absolutely sure. I'm not totally incompetent, you know.'

Roger and Mary avoided looking in Leblanc's direction. But Leblanc was too interested by Stephens's description to take umbrage. 'Leblanc here. What about a needle track?' he asked.

'Hi, Jean-Michel . . . how's the fiddling? No, I didn't see a track. Could have missed that, though . . . we didn't examine every section. But what's the deal with your case? He was *injected*?'

Mary broke in. 'Bob, I'll call you as soon as I get back. There's some funny business going on but we don't have the details yet. It'd be helpful if you'd keep this to yourself for a couple of days.'

'Okay, but don't forget, because at this point I'm mystified.'

'I won't . . . bye for now.'

After Mary hung up, the three of them sat there in silence for a few moments. Then Roger said: 'This is quite a puzzle. Both Hammond and Aconda became pathologically violent . . . with a sexual slant. Both have neuroblastoma cells in their brains, cells which couldn't have gotten there by any natural process. Hammond was definitely injected: We have the burr-hole and the needle track leading down to the spot where the cells are located. So surely Aconda must have been injected, too?'

'Perhaps he did indeed miss the burr-hole,' ventured Leblanc hopefully. 'Perhaps the operation was several years ago, and the hole had healed more completely?'

'But the cells were everywhere,' Mary interjected. 'Down at the bottom of the spinal cord, for heaven's sake. Could the cells have migrated that far?'

'I don't think so,' said Roger. 'I'm at a loss.'

'If we assume that they *were* injected into the hypothalamus, and the burr-hole healed over, perhaps some of the cells remained cancerous and spread through the bloodstream . . . they metastasized, in other words?'

'Tumors in the brain rarely metastasize,' said Leblanc. 'The cancer cells seem to have a hard time getting out of the primary tumor and into the bloodstream.'

'The bloodstream . . .' mused Roger. 'What if the cells were injected into the bloodstream in the first place?'

'Well, we know that's not what happened in John Hammond's case,' said Leblanc.

'Yes, yes,' said Mary, 'That *would* make sense. In Aconda's case, Albrick simply injected the cells into his bloodstream. That would be so easy. And that would explain why they're all over the brain, not just in the hypothalamus.'

'Yes, it all fits together,' said Roger. 'The fact that they're neuroblastoma cells gives them the power to migrate out of the bloodstream into the substance of the brain. And the genetic manipulation – the testosterone receptors on the cell surface – that makes them accumulate in the brain regions where testosterone-sensitive cells are normally located . . . the hypothalamus, the amygdala, the sacral segments of the spinal cord.'

'Why the sacral segments?'

'In men, those segments have groups of motor neurons that innervate the penis. They're testosterone-sensitive. Obviously, the injected cells accumulated anywhere in the nervous system where there were testosterone-sensitive cells. Albrick believes the receptor is a cell-recognition molecule, and not just a steroid transducer. Looks like he's right.'

'You know,' said Mary, 'Albrick's probably been injecting these cells into every cadet in the ROTC. I'm willing to bet that every one of the ROTC graduates who's been involved in the harassment incidents has got these cells in his brain. It's absolutely criminal. He's creating a band of zombies.'

'But why?' Leblanc interjected. 'Why would he be doing such a thing?'

'All kinds of reasons. First, he's eliminating any homosexual tendencies the cadets might have . . . and he really hates homosexuality. And second, he probably reckons he's making them more masculine, more macho, and so better soldiers.'

'But what a risk to take. If he were found out – and it looks like we have found him out – then he's going to face the most serious charges.'

'He's paranoid,' Roger chimed in. 'He's been thwarted before, more than once, when he's tried to put his theories into practice. And he has a strong sense that his research has a social purpose, a mission . . . the fulfillment of *his* goals for the human race. He probably knew it was hopeless to try and get permission. And it was just bad luck that he got found out. He had a great story, a great cover, his assistants are totally complicit . . . that guy James anyway. Probably a lot of them don't even know what's going on.'

'But how could he inject the cadets? Even an intravenous injection is something people take notice of. There'd have to be some reason for it.'

'Maybe they get some routine injections, vaccinations or whatever, and Albrick organizes that. He could just mix in the cultured cells.'

'An intravenous vaccine? I thought that vaccines were injected into muscles, or under the skin?'

'There is one vaccine that is given intravenously,' said Mary. 'It's an experimental AIDS vaccine called MAIT . . . it stands for Monoclonal Anti-Idiotype-T-cell vaccine . . . it's made of live T-cells. It's supposed to "educate" the person's own T-cells to resist HIV. I could find out if it's being used here. If so, it would be easy enough to add the neuroblastoma cells, or substitute them and not inject the vaccine cells at all. No one would be the wiser.'

'So what do you plan to do?' asked Leblanc.

'Blow the whistle,' said Roger. 'Put Albrick out of business once and for all.'

'But, excuse me, where is your evidence? You have these . . . a few pieces of broken glass. They could have come from anywhere. How do they prove anything?'

'And the burr-hole?' asked Mary.

'Cremated, the day before yesterday, up on Northern California.'

'What about Aconda's brain?'

'How can we pin that on Albrick?' said Roger. 'One

guy with a rare cancer. There's no evidence that it was caused by anyone, let alone by Albrick. We've got to find proof positive.'

'The proof is wherever they're injecting the cadets. Let me talk with Frinton,' said Mary. 'This may take more that we can do by ourselves. We need the smoking gun . . . or rather, the smoking syringe.'

CHAPTER FIFTEEN

Jeff stared blankly through the window of his room at the midday scene. The sun bathed the grassy quadrangle in glaring light. Students, singly or in small groups, strode purposefully to their prayers, their classes, or their lunch, casting hardly a shadow as they walked. Jeff, who until a week ago had been immersed in these same activities, now watched them from the shade of his room. He was suspended from almost every aspect of college life . . . evening prayers were the only time he spent with his fellow students. In a few days' time he would attend a Chamber hearing, and he would be expelled from Levitican. For doing something of which he had no memory.

The familiar sounds of a Judy Garland album, coming from the CD player behind him, did little to improve Jeff's mood. He turned away from the window and moved toward the mirror that was attached to the door of his closet. By bending his head down and peering upward, he could see part of the scalp wound that he had sustained in Albrick's vivarium. He prodded it gingerly . . . it seemed to be healing fine. His hand was healing too: Two fingers were still stiff and sore, but the bite marks were less distinct, and the swelling had mostly subsided. The doctor at the infirmary had cleaned and sewn up his wounds, and he had given Jeff a tetanus shot, while two campus policemen stood by. They had been intending to charge him with criminal trespass and hand him over to the Cabrillo city police, but Albrick himself came by and said he wouldn't press charges. 'He's been punished enough already,' Albrick had remarked cryptically. Jeff was kept under observation at the infirmary for twenty-four hours, in case his concussion had caused any internal bleeding, and then he was allowed to go back to his room. The University authorities started their own wheels turning, and Jeff was on the road to expulsion.

Jeff remembered what his plan had been: to join Many Sparrows on their break-in and to find the slides of John Hammond's brain. And the slides – or what was left of them – were in his pocket, so he must have succeeded in that part of the plan. But he had no recollection of that, or of how he got back to the animal quarters. He remembered nothing between the previous evening, when he and the others were making last-minute plans for the break-in, and the following morning when he was woken by a janitor, lying amidst the wreckage of Albrick's monkey room.

He had seen Scott briefly. Scott had told him that he and the other Sparrows had left without touching the monkeys. So he, Jeff, must have done it all. It was weird. It wasn't his style to write Nazi Butcher and stuff like that on walls. And why would he have done anything if the monkeys were completely healthy? He racked his brains, but he only exacerbated the headache that he had been suffering from, on and off, since the accident. He told Scott and the others to stay away, lest they incriminate themselves by being seen spending time with him. One martyr was enough.

Why had he gone off the deep end? There was only one explanation: It must have been what he had found out in Albrick's office. Something about John – evidence that Roger was right, probably, evidence that Albrick *had* injected brain cells into him. And now Roger was telling him that the slides showed exactly that – John's brain was full of foreign cells. He must have become enraged with Albrick and chosen this way to exact revenge. But it was so unlike him.

Yet it wasn't all bad, what had happened. Over the last twelve days Jeff's life had been on fast-forward, or so it seemed. It was as if some process of growing up, long blocked, had been released. He was gay, and he was going to remain gay – that much was clear to him now. For if it took more than psychotherapy or prayer or willpower to change – if it took replacing part of his brain – then Jeff knew that he was never meant to be straight. And maybe he was never meant to be Levitican, for that matter. He tried to imagine life outside the church: life without limits, but without guidance either. No Elders, no Dr Forrester – just his own conscience. It was scary, but not all bad.

Jeff meandered over to his desk, most of which was occupied by his computer and its numerous accessories. On the top of his printer was perched a photograph of a sculpture: Jean d'Aire, in sackcloth, noose around his neck, awaiting his death. Somber but unbowed, he stared straight ahead. He seemed unaware of his companions, who clutched their brows in despair or gestured their tortured farewells. In his huge hands, which dangled almost to his knees, he cradled a key, a key massive enough to open the gates of Calais. Jeff turned the card over and read: 'In his darkest hour, it turned out well for Jean. Jeff, may it do so for you too. Your friend – Roger.'

Roger, who had come into his life and changed everything! He had apologized, over and over again, as if he had been responsible for what had happened. He hadn't. Jeff knew that he himself had chosen his own way. Why, he had forced himself on Roger at the lecture, and afterward had volunteered to accompany him back to his rooms. He had made some feeble efforts to avoid him, at Dr Forrester's urging, but in reality he had wanted to be with him, right from the beginning. And the break-in: Roger never suggested that to him.

Jeff tried to visualize Roger's face. He had a poor visual memory, and he had a hard time summoning up the image, even though he went through their every encounter. He wished that he had a photograph, and then, suddenly, he realized that he could get one. He switched on his computer and logged on to the student activities bulletin board. The poster for Roger's lecture was still on file, and he downloaded it and printed it out. The bland publicity shot was in black and white. Roger pinned it up on the wall, then he went back to the computer, transferred the file to a graphics application, and began trying out different hair colors and skin tones. After four or five more-or-less naturalistic versions, Jeff started to go for more startling effects. Violet hair and green skin, with a pink and brown tie. Blue skin and bright red lips, with white hair against an orange background. Then he went back to the black-and-white version and started playing with Roger's features . . . shrinking or expanding his nose, tilting his ears, making him smile more or less. Soon the wall was plastered with twenty or thirty images of the scientist. Jeff walked up and down, trying to choose his favorite image. He settled on a freakishly colored version and stood contemplating it for a few moments. Then he kissed Roger's image full on his vermilion lips.

Jeff started backward, shocked at himself. He stood there in a daze for a minute or so, while Judy Garland crooned on in the background. He was shaking a little, and rocking on his feet, and his headache was throbbing.

After a while Jeff turned away from the psychedelic images. He went to his bathroom cabinet and found a bottle of aspirin; he took two and chased them down with a mouthful of water which he drank directly from the faucet. He lay down on his bed and closed his eyes, but the headache didn't get better. After a few minutes of tossing and turning, he got up again and started pacing up and down his room. 'Damn, damn,' he said to himself. 'Damn Roger, damn Albrick, damn Forrester, damn Levitican.' He clenched his fists and smashed them down on his desk. 'Why is this happening to me? Why?' Then he marched over to the tape player and ripped the Garland album out of the machine. He scanned the CDs and tapes that were arrayed along his bookshelf, next to his computer texts. He picked out a CD at random and loaded the disc into the player, dropping its plastic box onto the floor. A speed-metal beat filled the room, pounding in synchrony with his headache. 'Damn Roger!' he snarled again, and he began ripping down the images he had just taped up a few minutes before. 'Damn him!' He tore the pictures into shreds and threw them around his room. He stared blindly at the scattered fragments, and among them the broken CD box, with its title: *Motorhead*.

CHAPTER SIXTEEN

'This is our worst nightmare come true,' said Frinton, staring blindly at an ormolu clock on the mantelpiece. 'We thought something like this might become possible in ten or twenty years . . . that we'd have time to prepare against it, to have a national debate on the issue. We thought that by the time this thing became a reality, maybe homophobia would be a thing of the past . . . or at least that we would have had the chance to express our point of view. But it's here, now, and people are dying because of it. AIDS? Ha! That will seem like nothing by the time this holocaust is over. And I thought it was just Albrick giving speeches. What a fool I was! We must act now, and decisively – our whole community is at risk.'

A murmur of assent went around the table. Tony said, 'We must notify the Coalition.'

'I'll call Berson tonight,' said Frinton.

'Gentlemen,' said Mary, 'I have no desire to minimize what may be the dangers here. Indeed, I came here to impress them on you. But I ask you to consider carefully what may be the best strategy to deal with them. At this point, our hard evidence is very limited. I am convinced that one gay man, John Hammond, was subjected to a graft of genetically altered neuroblastoma cells in an attempt to change his sexual orientation. The attempt was successful, but he later became pathologically violent and committed suicide. I believe, as does Roger Cavendish, that this brain graft was performed illegally by Professor Albrick, but the evidence is very slender and highly technical. As things stand, there is no way we could pin this on him. We have one other man, the one who attacked me, who also very probably received neuroblastoma cells, but he was never gay, so far as we know, and he apparently did not receive a graft directly into his brain. We do know that he was formerly an ROTC cadet at Levitican. Again, there is no way we can make a definite connection to Albrick. Finally, we know that there is an epidemic of violence going on, violence against women and against gays and lesbians, and that the perpetrators of these violent acts are also former Levitican cadets. Our suspicion is that Albrick has been injecting these altered cells into the bloodstream of the cadets on a routine basis, under the guise of administering an experimental HIV vaccine. But we cannot prove any of this. That is why I am coming to you . . . an informal group of people, who might be able to provide informal assistance.'

'Cavendish,' said Luke, 'is he sound?'

'In his science? Yes, I believe so. Scientifically sound.'

'And his intentions? Isn't he just another Albrick, wrapped in a gay man's hide?'

'I don't believe so. Not anymore, anyway. He's been working hard to expose Albrick for the last two weeks. None of this would have come out if it weren't for him. But he probably didn't have much clue what was going to come out of his research when he started it. Probably never even thought about it. And that was not sound.'

'So what is this informal assistance that you want from us?' asked Frinton.

'We need a sample of the material that is being injected into the cadets. To see whether it indeed contains neuroblastoma cells.'

'Sounds like another mission for Marta,' said Ted, who was still wearing his moiré silk suit.

'I could ask her if she would be willing to help,' said Frinton.

'That would be very useful,' said Mary. 'The point is, though, we need to be very circumspect until we get this evidence. My request is that you treat the whole matter with complete confidentiality, until we have hard evidence in the bag. Otherwise, Albrick will simply clam up and put his program on ice until it's safe to start again.'

'And so we're to let the rapes and murders and gay-bashings go on?' asked Luke.

'Well, I'm not sure that nailing Albrick will do anything about the people he's already injected. We can't really uninject them. That's part of the problem.'

'But if they were identified, they could be examined, monitored, counseled, whatever. Detained if necessary.'

'Give us a couple of weeks, please. We have the opportunity here to really get to the bottom of things, and hopefully to put Albrick out of commission for keeps. What Cavendish and I can do, and your Marta . . . no police or gay-rights groups or anyone else can do. Give us the chance.'

Frinton's group gave their assent, and after a little more talk, they took their leave one by one. Sleepy chauffeurs snapped awake, and a procession of expensive automobiles glided down the bumpy grade to the Sunset Strip. Frinton and Mary watched them from the vine-covered balcony.

'Why are you doing this, Mary?' Frinton asked. 'You've been here ten days. You're endangering your job, your promotion, your whole career. Why don't you leave it to Cavendish?'

'I'm exorcising a demon, Jas,' Mary replied. 'I want the horror to go away.'

CHAPTER SEVENTEEN

Roger was tired, but not relaxed enough to go to sleep. He slumped into his armchair, turned on the TV, and opened a soda. 'Please give a warm welcome to . . . Chad!' said the talkshow host, and a multiply pierced and tattooed teenager, his head shaved except for five green spikes arranged Mohawk-fashion along the midline of his head, strutted onto the set, to be greeted by a chorus of boos and hisses. Disregarding the audience, he sat down in the one empty seat, next to a white girl with dreadlocks, broken teeth, and a syphilitic grin. 'Chad, excuse our audience,' said the host, 'but your fiancé Nora has just told us that you've been seeing someone behind her back and it's *her own mother*, Nelly. What do you have to say to her about that?'

Chad turned to his girlfriend 'You're a –*bleep*–ing liar! *You're* the one who's sleeping around . . . and with your own –*bleep*–ing father! I saw you giving him a –*bleep*–ing –*bleep*– in the garage last Sunday.' The audience jumped to their feet and erupted in cheers and synchronized hand-waving.

Just as Roger's mind was going nicely out of focus, there was a knock and a hesitant 'Roger?' from the corridor. With an effort, he got up again and opened the door. 'Jeff!' he said with a smile, 'How's things? Come in, come in, it's really good to see you.'

'How was the lecture?' Jeff asked. As he entered the room he looked back to see if anyone had been watching. Roger muted the TV.

'Fine, this time. No interruptions, no street theater, no ROTC. Everyone listened quietly, and they applauded politely at the end.'

'I came round an hour ago, but you weren't back.'

'Some of the Life Sciences faculty took me to dinner. We went off campus . . . so we could drink wine with our meal. Just as well: I had to listen to Angela Forte for an hour. You know what her research is? She's testing forty-five thousand different species of dung beetle for their ability to digest dog doo. It's her idea for cleaning up the streets of America. But so far, none of them can do it. There's something about dog food, apparently, that doesn't agree with them . . . the preservatives, she thinks. She has a grant from Ralston Purina to figure it out.'

'I think I'd rather step in dog shit than on some huge beetle and have that stuff come squishing out of it.'

'Well, yes, but she's thought of that. She plans to breed a beetle that only comes out between two and five in the morning. A sort of night-sanitation patrol. But she's having trouble holding on to her graduate students. They don't like cruising the streets of East Cabrillo picking up dog turds for their experiments. How's the headache?'

'Still there. It comes and goes. Pretty bad right now.'

'I'm sorry. Have a soda and watch some TV.'

Jeff took a can and wandered over to Roger's writing table, where several brain atlases were laid out.

'What are all these for?' he asked.

'I'm supposed to be helping Albrick with a project,' Roger said. 'But at this point, it's just a way of staying on here a while.'

'You're staying? I thought I would be saying goodbye . . . now you've done the lecture. I'm so glad.' Jeff flushed, and quickly added, 'But why?'

'We're going to try and get the dirt on Albrick . . . prove what he's doing here.'

'What he did to John?'

'That, and what he's doing to the ROTC cadets. Mary saw Jasper Frinton a couple of days ago . . . a gynecologist. He's gay, he lives in West Hollywood. He's connected with the Act Out! group . . . the activists who disrupted my lecture the first time around. The people who are responsible for bringing us together.' Roger laughed. 'Frinton and some of his friends bankroll their activities.'

'So?'

'So, Frinton's getting one of them to try to get evidence of what's happening with the ROTC. Maybe we can blow their whole cover. That would finish Albrick.'

'I hope so. Just don't involve me in it.'

'Jeff . . .' Roger put his arm on the younger man's shoulder. 'I'm devastated by what happened to you, you know that.'

'Yes, that wasn't what I meant. I just mean, I really can't help you, at this point. Unless with my computer somehow.'

'You know, if we can expose Albrick for what he is, that might change things for you. I mean, the break-in would be justified, kind of. Not the monkey part, but getting the slides. In fact, you could become quite the hero.'

'I'm not optimistic. I've been trying to make plans, for . . . for the hereafter.'

'You mean there's life after Levitican?'

'There's going to have to be.'

'So can you think calmly about that . . . about everything changing in your life?'

'I can't think calmly about anything . . . not Levitican, not my career, not the gay thing. Especially not the . . . the gay thing.'

'Tell me about it.'

'Everything keeps changing. One minute it seems like I really accept being gay, that it's really me and I'm proud of it and I want to stay that way; the next minute it seems totally disgusting, totally sick and perverted. Sometimes I really think maybe I'm not gay anymore . . . that it was all a crazy, crazy nightmare, and I'm waking up at last. And you're so tied up in it. When I feel like I'm not gay, then I get really mad at you . . . I feel like I hate you, almost like I want to smash your face in, actually. I'm sorry. And when I feel like I *am* gay, like right now, then I feel like I . . . that I really like you a lot.' Jeff blushed again. 'And these headaches on top of everything.'

'Well, I like *you* a lot. I certainly hope you don't smash my face in. I mean, I understand that you're in turmoil, it's not an easy transition to make after so many years of buying into the Levitican line.'

'I suppose that's what it is. Say, do you think you could give me a scalp massage? I think it might help my headache.'

'Sure. Sit down and watch Jerry Springer.' Jeff sat

down and focused on the show, while Roger stood behind him and started working on his scalp. 'I'm trying to remember my gross anatomy . . . let's see, this is the temporalis muscle here, starting on the scalp and running down to the jaw, and the masseter muscle is right here, in front of the ear. These two muscles are responsible for a lot of headaches . . . when you're so stressed out you start clenching your jaw a lot, and they go into spasm. They're certainly tense right now. Here, feel right here.' Roger took Jeff's hand and guided his fingers to a spot in front of his left earlobe. 'Feel here . . . now clench your teeth really hard . . . feel that? Now let your jaw go loose, let it just hang down . . . feel the difference? That's the way they should be all the time, except when you're eating. Now let me massage that a bit . . . how does that feel?'

'Good, thanks,' said Jeff. 'Hey, what's going on there?' he added, pointing at the TV screen. A fight had broken out on the stage, and technicians were trying to separate the combatants. Jeff grabbed the remote and clicked the sound back on.

'Sit down, sit down, everyone, please!' Springer was yelling over the roar of the audience. Some semblance of order was gradually restored.

'You don't need to avoid where the cut was,' Jeff said, keeping his eyes on the screen. 'It's healed fine; it's not sore anymore.'

'Okay, fine, I wasn't sure.' Roger's fingers started encroaching on the region of Jeff's wound.

'Mrs Metcalf,' Jerry Springer was saying, 'we have a problem here. Nora and Chad are making some very serious charges, charges that concern your husband Paul . . . Mr Metcalf, sit down please, sit down, thank you very much. Let me put it this way: You may not know for a fact what's been happening over the last few months, but to help us all understand better what's going on, tell us, is it *possible*, do you think, that your husband has been doing things with his own daughter . . . things that no father should even think of doing?'

'Naa, i' *ain't* bleedin' possible,' snarled the woman, who sounded like she was straight off the plane from London's East End. ''Cos that slut ain't 'is daugh'ah . . . I 'ad 'er wivve bloke wot installed de cable-telly.' Mr Metcalf collapsed to the floor, and the audience screamed their pleasure and began dancing in the aisles.

'A clean kill,' Roger commented approvingly. 'The crowd awards her both ears and the tail. How's it feeling now? Your muscles seem a bit more relaxed.'

'Good,' said Jeff, clicking off the sound again. 'You know, being gay would have to be pretty bad . . . to be worse than that.'

'Hey, there are plenty of good reasons for being gay, but cynicism isn't one of them. Anyway, I don't think Jerry's guests can be quite typical. Some of my best friends are straight . . . well, maybe not, but I do know one or two straight people. And what about Mary and her husband? They're happily married, as far as I know. And what about your parents?'

'They're fine . . . I mean they love each other and all. They've been together forever. Sometimes I think my Dad pays the price for it, though.'

'Like how?'

'Oh, you know, he's kind of downtrodden, as if he's given up on a lot of things . . . dreams and stuff. I think a part of him really wants to bust loose, but it won't happen.'

'Won't it shake them up, when they find out about you?'

'About my leaving Levitican?'

'Well, that of course, but I meant, about your being gay?'

'They know already.'

'They know? Since when?'

'Since about three years ago. I told them. Of course, I told them that I wanted to change, which I did then, and they supported that, of course . . . especially my mother. They met with Dr Forrester a couple of times. Now I'm going to have to tell them that I'm not going to change; that may be harder for her to accept.'

'If you're not a Levitican anymore, you won't be bound by their rules, will you? Wouldn't she see that?'

'I'm being booted out of the University, but not out of the Church. That's a decision that I have to make for myself, if I want to. Basically, I'm going to leave that till later.'

'So as for being gay, you're happy with that, right now at least?'

'Right now I am, yes, very much. You can massage harder there, maybe you'll break up some of the scar tissue.'

'That's what I'm trying to—'

'What?'

Roger fell silent. He was moving the scalp to and fro in the region of Jeff's wound, feeling the underlying contour of the skull.

'What is it?'

'There's a hole right here, at the back end of the scar.'

'A hole?'

'A small round hole in the skull, made by a drill. Oh, Jeff . . .'

'What, what?'

'They injected you!'

CHAPTER EIGHTEEN

Marta was standing in the line of cadets, trying not to draw attention to herself. She certainly looked the part; her camouflage uniform was the real thing, and she could pass as a man even without a disguise: The glued-on mustache was really unnecessary. She could talk something like a man too, if need be, though she hoped not to have to do too much talking. Only one thing worried her – she smelled like a woman. And in the hot, crowded mess hall she was working up quite a sweat. Even her breasts, bound severely to her chest with Ace bandages, seemed to be dripping small rivers of perspiration. Antiperspirant could do only so much. She tried to relax.

The ROTC had a strange notion of interior decoration, she thought. The centerpiece of the hall, dominating the south side, was an enormously enlarged, grainy photograph of a charging Marine, who had just jumped a muddy trench and was now plunging his bayonet into the guts of a surprised-looking Japanese infantryman. On either side of this inspiring work were arrayed all kinds of weapons of individual destruction: swords, rifles, carbines, and hand-grenades; even an ancient Gatling gun had somehow been riveted to the wall, its nine rusting muzzles pointed in the general direction of the college library. The opposite side of the hall was filled with long lists of names in ornate gilt lettering. Marta couldn't make out whether they were ROTC graduates who had made the ultimate sacrifice for their country, or merely the football teams of yesteryear. But she could read the inscription that ran along the top of the wall: A HUNDRED OF YOU SHALL PUT TEN THOUSAND TO FLIGHT.

The two men in front of her seemed oblivious to her presence. They were shuffling slowly forward as the cadets at the front of the line got their shots. 'Hey, Gary,' one of them called out to a cadet who had just been injected. 'How was it?'

'Painful, but worth it,' he said wryly, holding a piece of gauze in the crook of his flexed arm. Then he added, in a stage whisper loud enough for the whole hall to hear, 'Finally I can take it in the ass and not worry about rubbers.' There was a general uproar of laughter.

'Right on,' exclaimed a cadet further up the line. 'Nothing like the feel of a juicy tool slipping past that sphincter, eh, Gary?'

'Hey, how about a butt-fucking party tonight?' chimed in another cadet. 'HIV-positive personnel welcome.'

'Cut the crap, Sellings,' barked another cadet who was some kind of junior officer. He was standing next to the man who was doing the injections: His job was to rub the cadets' arms with alcohol swabs.

A third man was entering data at a terminal. He said: 'Who knows if this stuff even works? Are there any findings yet?'

The man doing the injections laughed. It was James,

who, like his boss, was an ROTC officer as well as a neuroscientist. 'This gives good protection against AIDS, believe you me. The best.' He was taking preloaded syringes one at a time from a cooler, fitting a needle, and injecting the cadets assembly-line style.

Marta peered over the shoulder of the man in front of her. 'Name and number?' asked the man at the terminal.

'Sir, Rawlings, sir. Forty-eight-oh-six-eighty, sir.' James put the needle into the antecubital vein with casual skill, and drew back some blood into the syringe. The blood made graceful swirling patterns in the yellowish, cloudy fluid. Then he undid the Velcro strap around the cadet's upper arm and slowly squeezed the syringe's contents into the vein.

'Give it a couple of weeks before you try that homo stuff, young man,' James said, as he reached for another syringe.

'Sir, yes, sir,' the cadet replied with a blush, and he stepped aside. Marta took a deep breath and moved forward. She hoped Jeff had done his job. 'Name and number?' asked the man at the terminal.

'Sir, D'Emilio, sir, sixty-fourteen-seventy-four, sir. Sir, special instructions, sir.'

James paused, the syringe in mid-air. 'Special instructions . . . what special instructions?'

The man at the terminal peered at the screen. 'Hemophilia, poorly controlled,' he read. 'Have D'Emilio take syringe to infirmary . . . they will administer under supervision. G.A.,' he finished.

'Hemophilia, poorly controlled?' asked James. 'You have hemophilia, poorly controlled?'

'Sir, yes, sir.'

'You're going to bleed out on me if I stick you?'

'Sir, it does go on bleeding for quite a while, yes, sir.'

'Sir, it does go on bleeding for quite a while, yes, sir,' James echoed, imitating her high-pitched voice. 'Listen, pretty boy, is that what you're going to tell the enemy when he's coming at you out of the bush with a machete? "Sir, I do go on bleeding for quite a while, sir!"'

As the cadets in the line behind her started to titter, Marta tried desperately to stay in control of the situation. 'Sir, when I'm serving my country, I'll take any risk that comes my way, sir.'

'Good answer, kid,' said James, softening his attitude. 'Not too many of your kind get to join the forces, that's for sure. But have no fear. I've injected any number of bleeders, and haven't lost one yet. Give me a twenty-seven-gauge, Tony.' While his assistant rummaged among his supplies, he began palpating for a vein in Martha's arm. 'Too much subcutaneous fat for a soldier,' he said disapprovingly. Then he dexterously flicked the old needle off the syringe and fitted the thinner one that his assistant had handed him.

Marta thought desperately. 'Sir, it's hemophilia Q, sir,' she blurted out at random.

'Hemophilia Q? . . . As in queer? Never heard of it!' As the cadets behind her burst into laughter, James slid the needle tip into the cubital vein, and pulled back. Marta's blood oozed reluctantly through the narrow needle into the syringe.

Marta panicked. She pulled her arm away, tearing the vein in the process. Blood drops spattered onto James's white coat. Before James could recover from his surprise, she grabbed the syringe, turned, and bolted for the door. Several cadets started after her.

'Let him go, let him go, the damn fool!' James shouted, as Marta disappeared out the door, and the cadets reluctantly gave up the chase. 'If he doesn't bleed to death before he gets there, he'll need all the help they can give him. Crazy kid. Next!'

CHAPTER NINETEEN

It was Saturday morning, and the pace of activity in the Department of Molecular Neurology was well below its weekday norm. Only ten or so people were there, and they were mostly postdocs and graduate students, not staff. They emphasized their weekend status by working in shirt-sleeves rather than labcoats, and by bringing large, inappropriate objects such as bicycles and surfboards right into the lab. A woman working at one bench had even brought a baby with her; it was crawling around inside a corral she had put together from Styrofoam shipping boxes and lab stools.

Albrick and Sue Forrester sat in Albrick's cramped office. Albrick wore combat fatigues, while Forrester had on the same shapeless black sweater and slacks that she wore every day of the year. Albrick looked like he would much rather be somewhere else, and after a couple of his feebly disguised yawns, Forrester seemed to catch on to the fact.

'You're off on maneuvers this weekend?' she asked.

'No, I'm prepping the corps for the reunion parade,' he replied. 'Got to be down there in a few minutes.'

'Oh, yes, I forgot. Your big day tomorrow.'

'I suppose you could say so.'

'I'm so jealous of you menfolk. Regression is actually

approved of. You can run around firing off pop-guns and driving go-carts around the campus . . . no problem, you're a credit to your sex. But what if my girlfriends and I decided to have a Barbie-doll-dressing party outside Moses Hall? I think our time at Levitican would be cut short, don't you?'

'Hah, maybe so, hmm. But you wanted to ask me something?'

'Oh yes. I've put together a manuscript for *Sexus*, and I was hoping you'd look at it. It's my theory.'

'Your theory?' repeated Albrick blankly.

'My theory of sexual identity development, you remember?'

'Oh, yes, how was that now?' No sooner were the words out of Albrick's mouth than he wished he had swallowed them.

'I've refined it quite a bit since we talked about it before. Basically, what I'm saying is, is that homosexuality isn't a state of *arrested* development, as Freud postulated, but a state of *hyper*development . . . in the Kleinian sense, sort of, but with iddystonic object relations, and with operant reinforcement from the mother, leading to pseudomaturation. There's a valorization of conflated libido goals . . . pre-oedipally . . . but later there's libido *fusion*, or even libido *extraction*.' Albrick's eyes glazed over a little too noticeably, and Forrester went on hurriedly, 'That's just my psycho-babbly way of saying, the mother makes her son grow up too fast, so that *she* can become *his* daughter . . . and thus become *her* own granddaughter.'

'Her own granddaughter?'

'Her own granddaughter! And you're wondering why?'

'I can't imag—'

'*To make her marriage incestuous!*' Forrester paused triumphantly, and there was a moment's silence.

'I'll take a look at it next—'

'It's the synthesis of psychoanalytic theory with behaviorism, I like to think. Psychobehaviorism, I'm calling it. The mechanisms are behaviorist, the structures are analytic. Now if you can just come up with the biology, we'll have the whole thing . . . the Grand Unification Theory of sex. Should have happened fifty years ago, but too many men with big egos got in the way . . . Plessey, Schuhmacher, Retzius. The proof is in the therapy.'

Albrick's mood of impatience was rapidly giving way to annoyance. This gerbil-brained psycho-groupie, he thought, with her pitiful notionettes cut-and-pasted from the 'What's Hot?' pages of *Psychology Today*. And to think that *his* vision, *his* years of labor, *his* success was going to make this ditzy nothing-woman an instant celebrity. Misogyny, jealousy, and wounded pride churned in his breast. How he looked forward to the day when he could trash her, dump her, tell her the truth. 'Of course, you have to realize—' he began.

'The proof is in the therapy,' she repeated. 'Covert sensitization for the operant control and analysis for the psychosexual re-entry. Since I started the combination approach, the results have been incredible. Eight successes in a row, and not one failure . . . not one, unless you count Jeff Galitzin.'

'Galitzin? Isn't he out of here? I thought he'd been expelled.'

'He will be soon. But right now he's sitting in his room, or doing brunch with your Roger Cavendish.'

'They're an item?'

'According to what I've heard.'

'Sick! Well, Cavendish will be leaving soon. And as for Galitzin, you may have done enough already. Wasn't he ready for his tests when this all happened? Give him a couple more weeks and you may find your work bearing fruit.'

'I don't think so. Your Cavendish started interfering with Jeff's treatment the day he arrived.'

'Stop calling him *my* Cavendish, will you?' Albrick snapped. 'He's the Halley lecturer this year, that's all.'

'Sorry. But however he got here, he totally poisoned Jeff's mind. The very first session after he arrived, Jeff's K-rating went down to baseline. And I wouldn't be surprised if he put Jeff up to the break-in, either.'

Albrick stared at Forrester. 'Put him up to the break-in? Why would he do that?'

'Who knows why? Maybe he loves animals too.'

'Loves animals? He's sent more macaques to monkey heaven than *I* have, for God's sake.'

'Well, then, maybe as a power trip of some kind.'

Albrick continued staring at Forrester, or rather through her, while his face went through a sequence of contortions. Then he raised his gaze to the racks of slide boxes over Forrester's head. 'If that faggot . . .' he began slowly, then he got up, and with a curt, 'Out of my way, please,' he began taking down box after box and checking the contents. He didn't find what he was looking for.

'What on earth . . .?' said Forrester.

'Hammond!' Albrick exclaimed, his anxiety building. He turned to the computer and began flicking through files. 'Dammit, he wouldn't dare.'

Forrester stared in bafflement as Albrick punched his way through the files. Meanwhile, she became aware that a man, also dressed in combat fatigues, was standing outside the doorway to the office. He was turned away from them and engaged in banter with the woman working at the nearby bench. 'How would Kev like to be our mascot?' he was saying. 'He looks like he's old enough to cling to the barrel of a howitzer.'

'That's sweet of you but no thanks, James,' she replied, 'I'm taking him to my macramé class tomorrow . . . they have a rag-doll workshop he's really into.'

James gave a choking snort and turned to enter the doorway of Albrick's office. 'Your battalion awaits you, Sire!' he declared, and did a heel-snapping salute. 'Lead us to glory, or the grave! Dr Forrester, good morning. You're giving the *Führer* some last-minute counseling?'

Albrick looked up at his assistant momentarily, then turned back to the computer. 'Hammond . . . Hammond . . . Hammond . . . where the hell is Hammond?'

'Your D'Emilio put on quite the little drama yesterday,' James went on.

'My D'Emilio . . . what the hell are you talking about?' Albrick responded, without even taking his eyes from the screen. 'Hammond . . . *HB 12!*' He jumped up and went back to the racks of slides, and began walking his fingers hurriedly from label to label.

'D'Emilio . . . the hemophiliac cadet you sent the note about. I was going to inject him anyway, but he grabbed the syringe out of my hands and dashed off to the infirmary, leaving blood all over me.'

James had succeeded in getting Albrick's attention at last. His fingers paused in mid-stride, and he turned toward James with a baleful glare. 'I sent no message, idiot. Who was this turkey?'

James stared at his boss. 'D'Emilio . . . D-apostrophe-E-M-I-L-I-O. Latino kid . . . a bit feminine look—'

'There's no cadet named D'Emilio and there's no hemophiliac in the entire corps . . . never has been and never will be. Who the hell did you give our serum to . . . the FBI?'

'D'Emilio . . . that's the . . . I . . .' James stuttered.

'Christ all-shitting-mighty!' Albrick swore, and he pulled a box out of the rack and tore it open. Seven slides were missing from the middle of the series.

'That fag swine!' Albrick burst out. 'That fucking fag swine!' He hurled the slide box across the office with all his force. It exploded into a million fragments of plastic and glass that seemed to rain down for several seconds onto the head of the terrified Sue Forrester. As entropy scored its final victory over John Hammond, the workers in the outside lab came rushing to see what had happened. 'It's over, James!' Albrick snarled, 'It's over with this pussy-shit science! Let's start playing hardball.'

He began to stride out of the room, grasping James's arm as he went. The students backed away in terror, but Forrester somehow held on to a sense of professional responsibility. 'Guy,' she pleaded to his receding back, 'You have issues we can work on . . . I can sense it.'

Albrick turned in the doorway and faced the distraught therapist. With pieces of glass and plastic adhering to every part of her hair and clothing, she looked like a Christmas tree decorated by a madman. 'Ignorant psycho-bitch!' Albrick snarled. 'Your therapy is *worthless*!'

James tried to pull him out of the room before he could say more, but Albrick thrust his arm away. 'It's *me* who cured those faggots,' he shouted, 'Me . . . do you hear me? Me!'

'Y-you?'

'Yes, me! With brain grafts! And you thought I was doing EEGs, you pathetic drivel-mongering dupe!'

'With grafts? Did you say grafts?'

'That's what I said . . . grafts. But no more, it's over. The field is yours, so therapy on, you clown. Albrick will rest when Albrick's work is done!'

CHAPTER TWENTY

'Company, present – *arms!*' yelled the drill instructor, and the thirty or so young men, clad in impeccable white uniforms, executed the salute with four precisely choreographed movements, accompanied by the slapping of palms on rifle-butts and the skull-cracking thud of boots on concrete. 'Company, at – *ease!*' The soldiers relaxed. 'Company atten – *shun!* . . . Present – *arms!* . . . Company, at – *ease!* . . . Company, atten – *shun!* . . . Present – *arms!* . . . Company, at – *ease!*'

The little group of soldiers continued to parade their salutes. They were a mere island in the tangled sea of men and vehicles that filled the quadrangle in front of the ROTC building. Used as an assembly area, parade ground, or practice battlefield as circumstances demanded, the quadrangle was the largest unobstructed open space at Levitican. Groups of men in a variety of uniforms mingled in informal groups, talked with old comrades, practiced routines, or engaged each other in a variety of blood sports. Some of the men were hard-bitten professional soldiers: A helicopter had just landed with a group of Marines from Camp Pendleton, and trucks carrying the insignia of fighting units from around the country were parked over toward the library. But many others were civilians – bureaucrats, upwardly mobile junior executives, or even shopkeepers or farmers – whose military activities were strictly a weekend affair. All had one thing in common: They had at one time been ROTC cadets at Levitican, and the annual reunion was the highlight of their year. Today was for rehearsal and briefing, and tonight was for partying, but tomorrow they would march through the streets of Cabrillo, dragging or driving enough firepower to topple a small nation state. They would end up right here, under the reviewing stand that the junior cadets were assembling out of a pile of planks and scaffolding. Senator Price himself, reliving the glory of his Vietnam days, would take their salute, flanked by dozens of lesser politicians, along with leaders of the Re-establishment Coalition, the Paul Revere Society, the Law of Jesus Foundation, the Daughters of God in America, the Family Values Task Force of Southern California, and of course the President and Elders of Levitican University.

As Albrick and James emerged onto the quadrangle, many of the men acknowledged Albrick with a salute or a greeting, or pointed him out to their comrades. Albrick marched briskly toward the front of the ROTC building. 'What's the plan now, chief?' asked James, as he struggled to keep up. 'Better have a good one, because you just sent us both into involuntary retirement, and I for one have mortgage payments to make.'

'A career change, James . . . or a continuation by different means.'

'Different means . . . what does *that* mean, if I may ask?'

'Wait and see. I'll be giving a little after-dinner speech tonight . . . it'll be clearer then. For now, let's do some male bonding. Get the orders for the parade.' James took a sheaf of documents from an aide, and Albrick began working the crowd. His memory for names and faces served him well. 'Totaled any more Humvees, Drayson? . . . I hear you guys took the Pershing Cup, you animals . . . If it can't make the turn, I don't want it in the parade, period . . . Sorry to hear about that reprimand, Stiegland, should have been a commendation, the way *I* saw it . . . Put your platoon in front of the horses, Brian, you don't want to be slogging through shit all afternoon . . . Frank, how's Frank Jr . . . the Cabrillo Creek bridge, Manes, every marching unit to break step, and any vehicle over five tons to use the beach . . . She *did*? Well, talk about an instant family, Markham! . . . Will it overheat if you stay in first gear the whole way? . . . All colors to be lowered at the Memorial, Hansen, make sure every unit knows it . . . Congratulations on your promotion, Vellacott . . . Give me that plunger, Orville, a fine gun should be treated like a beautiful woman, not like a whore . . .' Albrick worked his way gradually from group to group. The rage he had displayed on discovering Roger's perfidy was soon masked in comradely bonhomie.

CHAPTER TWENTY-ONE

Company, present –*arms*!' yelled the drill instructor, and the thirty or so young men and women, clad in impeccable white, gold, and lavender uniforms, executed the salute with fifty-seven precisely choreographed movements, spinning and tossing their painted plywood rifles, while at the same time flirtatiously wiggling their cutaway derrieres and lip-synching the words of Abba's *Mamma Mia*, all to the accompaniment of music from a portable tape-player that was sitting on a nearby park bench.

The drill instructor, Miles Brougham, was in his element. A rotund, perfectly bald man in his fifties, he sported a graying walrus mustache, set off by a ruddy complexion, twinkling eyes, and an ever-cheerful smile. Miles's life revolved around his three fetishes – for cigars, nipples, and uniforms. It was the last of the three that demanded the most of him, but it also gave him the most satisfaction. At the age of nineteen, while still a slender youth, Miles had won the all-Ohio collegiate baton-twirling championship, dressed in a get-up that would have out-sequined a toreador. His skill with the baton served him well during his three years in the Army, when he twirled his way from Heidelberg to Okinawa, followed always by a gaily outfitted marching band or by a troop of fresh-faced cadets in dress-uniform white. He had softened the heart of many a gruff military man along the way, and many a military wife too, in all likelihood, though he hadn't concerned himself too much with them. Since then, as his belly gradually filled out, his hairline receded, and his business obligations grew more demanding, Miles had had less and less occasion to indulge his passion, and had made fewer and fewer conquests when he did so. Often he had to be satisfied with chatting up policemen in local bars or trailing firefighters' trucks and offering to help haul their hoses, an offer that was spurned more often than not. But Miles wasn't bitter; on the contrary, a streak of indomitable good-nature enabled him to withstand the siege of time better than many a richer or handsomer man. And the West Hollywood Gay Pride Parade was the climax of his year, the late-spring day when his adolescent ardor flowered afresh, and his talents were fully appreciated.

Miles was satisfied with the troupe's preparation. He ended the drill, and the group gathered informally around a park bench onto which Miles lowered himself with a grunt. Against a fence behind the bench the group had propped up its banner, which read Gays In the Military – Serving With Flair. Miles was sweating lightly from his exertion in the warm afternoon sun, and he took off his marching-uniform jacket, revealing a singlet emblazoned with the slogan: Sometimes a Cigar is Just a Cigar, and then underneath, in smaller letters, But Not When *I* Smoke It. Suiting action to words, he produced a hand-rolled *presidente* and began performing oral sex with one end of it, while applying a lighted match to the other. As editor of *La Chaveta*, the newsletter of the Homophile Cigar-Smokers' League of America, Miles felt the responsibility to foster cigar awareness within the gay community, so he lit up whenever he could. In the city of West Hollywood, with its more-righteous-than-thou smoking ordinances, this wasn't very often. But West Hollywood Park was still a haven of deviance. The bluish smoke curled upward and drifted away among the trees, adding perceptibly to the afternoon smog and blurring the outlines of the Pacific Design Center that loomed up across San Vicente Boulevard.

'Could I ask you a personal question?' said Marta, loosening her own uniform slightly.

'Why certainly,' Miles replied genially.

'Are they, like a natural endowment, or did you do something to them?' With her gaze, Marta was indicating Miles's nipples, which were the size of small pillboxes. Riding on ample waves of adipose tissue, they spilled with artful spontaneity out of his singlet, drawing attention wherever he went.

'Only my gynecologist knows for sure, and he's not telling,' Miles answered with a smile. 'We like to keep a few secrets from our fans.'

'Oh, well, just curious. I mean, talk about nipple clamps . . . you'd need a pipe wrench to get ahold of those babies. Some of the women might appreciate a tip or two. But anyway, do you think we're set for tomorrow?'

'I think so, my dear. I just have a feeling we're going to win a prize this year. Isn't there a category for Most-Flippant-Presentation-of-a-Serious-Issue, or something like that?'

'There sure is, but the Dancing T-Cells always win that one. I'm pinning my hopes on the Least-Likely-to-Play-in-Peoria Award. Last year the Avengers took it with their Lesbian Wedding float, you remember? Well, this time they're doing a Lesbian Break-Up, complete with flying softball bats and a U-Haul truck.'

'A U-Haul truck?'

'To carry the winner off to her next partner . . . it's a girl thing. A neat concept, I have to say, but too much of a downer for a prize, don't you think . . . unless for Most-Politically-Incorrect, maybe?'

Miles's attention was momentarily distracted by two body builders who strolled by, wearing nothing but sunglasses, posing pouches and combat boots. He mentally dressed them as Prussian cavalry officers. By the time they receded from Miles's view they were flicking at each other's leather-clad buttocks with their riding crops. Miles took an extra-long pull on his cigar, exhaled with a theatrical sigh, and returned to the conversation.

'Is that arm giving you trouble?' he asked.

'Not really. Just a big bruise. If I'd only thought to undo that Velcro thingy it would hardly have left a mark. As it was, it went on bleeding under the skin till Roger Cavendish took it off . . . hence the lump. I'm not doing too well at Levitican, am I?'

'You're still alive.'

'That's true. And I accomplished my mission, in the face of unexpected difficulties.'

'So what is it you said they're injecting . . . some kind of anti-gay serum?'

'Cavendish is going to check what it is today. But according to what Frinton told me, yeah, it's something like that. They're inoculating the cadets against homosexuality.'

'That is far out, as we used to say. So how did you and Cavendish get on . . . did you apologize for disrupting his lecture?'

'No, but still, we had a good talk. His heart is in the right place, I have to say. He's really trying to stop Albrick's program. But the University is one hundred percent behind the man. Not only for the research, but also because he's a mainstay of ROTC. He'll be riding in a tank tomorrow, I'm sure of that. Maybe we should go down to Cabrillo, after our parade's over, and join theirs. They could probably use some light relief.'

'Or target practice, more likely. Marta, please recall that I do this purely as a hobby. I am not a political animal and I have no desire to lay my life on the line for this or any other cause. Take Act Out! down to Cabrillo if you must, honey, but find another baton-twirler, please.'

'I wasn't serious. This is our weekend off. After the parade Mave and I are going to boogie to k.d. lang at Girl Bar.'

CHAPTER TWENTY-TWO

Jeff and Roger glared at each other. It was Saturday evening, nearly twenty-four hours after Roger had discovered the burr-hole in Jeff's skull, and their relationship had been steadily deteriorating. The two men were once more in Roger's room, and Roger was close to desperation.

'Mary's a happily married woman,' he said. 'She's not the least interested in you sexually, and you frighten her. You've got to lay off it. We need to work together if we're going to beat this thing.'

'Well, you've had a day and you haven't come up with anything yet,' said Jeff. 'I mean, I find her really attractive sometimes, that's just the fact of the matter.'

'This is the graft talking, can't you see? It's not you.'

'Not me? It sure feels like me, when I get the feelings.'

'Is that now?'

'No, not really . . . I don't know what I'm feeling right now.'

'Mary was practically killed by one of . . . of . . .'

'One of us? One of my kind? Say it! I'm the enemy now, right? Is that what you're saying?'

'Jeff, have some understanding for how she feels.'

'I have some understanding for how *you* feel. Like you're losing me, right?'

Roger stared at Jeff. There was a pause. Then he said quietly, 'Yes, like I'm losing you.'

Jeff slid off the desk he had been perching on and started pacing up and down, without looking at Roger directly.

'I'm not straight,' he said. 'Not yet anyway. I don't know what I am . . . bisexual, confused, whatever. But you and I, we never . . . I mean, we weren't . . . God dammit, you know what I mean.'

'No, we weren't, I guess. Heading that way, maybe.'

'Hell, no. That's *you* reading something into it, Roger. We were friends . . . still are.'

'I hope so. But let's not get all wrapped up in you and me . . . let's try and solve the problem. You've got something very nasty in your brain and we've got to get it out of there.'

'Like how? Dig it out with a spoon?'

'Let's at least look at what's in the syringe Marta got for us. Maybe that will give us some ideas.'

'Where?'

'At Albrick's lab. He's shot off somewhere, Mary says, so the coast should be clear.'

'He shot off?'

'Yes . . . Mary ran into Sue Forrester. She was in a real state. Apparently she and Albrick had a row, and Albrick told her about the brain grafts. Then he said he was quitting his research and he dashed off somewhere.'

'Sounds like he's flipping out! Okay . . . yeah, let's do it, but remember, I can't get the door open this time.'

'No problem, I have a passcard now. I'm Albrick's collaborator, you remember?'

The two men moved toward the door, but before

they reached it they heard a brisk tapping. Roger opened the door. Jean-Michel Leblanc was standing outside. He was dressed in tails that, from their cut and age, might have been worn by Paderewski's grandfather, along with white silk gloves and patent-leather shoes. He was holding his viola case and some sheet music, and he was smiling urbanely.

'Jean-Michel,' Roger stammered. 'What – oh, the recital, I quite forgot!'

'Forgot? Ah, *dementia scholasticorum*, I fear. I would be most interested to see your hippocampus . . . a moderate atrophy of the dentate gyrus, I predict.'

'Actually I—'

'But no matter! There is still plenty of time for you to get changed. And your young friend . . . didn't we . . . yes, Jeff, the friend of John Hammond, of course. Are you an admirer of Franz Schubert? I am sure that there will be an extra seat.'

'Jean-Michel,' Roger broke in, 'we have a sample of the material that Albrick has been injecting into the cadets. We were just going to look at it. Please come help us . . . I think we could use your expertise.'

'Well, very well, I would certainly be interested to see that. We have time, thirty, forty minutes, maybe. But the warm-up is essential . . . all the more as one ages, I find. The spirit is willing, but the fingers, alas, are stiff. Forty minutes, yes.'

The three men left the guest house and made their way over to the Neuroscience Building. On the way over they heard music and laughter coming from far off. 'Is there another concert on the campus tonight? I hope we are not in a competition,' Leblanc said.

'It's the ROTC reunion,' said Jeff. 'It'll get louder.

But they're not a classical-music crowd, don't worry. Unless they burn down the campus, you shouldn't have any problem.'

'I hope not. To appreciate fine music one needs, above all, tranquility.'

Albrick's lab was empty. Roger soon found a tissue-culture microscope. He squeezed a few drops from the syringe into a culture dish, put it on the stage of the microscope, and started fiddling with the illumination. The microscope had two sets of binocular eyepieces, so that both Roger and Leblanc could observe the dish at once.

'You know, this does seem a bit familiar,' said Jeff. 'Isn't that Albrick's office over there?'

'That's right,' said Roger. 'Were you here any other time?'

'No, just that night.'

'Well, the amnesia must not be complete. And that figures, because you never had a concussion, just the effects of the drugs they gave you. If they gave you a veterinary anesthetic, ketamine-xylazine or some combination like that, then the retrograde amnesia would be incomplete. You get what's called a "cued-recall amnesia," when you can't remember stuff spontaneously, but if you're reminded of one thing, you can remember other things.'

'What do you see?' Jeff asked impatiently.

'Nothing much right now, the cells are still settling down onto the substrate. Give it a few moments.'

After a pause, Jeff said, 'Dr Leblanc, did John die peacefully, do you think?'

Leblanc took his eyes from the microscope and gazed off into the distance. 'I am sure of it,' he said. 'Dying is always peaceful. Only living can be otherwise.'

'Really, you think so? I can see that with John, because he wanted to die, it was suicide, but—'

'All death is suicide. You say to yourself, I think I will not bother with the next breath, and that is it. What brings you to that point, of course, can be unpleasant.'

'Jeff, come over here,' Roger said, and he led him over to the other side of the lab, out of Leblanc's earshot.

'You'd better not be thinking about suicide,' Roger went on emphatically. 'Are you crazy?'

'I didn't say—'

'Listen, if the very worst happens, and we can't get rid of these cells, so, you become straight. That's something you wanted to be, just a couple of weeks ago. Not worth killing yourself about, for God's sake.'

'Not for becoming straight, no . . . if that were everything.'

'That *is* everything, probably.'

'Not with John, was it? It wasn't an accident, what happened to his girlfriend, was it? I realize that now.'

'No, I don't think it was, but—'

'And the man who tried to kill Mary—'

'Jeff, there are hundreds of men who've gotten these cells, either directly into the brain like you and John, or via the bloodstream. Most of them are just fine, no problems at all. Some are acting up, yes, but they're a minority, there's no reason to think it will happen to you. You're a nice guy, nothing's going to change that.' Roger wished he could make himself sound more convincing.

'I hope not,' Jeff said.

Leblanc called over to them. He was looking down the microscope and gesticulating excitedly. 'Look at this,' he said, and Roger went back to his seat and peered down into the eyepiece.

The cells had settled to the bottom surface of the dish, where they had flattened out. Each cell looked like an egg that had been broken into a skillet: Its nucleus, like the egg's yolk, formed a glistening round hump in the center of the cell, and the cytoplasm flared out as a thin skirt around it. At first, the cells seemed motionless, but whenever Roger concentrated on a single cell for long enough, he could see that it was in ceaseless though ponderous motion. The edges of the cytoplasm formed ruffles that undulated, like the wings of manta rays, stirring the surrounding fluid into gentle eddies. Every now and then, some portion of the cell's perimeter would blister outward, forming a promontory. Cytoplasm streamed into the promontory, carrying particles and fibrils with it, and the promontory extended and lengthened. The tip of the promontory seemed to search and taste the environment: It carried a tassel of delicate, threadlike fingers that reached out to touch and grasp tiny flecks of dirt or the plastic surface itself. Sometimes the fingers withdrew again, to be replaced by others, but other times they got a firm grip of whatever they had touched, and then they contracted, heaving the entire promontory an almost imperceptible step forward. Thus, by the tireless efforts of these Lilliputian laborers, the promontories gradually became drawn out into snakelike processes, thin ropes of cytoplasm that extended ever further from their mother-cells, headed always by their tassels of restless, searching fingers. Sometimes the ropes would branch in two, and as more and more cells put on these ropes, and each rope branched and branched again, the bottom of the dish gradually became a dense interlocking web of cytoplasmic cables, like the tangled mass of roots at the bottom of a mangrove swamp.

'They're trying to form a little brain, right there in the dish,' Roger said.

'Let me see, let me see,' said Jeff impatiently, and Roger reluctantly gave up his place.

'They *are* forming a brain,' said Leblanc. 'Only, we don't now what it's thinking about.'

'I can guess,' said Jeff, as he stared with horrified fascination at the microscopic scene.

'Take a look at this cell, if you would,' said Leblanc to Roger, and Jeff had to give up his seat again. 'Here, I'm aiming the pointer at it.'

The cell seemed to be putting its growth processes into reverse. The long branching cables that extended from the cell were shortening. Where they formed contact with other cells, they seemed reluctant to part; the contract stretched out ever thinner until, with a sudden snap, the bond parted and the cable jumped back toward the cell body and was reabsorbed. And now the nucleus of the cell was starting to break up.

'It's dying!' Roger exclaimed. 'So they're mortal at least, thank God.'

'I wish it were so,' said Leblanc. 'Keep watching, please.'

As the cell's nucleus disintegrated, there appeared in its place a set of thirty or forty dark threadlike objects, the chromosomes, that moved around, pirouetted, and assembled in a line, as if they were taking part in a microscopic square dance. Then, as if tugged by magic webs, the chromosomes were drawn apart into two jostling groups, one at each end of the cell. Between them, the cytoplasm darkened and constricted, so that the cell took on the shape of an hourglass, whose neck became ever thinner and thinner and finally broke apart. Where there had been one cell a few minutes before, there were now two. After a brief rest, each of them began sending out its own snaking cables. Some of these formed incestuous links between the two sister cells, while the remainder reached out to make groping contacts with other cells in the vicinity.

'Neuroblastoma,' said Leblanc. 'Neurons, but cancerous . . . always ready to invade, to multiply, to subvert. In some of my infants, half the brain was replaced by these little monsters.'

Jeff shuddered, and buried his head in his hands.

'Jeff, that's *not* going to happen to you!' said Roger. 'We'll figure out a way to kill them.' He leaned his arm reassuringly over Jeff's shoulder's, but Jeff shrugged him off.

'Like how . . . how?' he said, half shouting, half sobbing.

'We'll figure out a way . . . we will.'

Leblanc gave Jeff a look of pained sympathy. 'They say, "Know thy enemy." Perhaps we can study the molecular characteristics of the cells, the surface properties, and so forth. Or the fine structure . . . we could take a look at these cells under the electron microscope . . . at that magnification perhaps we might find out something useful.' He looked at his watch, and added, 'Maybe tomorrow we could work on that.'

'Molecular characteristics . . . running gels and stuff?' said Roger. 'That would take forever. And electron microscopy . . . that takes forever, too. We'd have to fix the cells and embed them in plastic and who knows what. It would be the end of next week before we could even take a look at them.'

Jeff looked hazily at Roger. 'I seem to remember something. Can we take a look in Albrick's office?'

The three men walked over to the office. 'Sure is a mess in here,' said Roger, kicking at some of the debris on the floor. Albrick's computer was still running as Albrick had left it earlier, displaying the file on John Hammond's brain.

'It's right on the screen already,' Jeff said. 'How strange.'

'You're right,' said Roger. 'Evidently he took a sample for electron microscopy as well as for light microscopy. And it's been sliced already . . . box 45, grids 2B to 4F. Now we just have to find the box.'

'Maybe wherever the electron microscope is?' suggested Leblanc.

They went back into the lab, checking the side doors. Eventually they came to one that had a light above it and a sign: Do Not Enter When Light Is On. Opening the door, they found themselves faced by another door four feet ahead. The three men and the viola crowded into the narrow space. Roger closed the outer door and then cautiously opened the inner door. The small room inside was dimly lit by red safe-lights. It was warm, and there was a quiet humming of air pumps. In the center of the room stood the electron microscope, its tall vacuum column looming almost to the full height of the room. A heavy high-tension cable came down through a hole in the ceiling, bringing power from a voltage stabilizer in another part of the building. Attached to the column were all kinds of devices:

electromagnets, aperture controls, goniometers, and liquid nitrogen reservoirs. At the bottom of the column were heavy plate-glass windows, through which could be seen a tilted screen coated with yellowish fluorescent paint.

'A Philips 800B, with all the bells and whistles,' said Roger. 'I'm impressed . . . Mary's people really treated him well.'

'Over here,' said Leblanc. 'These must be the specimen boxes.' Roger went over to a set of drawers that contained plastic boxes about the size of credit cards. 'Box 45, here we are.' He took the box and slid back the cover, revealing an array of little numbered cavities. In some of the cavities were lodged tiny copper grids, a couple of millimeters across. The meshwork of the grids was almost too fine to discern. Roger took a pair of jeweler's forceps and carefully lifted one of the delicate grids out of its cavity. He placed it into the microscope's specimen carrier, a rodlike device that was sitting in a box on the console of the machine.

'I don't see anything,' said Jeff, peering at the grid.

'You're not supposed to. These slices are less than one ten-thousandth of a millimeter thick. That's about all the electron beam will travel through, and still make a decent image.' Roger secured the grid in place with a tiny locking ring, and slid the whole specimen carrier into its slot, about halfway up the column. There was a gurgling noise as the pumps swept away the air that had been carried past the seals. Then a light came on, and Roger hit a button marked with a lightning symbol. The screen glowed a fluorescent green. Now they could see the image of the copper grid, magnified a thousand-fold, on the screen. Roger started moving the specimen around with the X-Y micro-motors, looking for the tissue slices. 'Here we are,' he said. He increased the magnification to ten thousand, and turned up the beam current so that the screen was brightly illuminated.

'I still don't see much of anything,' said Jeff.

'Yes, look here, this is the edge of the specimen. Now as I move it to the right –' he lightly touched the X-Y motors again – 'now here's the neural tissue. You see this round thing, that's the nucleus of a cell, and this is the cytoplasm, here. The preservation is terrible, but that's what you get with autopsy material. He was dead for hours before Albrick took the specimen. Look, the mitochondria are shot, the endoplasmic reticulum has turned to soup. And the synapses are falling apart . . . look here, the vesicles have spilled out into the cleft, for heaven's sake. How are we supposed to tell which are John's own brain cells and which are the injected cells? Any ideas, Jean-Michel?'

'Well, from the nuclei, I think. The next cell, there, to the right. You see how the chromatin is condensed in that irregular way? Almost certainly a neuroblastoma cell, I would say.'

'Let's take a closer look,' Roger said, and he increased the magnification to fifty thousand. 'Ribosomes, Golgi apparatus, nothing too unusual, as far as I can see.'

'What are those specks?' Jeff asked. 'You see them, like little black dots everywhere?'

'A staining artifact, probably. Maybe one of the fixatives precipitated out during the processing . . . it's pretty common.'

'Compare the two cells, though, Roger,' said Leblanc. 'You see the normal brain cell on the left: It doesn't have any of them. It seems to be something peculiar to the blastoma cells.'

'Well, yes, it does look that way. But even so, sometimes these precipitates are capricious, they'll hit one cell and not another. Let's get a bit closer.' Roger upped the magnification to one hundred thousand, and the image began to lose crispness as the machine approached the limits of its resolution. 'They're extremely electron-dense . . . got to be a heavy metal of some kind. That's what makes me think it's the osmium fixative. They're perfectly round, and I'd say they're about . . . well, let's get an exact measurement,' and he lowered a micrometer bar onto the screen. 'Twelve point five nanometers . . . that is *small*.'

'So what are they?' asked Jeff.

'I have no idea,' said Roger. 'But we can find out.'

'How?'

'With this little gizmo.' Roger pointed to a bulky cylindrical device that was attached to the main column of the microscope, right above the level where the specimen was inserted. Multicolored cables led from various points on the object down into the base of the microscope. 'Backscatter ion spectrometer,' he said. 'What we do is, we focus the entire electron beam down to a tiny, very intense spot, less than a micron across. We aim it at the place we're interested in, and the irradiation ionizes some of the atoms in the tissue slice . . . puts a charge on them and vaporizes them. They go boiling off out of the slice, and then these magnets draw them into the spectrometer at high speed, twisting them as they go. The lighter atoms twist more easily, so they get spread out into a kind of rainbow according to their atomic weight. At the far end of the spectrometer, here, they hit an anode, and they generate a current which we can measure. The anode scans across the rainbow, measuring how many atoms are present at each atomic weight. So we get a series of peaks in the current, corresponding to the atomic weights of the various elements that were present in the slice. This screen down here should display the peaks.'

'Well, let's do it.'

'We shall. First, let's look at the normal cell though, so that we can see what elements are there.' Roger moved the specimen slightly so that the cytoplasm of the normal brain cell occupied the center of the field. He then bundled the beam to a tight spot, and threw a few switches. The screen below started displaying a horizontal line that gradually developed several peaks that grew upward over a period of half a minute or so.

'Okay,' Roger went on, 'This first peak at the left is at 190.2 . . . oh, and neat, it prints a little symbol, *Os*, that's osmium. They don't make us go running to find a chemistry textbook anymore. It's from the osmium tetroxide, the fixative used to prepare the tissue. Now this next peak is, let's see, 207.2 . . . *Pb*, that's plumbum, lead. The sections are stained with lead citrate . . . a nice electron-dense stain. And it looks like there's one more peak coming out, yes, 238.0 . . . *U*, that's uranium. That's from the uranium acetate, another stain. That's it, just the three peaks in the heavy-metal range . . . just what I'd expect. Now let's look at the blastoma cell.' Roger moved the slice over slightly, until a patch of the cytoplasm of the neuroblastoma cell, with some of the dense particles in it, was centered on the fluorescent screen. Then he refocused the beam, and switched on the spectrometer again. Soon another graph was emerging. 'The same three peaks, it looks like . . . osmium, lead, uranium. No, wait, there's a new peak, I think, a small one, kind of indistinct, between the osmium and the lead. The computer isn't buying it yet, but I think, yes, here we go, wow, 197.0 . . . *Au*.'

'*Au*?' Leblanc and Jeff asked simultaneously.

'*Aurum*. Gold.'

CHAPTER TWENTY-THREE

The ROTC mess hall, where just the day before the cadets had lined up for their high-tech AIDS vaccines, was now transformed into a medieval hostelry. The carousing soldiers sat or slumped at long trestle tables that filled the room from end to end. Each table groaned under the weight of an enormous platter that carried the remains of an entire suckling pig, its dismembered carcass still clinging to the metal spit it was roasted on. Other dishes and plates lay scattered around, some on the tables, some on the floor. The linoleum floor itself had been strewn with hay, perhaps to soak up any spills, or perhaps to give the scene a more Breughelesque character.

Although the soldiers' hunger had been satisfied, their thirst remained unquenchable. Serving wenches hurried to and fro, carrying six huge pewter tankards at a time. They slapped the tankards down on the wooden tables, spilling the frothy ale in generous floods and earning curses from the men whose uniforms were soaked. The wenches, who were supplied by a local agency, were done up in traditional serving-wench garb, their bosoms amply exposed and prettily framed in flouncy lace. As they moved among the tables, they had to run a gauntlet of bottom-pinches and tittytwisters, which they attempted to ward off by striking the offending hands with loaded tankards, a maneuver that led to further spillage of beer.

At one end of the hall a raised platform was doing service as a minstrels' gallery. A group of musicians, attired in Robin Hood outfits complete with feathered caps, were turning out country-western numbers. Although amply provided with microphones, the musicians could barely be heard over the sounds of general merriment, as the soldiers laughed and shouted, or engaged in food fights. Some of them had even started up their own drinking songs, accompanied by the rhythmic pounding of booted feet on the floor and the crashing of beer mugs on the tabletops. Over to one side of the hall an entire roasted pig, which had somehow escaped being eaten, had been sat upright on a table, a World War II era helmet perched incongruously on its head. Somebody had produced a bayoneted rifle, and soldiers were taking turns leaping from an adjacent table, weapon in hand, attempting to spear the animal as they landed. They were trying to imitate, as closely as possible, the scene depicted in the giant picture behind them. A photographer was capturing the soldiers' efforts, and raucous applause burst out when one soldier, perhaps not quite as drunk as his comrades, managed to drive the bayonet through the pig's midriff. The soldier tried to lift the entire animal into the air, still spitted on the end of his rifle, but before he could raise it more than shoulder high he fell laughing off the table onto the floor, and the pig, rifle and all, came tumbling down on top of him.

At one table near the middle of the room, a soldier

in the uniform of the third Kentucky Light Infantry had taken an interest in one particular serving wench, a large, flaxen blond maiden who looked as if her ancestors might have been Norwegian. 'Here, Brunhilda, give me a kiss,' the soldier exclaimed as she hustled by, and he grabbed her by the wrist and attempted to seat her on his lap.

Remembering what she had been taught at the agency, she shouted, 'Unhand me, varmint!' and, when that had no effect, she added, 'Desist, arrant knave!' while attempting to shake her arm loose from his grip. Some of the wenches in other parts of the hall heard her shouts and started making their way over to the scene of the fracas. But the infantryman was not to be denied: He seized the woman by the hair, pulled her head brutally backward, planted his lips on hers, and plunged his tongue deep into her mouth. She bit fiercely down, severing his tongue two inches back from its tip.

The infantryman leaped back and let out an agonized scream that quickly ended in a fit of choking, as his throat filled with blood. The serving wench spat out the severed tongue onto the table, where it lay, still quivering, next to a half-empty bowl of apple sauce. She turned to run, but she was seized by the five other men who had been sitting at the table. Plates, dishes, and tankards went flying as they manhandled her facedown onto the table and pulled her legs down over the end. In a moment her dress had been pulled up above her waist, and her panties were torn off in shreds. Her screams could hardly be heard amid the general uproar. While four of the men held her down and tried to gag her mouth, the fifth unzipped his pants, exposing a penis that was not yet fully erect. He smeared it with a mouthful of spit and worked it for a moment or two, while kneading and slapping the woman's buttocks with his free hand. Meanwhile the other wenches, who had come to the woman's aid, had themselves been seized by soldiers at nearby tables, and were trying vainly to fend off similar attacks.

Just as it seemed that nothing could save the women, a bellowing roar filled the hall. 'Men!' yelled a voice that shook the walls, and again, 'Men!' It was Albrick, who had seized a microphone from one of the musicians and was shouting into it with all his force. Somehow his authority percolated into the consciousness of the riotous soldiers. The noise abated slightly, and Albrick was able to shout some orders. 'Let the women go! Let them go! Get that man to the infirmary!' The women were released, and, shaking and crying, they ran for the exits. The wounded infantryman, whose entire front was now stained by a river of clotted blood, was carried out by four men, while two others began searching for his severed tongue amid the debris on the floor. The remaining soldiers, two or three hundred of them, stood or sat motionless, uncertain what to do.

'Are you out of your minds?' Albrick shouted. 'Are you insane? Is this what you came here for . . . to rape a few defenseless girls?'

'Sure was, sir!' came a voice from the middle of the throng. Some of the soldiers laughed raucously or shouted, 'Right on!' or 'Bring the bitches back!' But they were silenced by others, and the hall quieted down again.

'Men!' Albrick continued, 'I have work for you . . .

here, now, tonight.' There was a chorus of groans. Somebody shouted, 'I'm not cleaning up this mess!'

'Not to sweep the floors. Not to wash the dishes. To do what you were born for . . . to fight!'

'All right!' came from a host of voices, followed by a chorus of 'Fight! Fight! Fight!' and a clashing of beer tankards. For a moment it seemed like the riot was about to break out again, but Albrick kept going.

'Have you sworn to fight for your honor?'

'To the death!'

'Have you sworn to fight for your country?'

'To the death!'

'Have you sworn to fight for your God!'

'To the death!'

'Then listen! We are at war! The enemy is at our gates!' There was a roar of approval, and a renewed chorus of 'Fight! Fight! Fight!'

'Quiet! Listen! How many of you went to Ireland?' Fifty or so voices shouted, 'I did!'

'And what did you do there?'

'Nothing!'

'Nothing, right? Nothing, except let yourselves be shot at by some two-bit terrorists and say, "Thank-you very much, sir!" Nothing, except take orders from some dolled-up French brigadier who couldn't even speak straight English. Nothing, except wear those fag blue berets, right? And then, when the going got tough, why, you were all brought running back home to mother. Is that the way to fight?'

'No!'

'Is that what you were trained for?'

'No!'

'Well, listen. The Irish aren't your enemy!'

213

'Love the Irish!'

'And listen. How many of you worked on the Mississippi levees?'

A chorus of 'I did!'

'You filled sandbags for six weeks. You carried hogs around. Then you filled more sandbags. And you took orders from who? From the Red Cross, for God's sake! Is that what you were trained for?'

'No!'

'The Mississippi River isn't your enemy!'

'Love the Mississippi!'

'And listen! How many of you missed a promotion, for no other reason than that you're male and you're white?'

'I did!'

'And how many of you have had to face committees of inquiry? How many of you have gotten a reprimand for "sexual harassment," when all you did was show your appreciation for the opposite sex, the same as every other red-blooded heterosexual American is entitled to do?'

'I did! Bring the bitches back! Bring 'em back!'

'Quiet! Listen! You men are the best! America's best! But evil people are trying to weaken you . . . to castrate you!'

'Ouch!'

'Evil people in places of power. In Washington. In Hollywood. In San Francisco. Evil, godless people who are trying to destroy our great country . . . from within! By reducing our armed forces to a gaggle of Sunday-school do-gooders, armed with sensitivity manuals and equal-opportunity statements. By laying down rules of engagement. Rules of engagement! Thou shalt not shoot unless thou hast been shot at! Is that the way to fight?'

'No!'

'Is that the way to win?'

'No!'

'And who are these evil people, I ask you . . . who are they?'

'Who are they, who are they?'

'*Homosexuals!*'

'Ughhh!'

'Homosexuals! Sexual perverts! Disgusting sodomites who've brown-nosed their way into positions of power, all across our country. They're sitting in the President's cabinet. They're teaching in our schools. They're making our movies. They're even preaching in our churches! Seducing our children, destroying families, uprooting our traditions, undermining our faith!'

'Shame!'

'And now they're demanding to be let into the military! To serve alongside of you! To eat and sleep and fight alongside of you! To bring disease and corruption into your mess halls and your barracks! Can you imagine what it'll be like? When you can't take a shower without having one of them come on to you, offering to soap your back and who knows what else afterwards? When you can't arm wrestle with a comrade, without him thinking you want to suck his dick?'

'Ughhh!'

'And the government is going along with it! And the courts are going along with it! They're creeping in, and soon they'll be rushing in. And soon it'll be affirmative-action time. Quota time. Promote more homosexuals! "You're not gay? Step back, please! Let the fairies through!" I ask you . . . is that the way to fight?'

'No! No! No!'

Albrick paused, and softened his voice. 'Men, we are the few, the happy few, who are not yet contaminated. This corps and this college still guard the noble principles that made our country great. We still stand for something . . . for our country's past, and for our future. We have sworn our oath, and we will stand by it till our dying breath. But we are under siege. Just two weeks ago a verminous crew of perverts stole onto our campus and interrupted a lecture. They tried to put on some obscene Punch and Judy show, to make a mockery of everything we stand for. Some of you helped round them up, and taught them a little lesson in the process. Well done, well done! But what happened then? They were let off! No prison! No probation! Not so much as a fine! A slimy fag lawyer and a corrupt judge conspired together to let them off scot-free!'

'Shame! Shame!'

'Shame indeed! And where do these people come from, do you think? Not from Levitican—'

'No!'

'Not from Cabrillo, not from Orange County! They come from the deepest cesspool of vice in the Western world. From the most depraved pit of iniquity since Sodom and Gomorrah. From a hellhole of perverted lust, where men with men do that which is an abomination, and women with women too. And not just in their bedrooms, not just in their own homes, but in the bars, in the bathhouses, the gyms, the hotels

. . . yes, they do it in plain view in the very streets of the city! Sex everywhere, sex for money, sex for drugs, you name it. And nothing done to stop it, because the very mayor, the councilmen, the police . . . they're perverts, all of them. And what's the name of this festering swamp of evil, this city of atheists and antichrists, this—'

'Bakersfield?' came a suggestion out of the crowd.

'West Hollywood! West Hollywood! A city of nothing but fags and dykes, doing whatever they wish with each other. And that means a lot, let me tell you, a lot, more and worse than you can possibly imagine. But don't take it from me – you wouldn't believe it! – Get it from them! Listen! This is them talking!' Albrick pulled out a copy of the *West Hollywood Blade* and began reading from the personal ads. '"Ted – into restraints, cuffs, ropes, chains, dildos, whips, paddles, devices, blindfolds, hoods, gags, tit clamps, cock-and-ball torture, hand-ball hard or easy – $50 mornings, $75 till midnight." Here's another: "Handsome, trim, muscular toilet bottom wants to give total toilet service to hot masculine tops." Toilet service! Here's another: "Huge nasty nine-and-a-half inches wants to hose you down. Golden showers from hung, big balls, Italian." And this one: "Fisting boy – toys, holes, and poles – let's do it!" Hundreds and hundreds of these. Here, read them for yourself, look at the pictures . . .' He threw the magazine into the crowd of soldiers, who ripped it to shreds. 'That's what's going on there. Is that the America you want for your children to grow up in?'

'No!'

'Is that the America you want to fight for?'

'No!'

'Is that the America you want to die for?'

'No!'

'Or is that the America you want to wipe off the face of the earth?'

'Yes! Kill them! Let's get 'em! Let's go!' The soldiers broke into an uproar of excited shouting and pounding.

'Men, listen!' Albrick yelled. 'Tomorrow is the high holy day of that evil empire. The Gay Pride Parade. Pride! That's good, isn't it . . . pride? Pride in sucking dick? Pride in pissing all over each other? Pride in molesting children and God knows what else? That's what they're proud of! And they're going to march down Santa Monica Boulevard . . . every fag and dyke in Southern California, tens of thousands of them . . . they're going to march down the Boulevard tomorrow morning and they're going to tell the world all about it. Floats promoting every perversion you have ever heard of and a good many more . . . and all this broadcast on national television, there for every boy and girl in America to see, from Anchorage to Virginia Beach, this smut spread nationwide, poisoning the minds of our children, mocking everything their parents have ever taught them, destroying their resolve to lead clean and decent and upright lives. It's an abomination! It's sick and evil! *Let's put a stop to it!*'

'Kill them! Kill them!' screamed the soldiers in a frenzy of excitement.

'They want their asses whipped?' Albrick shouted. 'We'll whip their asses!'

'Yes!'

'They want to be hosed down? We'll hose them down!'

'Yes!'

'They want to be chained up? We'll chain them up, and we'll bring them down here as trophies for our parade, and then we'll throw them in the ocean and let them swim to Japan or Thailand or wherever their kind are welcome!'

'Yes!'

'Men, we'll go up tonight and station ourselves along the route, on the rooftops, hidden. And tomorrow, when that pansy parade comes prancing down the street, we'll give them such a fight, they won't stop running till they reach the Colorado river!'

'Yes! Kill them! Kill them!'

'But men, listen carefully! There is danger for you there! Not those fags and dykes, don't worry about them. But there's AIDS! Most of those homos have AIDS, and they'd love to pass it on to you.'

'Kill them!'

'Only those of you who have had the AIDS vaccine are to take part in this mission. This is an order! The others, guard the campus! Who knows what they might be plotting?'

'Kill them!'

'Now, to the armory! And then, to your vehicles!' The men rushed to the west side door of the hall. Albrick, with James at his side, followed them.

'This is just a show of force, right, chief?' said James.

'A show of force, yes,' said Albrick, without glancing at his sidekick. 'A show of force.'

CHAPTER TWENTY-FOUR

'Gold?' Jeff asked.

'That's what it says,' said Roger. 'And I'm sure it's nothing to do with the fixation or staining. Those particles were already in the cells, for some reason.'

'You mean, Albrick put them in?'

'That's how it looks.'

'How could he do that? And why?'

'Beats me.'

'Maybe as a label?' suggested Leblanc. 'Maybe he wanted some way to tell which were the grafted cells, when he came to look at brain tissue like this.'

'Not a very good label, though,' said Roger, 'if it takes electron microscopy to see it. There are much simpler methods . . . he could have added an indicator gene of some kind . . . you know, a gene that would promote a histochemical reaction that one could see in the regular light microscope. But wait . . . talking about adding genes . . . these cells *do* have an added gene. It's for the altered testosterone receptor, you remember. That's what Albrick told me, anyway. This is why the cells migrate preferentially to the sexual parts of the brain. Maybe the gold particles are somehow involved in the genetic alteration of the cells.'

'You mean they have some kind of genetic effect on the cells?'

'No, but listen . . . I asked Albrick's assistant how he got the synthetic genes into the cells. I asked him whether he was using a virus to carry the genes in, and he said no, he was using physical methods, but he didn't explain what he meant. Maybe he was using the gold particles instead.'

'How would that work?'

'I've heard of people trying something like this. You take a solution of the DNA you want to put in the cells, and you mix it in a test tube with some kind of dense particles . . . in this case Albrick used a suspension of gold particles, evidently. The DNA molecules stick to the gold particles, sort of coat them. Then you load the suspension into a brass cylinder with a small opening at one end, and you load the cylinder into something like a staple gun. You fire the gun at the cells, but the trick is, the brass cylinder is stopped dead by a flange, about a centimeter away from the cells. The contents of the cylinder go flying out of the opening in an extremely fine spray. The droplets are so small, the liquid part evaporates before they hit the cells, but the gold particles hit the cell membranes, still traveling at supersonic speed. They go through the membranes into the cells, but once they're in the interior of the cells they slow down and stop almost immediately, they're so small. It's kind of like cannonballs going into molasses . . . the viscosity is too much for them. Then the DNA wanders off into the nucleus and does its stuff, but the gold just stays there in the cytoplasm.'

'Forever?' Jeff asked.

'Forever. It doesn't do any harm, and it can't be

broken down. It dilutes out a bit, as the cells divide and grow, but basically it's there permanently.'

'That's wild . . . sort of like cells with dental fillings.'

'But the important question,' said Leblanc, 'is how can you use this information? Do these particles make the cells vulnerable? Have you found the heel of Achilles? Is there—'

'Magnets!' Jeff broke in. 'Get a really strong electromagnet that reverses polarity at high frequency. It would make the particles vibrate so much they would destroy the cells they're in.'

'Magnets?' Roger laughed. 'Gold isn't magnetic. That's why people with gold fillings can be put in MRI machines and not have all their fillings jump out when the machine's turned on.'

'Oh yeah, right, I forgot,' said Jeff with embarrassment.

'That's okay, we're brainstorming,' said Roger, wishing he hadn't laughed.

'If not magnetic fields, what could act on gold?' asked Leblanc.

'Gravity's the obvious thing,' said Roger. 'The density difference between gold and biological tissue is enormous. In principle, you could put a person in a centrifuge, and the gold particles would migrate under the g forces and destroy the cells they're in. But it wouldn't work.'

'Why not?' asked Leblanc.

'Because the particles are so small. At that size, the normal thermal motion would be much greater than any motion you could induce by g forces. The person's brains would fly out his ears before the gold particles moved significantly.'

'Thermal motion?' said Jeff. 'How about increasing the thermal motion? Heating the particles somehow?'

'How?' asked Roger.

'What about microwaves? Gold should absorb microwaves really well.'

Leblanc looked at his watch. 'Gentlemen, I have to leave you. I should be getting ready for the recital.'

'Jean-Michel, stay a few minutes, if you can. Let's see if we can't figure something out – it's pretty urgent.'

'A few minutes only, then. Without the warm-up, I am – what's the word? – a "klutz"?'

'Let's try it!' said Jeff impetuously. 'There must be a microwave oven around here somewhere. Let's get some of the cells and zap them – see what happens.'

Jeff led them out of the electron microscope room, and they prowled around looking for a microwave oven. They soon found one in the lunch room that was next to the library. They brought it into the main lab and set it on a bench.

'Obviously if we overdo it, we're going to kill everything,' said Roger. 'We need some sort of comparison cells that don't have the gold in them. Then, if we kill the neuroblastoma cells but not the comparison cells, we know we're in business.'

'There were some cells in there that looked like blood cells,' said Leblanc.

'Oh, right,' said Roger. 'Marta . . . the woman who got the syringe . . . she told me that some of her blood got into the syringe. That must be where they're from.'

'Okay, let's do it,' said Jeff.

Roger put a few drops from the syringe into a vial, and put the vial in the oven. 'What shall we try? We have a choice of, let's see, hot dog, coffee, soup, hamburger, popcorn, or baked potato. No button for neuroblastoma.'

'You can just enter the time,' said Jeff impatiently.

'Okay, how about five seconds?'

'Do it!' said Jeff.

Roger hit five seconds. After the oven stopped running, he took out the vial, and put the contents under the microscope. 'Everything looks as healthy as ever,' he said after a few minutes observation.

'Try longer!'

Roger repeated the experiment with a fifteen-second zap. Again, there seemed to be no effect on the cells. He repeated it again, heating the cells for thirty seconds.

'Total destruction,' he reported.

'It worked?' asked Jeff excitedly.

'It certainly did not work. Everything is cooked . . . the blastoma cells, the blood cells, everything. This doesn't seem to be the magic bullet we imagined.'

Jeff groaned and slumped his head on the bench.

'We're going to have to think of something else,' said Roger glumly.

'Wait,' said Leblanc. 'Permit me to make a small demonstration.' He took the viola case, which he had not let go of once since entering the lab, and laid it on the bench top. He opened it, revealing an instrument whose elegant curves and mellow varnish matched Leblanc's attire. He did not take the viola out of the plushly lined case, but instead took Roger's hand, and laid one of his fingers on a string. 'Rest it there gently, and tell me what you feel.'

'Nothing,' said Roger, puzzled.

'One moment.' Leblanc took a deep breath, and

began to sing an ascending scale in long, sustained notes. 'Do, re, mi, fa, so, la, ti—'

'La . . . that's it!' said Roger with a laugh. 'That tickled! I get you. Do it for Jeff.'

Jeff also laid his finger on the string, and also felt the vibration as Leblanc reached 'La.' 'Resonance?' he asked.

'Resonance,' said Leblanc. 'You must match the frequency of your stimulus to the resonant frequency of your target, am I not right?'

'You're right,' said Roger.

'With that, gentlemen, I must regretfully say good evening.' Leblanc closed the viola case and turned to leave.

'Wow them!' said Jeff.

'I shall do my best. As you will too, I am certain.' He shook hands with Jeff and Roger and left the lab.

'I remember now from physics,' said Jeff. 'The energy transfer is maximal at $f=w/2dc$, where f is the frequency, w is the atomic weight, d is the particle diameter, and c is the velocity of light. So let's see, we have a particle diameter of, what did you say?'

'Twelve point five nanometers.'

'And the atomic weight?'

'One hundred ninety-seven point zero.'

'That gives, hold on . . . make it fourteen point three gigaherz.'

'That's a high frequency.'

'Yeah, but do-able. We need a waveform generator.'

'Albrick does physiology, he'll have one.' The two men went rummaging in among the side rooms again, and eventually came out with a black box that they set next to the microwave oven.

'Shall we take the magnetron out of the oven?' asked Roger.

'No, let's just get the back off, and I'll wire the WaveTek directly to it. Bypass the electronics.' The two men had begun working with screwdrivers at the back of the oven when they heard a banging on the main door of the lab. They both jumped as if caught red-handed while cracking a safe.

'Roger!' came a muffled voice.

'It's Mary,' said Roger, and he went to open the door.

'Roger, I've been looking for you everywhere,' said Mary as she strode into the lab. 'Luckily I ran into Leblanc, and he told me you were here. Something terrible is happening . . . Albrick and the ROTC are going up to West Hollywood.'

'To West Hollywood? Why?'

'To disrupt the Gay Pride Parade. And they mean business . . . they've taken every gun in the place.'

'How do you know this?'

'I saw them leave the campus, shouting and all. So I went over to the ROTC building and talked to some women who'd been serving their dinner. They overheard Albrick giving some kind of rabble-rousing speech . . . really homophobic. They're going to lie in wait on the parade route, and give them hell . . . probably kill a bunch of them, if they're still in the same mood tomorrow morning. And at the dinner it was Tailhook all over again, only ten times worse. So I called Frinton, and he's going to see what he can do at his end. But I'm really scared. They have enough firepower to knock out the entire Los Angeles Police Department if they want to.'

'They should cancel the parade.'

227

'That they will never do, Frinton told me. Gay pride, you know.'

'Gay suicide, it sounds like. What the hell are we supposed to do?'

'I don't know. But I'll call Marcus, see if he can do anything.'

'Okay, but hold on. We've got another twelve hours or so. Jeff and I are trying to figure out a way to kill the neuroblastoma cells.'

Mary surveyed the apparatus in front of her. 'Let me guess. You're building a time machine, and you're going to travel back and tell Jeff not to break into Albrick's lab after all.'

'If only it were that easy. But listen, we found gold particles in the neuroblastoma cells . . . Albrick put them in when he was doing his genetic tinkering. Jeff suggested using microwaves to heat them, and we're adapting this oven to produce the right frequency of microwaves.'

'You're going to put your head in that oven and turn it on?' Mary asked Jeff incredulously.

Jeff looked at Mary, who had barely acknowledged his presence up till then. Something stirred in him, but he simply grunted, 'Yeah, I guess.'

Roger picked up on Jeff's unease. 'Let's get on with it,' he said. The two men continued working on the oven, connecting it to the waveform generator. From time to time, Jeff looked up at Mary, but she didn't return his gaze. When they had finished, Roger said, 'Okay, let's give it a try.' He squeezed out another few drops from the syringe. 'Set it at fourteen point three,' he said. He closed the oven door and made to hit the timer.

'No, turn it on from the WaveTek,' said Jeff. 'The buttons are out of the loop.'

Roger pushed down the toggle-switch. Nothing seemed to happen. 'It's on,' he said, 'but at this high frequency it doesn't make any sound, I guess.'

'And the fan's disconnected,' Jeff added.

After fifteen seconds Roger let go of the switch, took out the vial, and put it under the microscope. While Roger was waiting for the cells to settle, Jeff turned to Mary. 'Mary,' he said, 'You used to like me.'

'I still do,' she said. 'But it makes me uneasy being with you, for reasons I think you can understand.'

'I would never harm you.'

'I know, I know, but—'

'And I have to say, you are an extraordinarily beautiful woman.'

Mary and Roger both tensed up. Roger said, 'Jeff, let's concentrate on what we're doing, shall we? Could you inactivate the door switch on the oven, please?'

'It's out of the loop, like everything else, dummy,' Jeff said. 'And Mary, I thought I should tell you, I've never had sex with anyone my entire life, not with any woman, not with John, not with Roger. I'm a virg—'

'Jeff, I don't want to hear this from you,' said Mary. 'I'm not interested, and please don't—'

'It *worked*!' shouted Roger. 'Look here!' He pulled Jeff over to the microscope, and Jeff reluctantly took his eyes from Mary and applied them to the eyepieces. The neuroblastoma cells lay in shriveled, barely recognizable fragments, while Marta's blood cells looked as healthy as ever.

'Yeah, looks like it worked,' he said distantly, and

turned his gaze back to Mary.

'I'm going to put *my* head in the oven first,' Roger said, 'to make sure there are no unexpected effects.'

'Are you sure you know what you're doing?' asked Mary, now prey to two separate anxieties.

'Yeah, I'm pretty sure it's harmless at this frequency.' He put his head into the oven and reached for the WaveTek. 'A little tight in here . . . I feel like Alice in Wonderland, when she got big. And it smells of instant noodles. Well, here goes.'

Swallowing hard, he pushed down the toggle-switch and held it down while counting to fifteen.

Mary watched nervously, but Jeff seemed to have lost all interest in the proceedings. He moved closer to Mary and said, 'You know, Mary, I feel like I've been saving myself for you the whole time, though I didn't know it.'

'Stop it, Jeff, will you?' she said. 'I don't want to hear any more of this.' She moved over so that she was on the other side of Roger, away from Jeff.

Roger pulled his head out of the oven. 'Everything's fine . . . didn't feel a thing. Now, Jeff, it's your decision, are you ready to try this?'

Jeff didn't seem to hear him. 'The Virgin Mary and the Virgin Jeff,' he was saying dreamily. 'I like that concept, don't you?'

'The Virgin Mary?' said Roger. 'You better check with her husband.'

Jeff at last turned to Roger. 'You asshole! You don't know anything about her sex life. I've been praying to the Virgin Mary all my life, and now I realize that this is her, come down to earth, to be mine!'

'Jeff, the graft is making you crazy. You must see

that. The only way to get better is to put your head in—'

'To get better? *Better?* That's what you think is better! Because that's the way you'd like me to be . . . a fag like yourself, right?'

'Jeff, he's right,' said Mary. 'He's only thinking of what's best for you. You must make the decision for yourself, but you must realize that your brain has been tampered with, and some of the thoughts you're having are not your own real thoughts, they're not you. And—'

'Not me?'

'Not when you're well, when you're healthy.'

'I *am* healthy. How dare you say I'm not healthy? Let *me* be the judge of that. I'm straight, and that's healthy, isn't it?'

'Yes, healthy for some peo—'

'Healthy for me! Healthy for us . . . for you and me!'

'Jeff, I'm married and I'm not in the least interested in—'

'Well, Mary, Virgin Mary, Virgin Jeff has the hots for you, and—'

'Jeff,' pleaded Roger, 'there's nothing to be afraid of. I did it already.'

'I'm not afraid. I'm just happy the way I am.'

'You are afraid!'

'Crap! Mary, I—' He reached toward her invitingly, and she shrank back in fear.

'You're claustrophobic!' said Roger.

'Claustrophobic? Are you crazy?'

'You're scared to even put your head in the oven, it's so tight in there.'

'Scared, you cocksucker? Watch this!' Jeff grasped

the door of the oven and ducked his head inside.

Roger leapt onto Jeff's back, reached around his head, and grabbed hold of both sides of the oven. Jeff's head was jammed tightly into it. He immediately started thrashing and cursing.

'Mary!' shouted Roger. 'Quick, the switch . . . push it down . . . the switch on the WaveTek!'

'Roger, I can't . . . Oh my God, I can't, it's not right, it's his decision!'

Jeff was flailing madly with his arms, trying to get loose from Roger's grip, and trying to find the WaveTek or the cables that connected it to the oven.

'Mary, for God's sake, I can't hold him! *The switch, the switch!*'

'I can't!' Mary screamed. 'He doesn't consent! Oh God!'

'Let me out!' came Jeff's muffled shouts. 'Let me out, or I'll kill you!'

'Consent?' shouted Roger, desperately trying to hold on to Jeff's squirming body and to avoid his kicks. 'Did he consent to what Albrick did to him? We're just reversing that!'

'I know, I know, but . . . Oh God! I don't know . . . I can't!'

'Mary, I can't hold him! The switch! Press the switch!'

'Let me out! I'll kill you, both of you!'

'Oh God forgive me!' cried Mary, and she lunged for the switch and held it down. Jeff began roaring and thrashing crazily. Then the roaring diminished to a groaning, and the thrashing to a trembling, and then he was silent and limp.

'We've killed him!' cried Mary, and she let go of the switch and stared horrified at Jeff's lifeless body. Roger pulled him away from the oven and lowered him onto the floor.

'He's breathing,' he said. 'Oh God, don't let him die!' Roger stood back and leaned heavily against a bench, fighting to regain his breath.

Jeff's eyes opened slowly. He looked at Mary. He looked at her long and hard, as if in puzzlement or forgetfulness, and Mary began to cry. Then, Jeff's unseeing eyes lifted themselves from her and traversed an arc across the lab, not jumping from object to object but sliding smoothly, as if following some drifting apparition that was visible only to them. Finally, they landed on Roger, and Jeff stared at his face, first in puzzlement, then in recognition, and then with a growing smile.

'Roger!' he whispered.

'Jeff!'

'I feel like—'

'Like what?'

'Like I woke up . . . like I woke up from some terrible dream.'

'You did.'

'Let me get up.'

'Sure, but take it easy.' Roger and Mary helped Jeff to his feet, and he stood up, leaning groggily against a bench.

'I feel a bit light-headed,' he said, 'but I'll be fine. Mary, I can't believe . . . I can't believe I said all that stuff.'

Mary smiled. 'It's okay, I understand the reason.'

'I'm really sorry.'

'It's okay. It's all over. Don't think about it. We have other things to worry about.'

'You mean Albrick?'

'Albrick, yes, and his zombies.'

'You said they went up to West Hollywood?'

'Yes, all of them. All the ones who've had the injections. They're planning to attack the parade tomorrow morning.'

'Well, we know how to destroy the cells now,' said Roger. 'Zap them with microwaves. The only problem is persuading all those guys to put their heads inside this thing. Somehow, I think they'd be even less cooperative than Jeff was.'

Jeff blushed. 'If we could set something up,' he said, 'you know, like the metal detectors you walk through at airports. And they'd just walk through and get zapped. Some kind of trick like that. Or, you know, step into this telephone booth, there's someone wants to speak to you, and presto, zap them.'

'I don't see how we could do anything like that before tomorrow morning. They're under Albrick's command, and they going to be scattered over West Hollywood, probably. How on earth are we going to rig anything up like that? We'd need to irradiate the whole city.'

Mary was seized by a thought. 'Microwaves work from a distance, right?'

'Right,' said Roger, 'but you're going to have a power problem as soon as you get more than a foot or so away. Inverse square law. And, there's going to be a big power loss at that frequency anyway, because most of the energy is reflected away at the surface of the head. Only a tiny fraction makes it through into the brain.'

'But I remember something. Have you been to Mount Wilson, either of you?'

'Mount Wilson?' said Jeff. 'Yes . . . you mean up the Crest Highway, where the telescope is, behind Pasadena?'

'Yes,' said Mary. 'Can you remember, when you're looking out over the city from there, can you see West Hollywood?'

'Um, I think, well, I remember seeing the Pacific Design Center . . . I remember picking it out with my binoculars once when I was up there. But why?'

'The Pacific Design Center . . . that's in West Hollywood?'

'Yes, on San Vicente, near the Beverly Hills end of the city.'

'And the rest of West Hollywood?'

'It's pretty much hidden, I think. Griffith Park juts out and cuts off the view. The way I remember it, you can see the little observatory in Griffith Park, and the Design Center is just above to the right of it, but much further away. You can't see the eastern part of the city at all. But why?' Jeff felt light-headed again and grabbed for the bench to steady himself.

'Roger,' said Mary, 'why don't you help Jeff get upstairs . . . the fresh air would help him, I think. There's something Marcus told me once. I need to call him. I'll follow you up in a couple of minutes.'

'Sure,' said Roger. 'Anyone would feel better getting out of this lab.'

The two men moved slowly toward the elevator. Roger was holding his arm around Jeff in a precautionary way, without actually taking his weight. 'You're not going to fall down on me, are you?' he said. 'You put my back out in that little tussle. I'd rather not do any heavy lifting.'

'I'm feeling good,' Jeff said. 'Let me just rest my arm around your shoulder, like this, there we go.'

The elevator took them up to the first floor, and they walked out of the building into the dark, deserted courtyard. Jeff and Roger walked over to a bench, and sat down. The inscription on the back of the bench read: THOU SHALT NOT LIE WITH MANKIND, AS WITH WOMANKIND: IT IS AN ABOMINATION, but neither man noticed it.

Now that they were sitting down, it was no longer necessary for Jeff to rest his arm on Roger's shoulder, but he did not take it away. After a few seconds, Roger turned to look at Jeff. Their eyes met, and they looked at each other for one moment longer than is permissible between two persons who are not lovers.

'Jeff!' said Roger in a choked voice.

'Roger!'

The two men drew each other closer, and their lips touched.

The faint sound of music drifted across the courtyard. It was Leblanc's quartet, launching into the slow movement of *Death and the Maiden*.

CHAPTER TWENTY-FIVE

The convoy of twenty or so vehicles turned off the
405 Freeway at the Westwood exit, and rolled onto
the grounds of the Wadsworth VA hospital. The trucks
stopped in one of the back parking lots, a tree-
shadowed space between the cemetery and the
stadium, where they were least likely to be noticed. It
was about 2:00 a.m. Albrick had stopped the convoy
once already, at a freeway rest stop, to let his men sober
up. They had stayed there for two hours, and some of
the men had slept. When they set out on the second
leg of the journey, the men were much quieter, and by
the time they reached Westwood, their mood was one
of grim determination.

Albrick called his company commanders together,
and they went over their plans and set up
communications. Then Albrick, James, and two aides
broke into a private car and drove it down Wilshire
and Santa Monica boulevards to reconnoiter the scene
of their planned action. The streets of Westwood and
Beverly Hills were already quiet, but as they came into
West Hollywood there were still plenty of people about.
The bars of Boystown, clustered around the intersection
of Santa Monica and San Vicente Boulevards, were just
closing. Groups of young men were milling about,

talking, and laughing. Some were making use of the bleachers that had been erected on the grassy median strip to continue the conversations they had been having in the bars. Some were relieving themselves in corners or throwing up in gutters. Other were heading off for the all-night clubs or desperately trying to make last-minute pick-ups before the crowd dispersed.

The sight of four men in military uniforms, even in a private car, attracted some attention from the men on the sidewalk. There were even a few wolf-whistles. Albrick cursed, and told the driver to drive on. They continued eastward to Crescent Heights Boulevard, where the marshaling stations and announcer's platform for the start of the parade had already been set up. Then they turned around and drove slowly back westward along the route of the parade, checking out the buildings and side streets. At one point they took a detour down an alley, so that Albrick could inspect the backs of the buildings that fronted onto the Boulevard. This part of the city was much quieter, although there were still a few people about.

When they got back to the convoy, Albrick briefed the remainder of the group on the locations that were to be used. Then small groups of men were ferried down to West Hollywood, again in private cars. They went by Wilshire Boulevard to avoid the late-night revelers, and then drove up the side streets to reach the buildings they were aiming for. The car stopped briefly at a dark back door, two or three men got out, forced the door, and were inside within a few seconds. Then they found the stairwell, climbed to the roof, and set up their weapons and their communications equipment. By 4:30, a hundred and fifty men were stationed on rooftops along the quarter-mile stretch between Sweetzer Avenue and La Cienega Boulevard. Once they had set up their equipment and reported their locations, the men stretched out and tried to get some sleep before dawn.

Back at the VA hospital, Albrick briefed the remaining hundred or so men on their roles. Two communications engineers were checking with the men on the rooftops by radio. They were also monitoring police and military channels, but none carried any reports about their activities. They seemed so far to have evaded notice. Around 4:30, however, one of the radiomen came over to Albrick. 'Just got a message from a colleague in Washington, sir,' he said. 'Don't know whether it's something you should know about. General Braddock at the Pentagon to PAVE-PAWS Mount Wilson. The staff there is to admit his wife, Mary Braddock, and cooperate with her. They're supposed to call back to the Pentagon for further orders when she arrives.'

'PAVE-PAWS . . . that's the phased array?'

'Yes sir.'

'What in heaven's name—? James!'

James walked over sleepily from the Jeep where he had been dozing.

'James, Mary Braddock has taken it into her head to go visit Mount Wilson in the middle of the night.'

'Spunky gal! The stars are incredible, and the view of LA. Did you ever see *E.T.*?'

'Did you tell Cavendish about how we got the TR gene into the blastoma cells?'

'Um, hold on, this is too abrupt a change of conversation for four in the morning . . .'

'Did you tell him?' Albrick demanded. 'Yes or no?'

'Er, no . . . that is, I told him we were using physical methods.'

'Well, he must have figured it out.' Albrick turned back to the radioman. 'Your colleague . . . can he do a countermand?'

'I can do it from here, sir. We have the codes.'

'Okay, then countermand. No one to be admitted under any circumstances.'

'From General Braddock, sir?'

'That's it.'

'Yes sir. And sir, if you wish, we can follow that with a channel block. Stop any further communications in or out, if that's what you wish, sir.'

'Do it. And call back to Levitican. Put the helicopter crew on alert. We may need them.'

CHAPTER TWENTY-SIX

A deer darted into the road, gazed vacantly for a moment at the car's headlights, and bounded off into the chaparral. It barely escaped having its tail clipped. Roger swerved but quickly regained control. 'Sorry about that,' he said, 'I guess this is wilderness, even if we're only fifteen minutes out of LA.'

'What happened?' came Jeff's sleepy voice from the backseat.

'A deer,' said Mary. 'Have you been sleeping?'

'Yeah, I guess, some. Deers are nothing. I saw a bear at the side of the road once, up at Newcomb Ranch. It was dumpster diving. And they have mountain lions . . . an off-road cyclist was attacked by one not far from here . . . on the Jeep trail up to Mount Wilson.'

'Was he hurt?'

'Bit his head . . . he needed quite a few stitches. And the next day, he went up the same trail, with a wooden club to protect himself.'

'Bet he wished he had one of the old hard-shell helmets. Styrofoam is fine for when you hit the pavement, but for mountain lion teeth . . . maybe not.'

In the cool night air, the car was making easy work of the long climb. Since leaving the lights of La Cañada behind them, they had seen nothing except what was revealed by the car's headlights: an ever-winding strip of tarmac framed by bushes and boulders. Reflector posts cropped up monotonously every hundred yards or so. Occasionally they drove between tall rock walls where, generations ago, the road's builders had hewn a path through an obstructing hillside, or else they found themselves suddenly on a bridge that vaulted audaciously over invisible depths. For a road to nowhere, the Crest Highway was over-engineered.

'Anyway,' Mary went on, 'I heard about the phased array here sometime in the eighties. Marcus was involved in some of the logistical work. But it was secret, and he didn't tell me a whole lot about it, even though he had to come out here quite a lot.'

'Why was it secret?' asked Roger. 'I've seen the one on Cape Cod . . . there's nothing secret about it . . . you can see it from the road and anyone will tell you what it is.'

'It was in violation of the SALT II agreement. What they agreed was that each side should have no more than seven of them, and they should be placed at the perimeter of the country, facing outward. The Cape Cod machine was one of the seven, and it was perfectly legal, but this one was the eighth. And, it is sort of on the perimeter of the country, but it's still inland from LA.'

'What difference did that make?'

'Well, the idea was that they should provide long-range warning against ICBMs or submarine-launched missiles, because that's what they call "stabilizing": It increases the likelihood that you'll have time to retaliate before you get incinerated, and so the other side is less likely to fire off its missiles in the first place. But if you have one inland, or near a large city, you could use it to guide anti-ballistic missiles, in other words to provide an umbrella against attack, and that's *de*stabilizing, because then you might be able to launch an attack and yet protect yourself from the enemy's response. At that time, everyone thought anti-ballistic missiles were just around the corner, you remember. We were going to be able to knock the ICBMs out on their way down, and the phased-array radars would be the eyes and ears of the system. So the treaty was to prevent that . . . but we cheated.'

'What are phased arrays, anyway?' asked Roger. 'I'm a bit hazy on the—'

'I can tell you that,' Jeff broke in. 'They had an article in *Scientific American* about them. They're like the old rotating-dish radars, basically, but they're stationary. You have a whole lot of antennas, set up in a rectangular array . . . maybe thirty by fifty for a big one. Each antenna is sort of like the magnetron in a microwave oven. The trick is, you adjust the phases of the signals going out of the different antennas across the array. The waves coming from neighboring antennas interfere with the others, either constructively or destructively, and that controls what direction the beam goes out in. If they're all in phase, the beam goes out straight ahead. If you phase advance the waves from the antennas at the left side, the beam will go out to the right, and so on. So you can guide the beam around electronically, and that means instantaneously. In fact you can flick it around so fast that you can have what amounts to several different beams going out at once. That would be useful if you're tracking a lot of missiles. And the power is greater, of course, because you can make them as big as you want, and because the beam is so focused.

They have them at airports now.'

'Yes, that's right,' said Mary, 'but these PAVE-PAWS radars are much larger. Anyway, after the Berlin Wall came down there was a big re-think about missile defense. They decided that the main threat was an attack from a rogue state . . . from some fanatical dictator who had a few missiles and didn't care what the consequences were. So they decided they really needed an anti-missile system now, because deterrence might not work. But the ABM missile thing was out the window. Too expensive, and it didn't work . . . they couldn't even hit a Scud, let alone an ICBM. So they went for lasers, particle beams, and what have you . . . whatever was left over from the Star Wars program. But they had problems with those, too. Then, finally, they came up with the notion of modifying the phased arrays . . . mainly by increasing the power . . . so that they wouldn't just detect missiles, they'd knock them out, too.'

'That would have to be immense . . . the power, I mean, wouldn't it?' asked Roger. 'If—'

'Here, look!' Mary interrupted. 'Mount Wilson, five miles. Turn right.' A few yards beyond the sign, just beyond a ranger station, a narrow side road became visible. Roger turned the car onto it. As the car turned, a distant mountain became visible to the east, its blackness silhouetted against a deep red band of sky . . . the very beginnings of the dawn. 'Spectacular, isn't it?' said Jeff. 'It's like there's a fiery furnace behind Mount Baldy somewhere.'

The Mount Wilson road was much slower going than the Crest Highway. The grade was steeper, and the turns tighter and less predictable. In places, the road was cut into the side of the nearly sheer cliff. The headlights illuminated walls of black granite, crisscrossed by veins of lighter rock in crazy patterns, as if the rock had been fractured and filled many times over. Just when it seemed like the road was going to terminate in blank rock, it would take a last-minute turn and dodge under an overhang or around a crag. Little rivers of melt-water crossed the road from time to time, spreading gravel and rocks across the asphalt. Tired and anxious, Roger drove the car at a crawl.

'But the power thing,' Mary went on, 'this is the interesting part. Marcus told me they built a power line all the way from a nuclear power station down the coast . . .'

'From San Onofre?' asked Jeff.

'San Onofre, yes. It's a dedicated line.'

'Yeah, you can see two lines crossing the freeway, coming out of the power station. So one of them comes up to Mount Wilson?'

'That's right. And the entire output of the station can be switched to that line at the throw of a switch. It's controlled remotely from Mount Wilson.'

'Wow,' said Jeff. 'But what happens to the people who are getting power through the other line?'

'Civilians,' said Mary. 'They don't count. But actually, the system has only been tested once at full power, according to what Marcus told me, and that was in 1994, right after the Northridge earthquake.'

'After the earthquake . . . how so?'

'There was a power outage, all over LA, right? It lasted, I don't know, a few hours?'

'Different times in different places.'

'Well, they had planned for just such an outage . . .

when they could take it to full power and not be noticed. Within an hour after the earthquake, they revved up the radar and knocked out a TRANSIT satellite. Marcus's people had a list of expendable satellites and this was the first one that popped up over the horizon. The Navy wasn't too happy about that, even though they're out of date, apparently. At the time, all they knew was that the satellite went dead, but in '95 they retrieved it with the space shuttle. Its electronics were fried, Marcus said. And they did several more during the day . . . they kept the power out deliberately. I shouldn't be telling you this.'

'Damn,' said Jeff. 'So while my parents were huddled in their backyard around a candle and a pocket radio, the US Government was borrowing their electricity to take pot shots at its own satellites?'

'Something like that.'

'So are you pretty sure that it can do what we need it to do?' Roger asked. 'I mean to aim at West Hollywood and have the right frequency and so on?'

'Not sure, but it seems like our best chance. There's going to be two people there, Marcus said, and he's told them to help us.'

'Well that's good, because unless there are buttons saying, you know, HOT DOG, BAKED POTATO, WEST HOLLYWOOD, I wouldn't know how to proceed, would you? I mean, I can't help thinking we'd be more useful down on Santa Monica Boulevard with a pile of paving stones.'

'Well, I'm hoping Frinton is organizing resistance down there. And I told him to try to make sure that Albrick's men went down toward the Design Center. I hope to God Jeff's right about the sight-lines.'

'I am right,' Jeff said, 'unless Griffith Park lifted up in the meantime.'

'It did lift up . . . in the Hollywood quake,' said Roger. 'But only by five millimeters. Hey, looks like we're here.'

As the car took a sharp right-hand turn, the winking red lights of a small forest of transmitters loomed up ahead. And at the same time, the ground fell away to the right to reveal the entire Los Angeles basin, still swathed in darkness. From their six-thousand-foot viewpoint, the city looked blissfully peaceful. The regular grids of street lights converged toward the ocean. The highrises of downtown LA were easily spotted, as were the mini-downtowns of Pasadena, Glendale, and, far off to the right, Century City.

They came to a junction where several roads came together, and Roger paused for a moment. Mary said, 'It's a building with a sign saying National Weather Service, Marcus told me.'

'It's too dark to see any buildings, let alone any signs. They don't have a single light up here.'

'Probably because of the telescopes,' Jeff said. 'They don't want any stray photons bouncing around. Let's cruise around here.' Roger took a right-hand turn, marked MT. WILSON CIRCLE. The road led them around the peak of the mountain, always with a view of the city on their right. After half a mile the road curved sharply to the left, and they passed some locked gates.

'That's the entry to the park, where the telescopes are,' said Jeff. 'And that other gate is the head of the trail down to Altadena.' Roger continued, and after another half mile they looped back to the junction again, without seeing any buildings.

'What about those other roads,' said Mary. 'What do those signs say?'

Roger maneuvered the car to illuminate the street signs. 'Er, let me see, this one is Audio Drive, and it's one-way the wrong way. And this one is Video Drive.'

'I think it's another loop,' said Jeff, 'like Mount Wilson Circle, but inside of it and higher up.'

'Okay, let's try it,' said Roger. 'This seems to go closer to where the transmitters are.' He took a sharp left turn and headed the car up toward the very peak of the mountain. The road was flanked by sheds and service buildings, and by transformers that were humming away inside chain-link cages. The concrete footings of the transmitters jutted out into the road, and the pylons themselves extended upward into the darkness. Roger stopped to point a flashlight at a sign at the side of the road. It read: Caution – High-Level Radio-Frequency Energy Area – No Loitering.

'Hard to believe that there's anyone around here . . . the whole place looks deserted,' he said. 'Let's go on.' He drove slowly forward. After about another hundred yards they came to a building on the left. The bottom part of the building was constructed of concrete, but the upper part, ranging perhaps sixty feet in the air, was covered in corrugated fiberglass siding. There were no windows, just one doorway facing onto the road, and what looked like the entry to a pair of garages. Both the doorway and the garages were secured by metal doors. A small notice fixed to the building read: US WEATHER BUREAU. 'This looks like it,' said Roger. He pulled the car over to the right-hand verge and parked. After he had done so, he noticed that the right-hand side of the car was overhanging a steep slope that seemed to lead down to Mount Wilson Circle. 'Stay in the car a second,' he said. 'I'll go see if I can rouse anyone.' He walked over to the doorway of the building, where he found an intercom. He pressed the button, and after a moment a voice said, 'Weather Bureau.'

'This is Mary Braddock's party,' Roger said.

'I'll be right with you,' the voice said. Roger turned and gave a thumbs-up signal to Mary and Jeff. After half a minute the door opened, and a man in jeans and a plaid jacket came out. 'Where's Mrs Braddock?' he said.

'Over there,' Roger said. They walked over to the car. The man shone his flashlight into the interior. Seeing Mary in the passenger seat, he walked around the car, edging his way along the top of the slope. Mary rolled down her window.

'Good morning, ma'am, your husband told us to expect you. Your ID, please.'

Mary reached for her purse. While she was rummaging around in the darkness, the man said, 'This is a real mystery to us, ma'am. I can't imagine that this is just a pleasure trip, at this time of the night, is it?'

'No, it certainly isn't,' Mary said. 'We have some serious work for you.'

At that moment another figure appeared in the doorway of the building. 'Greg . . . a countermand,' the person shouted. 'A countermand, from Washington. Get back in here . . . no one to be let in.'

Greg pulled a gun from under his jacket. 'What's going on? Get out of the car,' he ordered.

'Come back in!' the person in the doorway shouted, even more urgently.

'Damn it—' said Mary. Then she released the door catch, got her foot against the door, and heaved the man away from the car. He lost his balance, but hung on desperately to the door frame with one hand. Roger seized the hand and prised it loose from the door. The man tried to grab onto Roger's hands, but they slipped through his grasp, and he fell backward down the slope into the darkness. There was the sound of an impact, followed by a scream so loud it seemed it must have wakened the whole of Los Angeles. Finally it tailed off into a muted groaning.

Roger ran toward the door of the building, but it slammed closed before he had even got halfway across the road. Jeff got out of the car and ran over to join him, but Mary remained in the car, shaking and crying. It seemed like the Aconda episode all over again.

Roger and Jeff hit the intercom and pounded on the door, but there was no response. The groaning from down the slope ceased, and it was eerily quiet again. 'What the hell do we do now?' asked Roger. They inspected the building, but as far as they could make out in the darkness, there was no other way in. The side walls were solid concrete, and the back was buried in the bedrock that reared up behind the building. 'Let's go see what happened to that guy, anyway,' Roger said. 'I hope to God we didn't kill him.' Roger grabbed the flashlight out of the car. 'Mary, hang in there,' he said. Then he pointed the flashlight down the slope. 'Can't see a thing,' he said.

'He must have fallen right down to Mount Wilson Circle,' said Jeff. 'Do you think we can climb down?'

'Not in the darkness. Let's drive back down and see if we can find him from the road.'

They got back into the car, turned, and drove back to the junction, and then turned left along Mount Wilson Circle. They drove slowly along, scanning the left-hand verge with the flashlight as they went. Then, as they rounded a curve, Roger shouted 'Oh my Christ! Mary, don't look!'

The car's headlights were illuminating a giant century plant at the side of the road. The body was spread across it, lying on its back; the head dangled upside-down on the side facing the car, and the open eyes seemed to be staring accusingly at them. Roger and Jeff got out and walked over to him, trying to brace themselves for what they were going to see. At least a dozen of the plant's barbed spines had gone clean through the man's body. Blood was running down his face and into his hair, and was dripping from there onto the pavement. 'He's dead,' Roger said, stating the obvious.

'Jesus forgive us!' said Jeff faintly.

'Indeed,' said Roger. 'So far this trip has been an unqualified disaster. We've killed a government employee and we haven't accomplished anything. Maybe we should just wait to get arrested.'

'Roger,' Jeff said, 'we've got to do something. In a few hours, Albrick's going to be attacking the parade.'

'There's the gun,' said Roger, and he walked and picked up the weapon. 'If it's still working, maybe we could shoot the lock off the door.'

'It was a solid steel door,' said Jeff. 'I'm sure we're not going to get through it with a pistol. For a so-called weather bureau, they are very security conscious. They even had an ocular scanner, did you notice?'

'You mean the thing where you look into it and it

checks the blood vessels in your retina?'

'Right. The eyepiece was right above the intercom.'

'Oh, yeah, I saw that, but I thought it was some kind of spyhole, for them to look out.'

'No, it's a scanner. I downloaded some pictures of them once, when I was really into that stuff.'

Roger looked at the dead man. 'Well,' he said, 'I think we have to do some emergency ophthalmic surgery. Get the flashlight. And tell Mary not to look!'

'You're going to cut the eye out? Jesus!'

'That's right. And see if Mary has a pair of tweezers, will you?'

While Jeff went back to the car, Roger fished a penknife out of his pocket. He checked both the dead man's eyes: They were in good shape. Then he tried to visualize the anatomy of the eyesocket, as he had learned it many years ago.

'She doesn't have any tweezers,' Jeff said as he returned with the flashlight.

'Damn, I need something.' He walked back to the car, opened the trunk, and found the toolbox. Inside he found a pair of needle-nosed pliers. Mary was curled up in a fetal position on the passenger seat. 'Mary, I've got to get one of his eyes,' he said. 'It's the only way we can get in.'

'Do it,' Mary said. 'Just don't let me see it. This is too awful.'

Roger returned to the body. While Jeff held the flashlight, he grasped the lower eyelid of the right eye with the pliers, inserted the knife blade and extended the eye slit laterally. Then he cut around the base of the eye, back toward the nose, until the whole of the lower eyelid was cut away. He did the same with the upper lid. Freed of the lids, the eye looked enormous and even more grossly accusing than before. Now Roger tried to get a purchase on the conjunctiva, but the pliers refused to hold onto the slippery membranes. Eventually, he simply grasped a fold of the tissue between his fingernails, and pulled the eye over until the pupil was buried out of sight next to the root of the nose. He cut through the conjunctiva, and worked his way around the eye until it was attached only by the eye muscles and the optic nerve. He began diving for the eye muscles with the pliers, cutting their attachments to the eyeball. '*Rectus lateralis, no, medialis,* I keep forgetting it's upside-down . . . *rectus inferior,* I mean *superior* . . . *obliquus* . . . shitting hell!' Roger had accidentally stabbed the globe of the eye with the knife. The eye jelly burst out of the eye, forming a quivering wet mound on the blade of the knife. The remainder of the eye collapsed to a shapeless mess. Jeff turned pale and vomited onto the asphalt.

'Sorry, I'm not in good form at five in the morning with no sleep,' Roger said. 'Are you okay? Well, that's one down, one to go.' He flicked the eye jelly off the blade, and began afresh on the left eye. This time, he cut all the eye muscles without incident, until the eye was dangling only by the optic nerve. 'Need one of those grapefruit knives,' he said. 'I can't get behind the eyeball with a straight blade.'

'Here,' said Jeff, wiping his chin. He was glad of something to do. He took the knife out of Roger's hand and found a small round stone. He laid the knife blade broadside on the stone and began pounding it with a rock. 'It would help if this was red-hot,' he commented dourly, as the blade reluctantly began to bend.

Eventually he had the blade curved into something like a grapefruit knife. Roger slipped it behind the eyeball and neatly severed the nerve. The eyeball fell free into his hand. 'Let's hope this works,' he said. 'It's kind of distorted a little.'

'It's intelligent software,' Jeff said. 'It looks at the hierarchy of branch points, not the absolute geometry.'

'Before we go back up, we should hide the body a bit. Someone's sure to come by . . . the astronomers must be going off duty.'

Roger took the eyeball and placed it on the dashboard of the car, again warning Mary not to look. Then he walked back to the body. It was a truly frightful sight: the empty, bloody eye sockets and the impaled, back-curving torso suggested the most barbarous of martyrdoms. With difficulty they heaved the corpse up off the century plant and let it fall onto the ground behind, where it was out of the sight of a casual passerby. 'This is about as good as we're going to do right now,' Roger said. 'Now let's see how well our key fits.' He picked up the gun and they went back to the car. The darkness was beginning to give way to dawn, and as they drove back up Video Drive they could dimly make out the mist-shrouded forests falling away toward Altadena.

'Okay, you two stand to either side of the door,' Roger said as they got out of the car. 'I don't want the guy taking shots at either of you.'

'What about you?' asked Jeff anxiously.

'I'll be careful,' Roger said. They came up to the front door, and Roger held up the eyeball to the scanner with his right hand. His left hand held the gun pointed at the door. A little screen lit up: MISREAD, TRY AGAIN.

'Damn,' Roger said. He took a careful look at the eyeball. He couldn't remember which side was up. Eventually he figured it out from the layout of the muscle attachments, and he held it up to the scanner again. This time the screen said ENTRY GRANTED, and there was the click as a magnetic latch opened. Roger pushed on the door and it swung inward. A woman was running along a corridor toward the door, but when she saw Roger, the eyeball, and the gun, she let out a faint scream and stopped in her tracks. Roger rushed forward. He threw the eyeball down and held the gun to the woman's head. 'Put your hands up,' he said curtly, as Jeff and Mary came in through the door behind him. Roger had a vivid fantasy that he was acting in some third-rate thriller, and he imagined the director saying, 'Cut, cut . . . that was just hopeless, Roger, could you try it again with just a little more panache?' While he was in this fugue state, Jeff and Mary grabbed hold of the woman, frisked her for weapons, and marched her back into the main control room of the building. They sat her down on a swivel chair and tied her to it with a roll of duct tape that lay conveniently nearby. She had not said a word.

Mary surveyed the room; it was packed with enough screens, consoles, and computers to run a moon mission. 'This is boy stuff,' she said. 'Let me know when you have figured it out.' She took the gun from Roger's hand and slumped down in a chair. She fell into a half-doze, but kept the gun pointed at the bandaged woman.

CHAPTER TWENTY-SEVEN

'I'm a Dancing T-cell and I lost my mommas!'

Mavis Trautheim peered down at the anxious little fur-ball standing in front of her kiosk. 'Okay, sweetie, hold on,' she said, and she scanned down the printout. 'Los Angeles AIDS Foundation . . . mmm . . . number 142. It should be about three blocks up, after the Rubber Queen. Say, Anthony, could you hold the fort for a few minutes? I'm going to take this kid up to the LAAF contingent . . . she lost her blood group.'

'Her blood group?' asked Anthony sleepily. He was slumped in a folding chair.

'Yeah, her blood group . . . she's a T-cell. Hint, hint, nudge, nudge. I'm trying to make you laugh. You know, laugh . . . as in LAAF.'

'Mavis, it's seven thirty in the morning, I don't laugh before lunch. I don't even smile before ten thirty. Just pick me up a double espresso on the way back, will you?'

'Honey, just sit here and look like you're awake for five minutes, please.' Mavis eased her enormous bulk off the seat and hopped down onto the sidewalk. 'What's your name, sweetie?'

'Boudicca Hensley-Ferraro,' said the fur-ball.

'Boudicca, that's a nice name. I'm Mavis. Your

mommas are up the street, come along.'

'I'm seven and a quarter. I was conceived by oocyte fusion.'

'That's neat. And is this your first year as a Dancing T-cell?'

'It's my third year. But the first year, I only danced part of the way. Then I rode in my one momma's backpack.'

Mavis waved at a studly, bare-chested man who was polishing an immaculate 1974 Thunderbird convertible. 'Hey, Max!' she shouted. 'Who are you driving this year?'

'Hi, Mavis! Dirk Zamboni and his boyfriend-du-jour.'

'Dirk Zamboni? With his saxaphoni? You mean he finally came out of the closet? I gave up on him in 1976.'

'Yeah, I think now he's out, they're going to clean out the closet and donate it to the Smithsonian.' He returned to his polishing.

'Did you make your costume?' Mavis asked Boudicca, as they continued up Crescent Heights Boulevard.

'Me and my boyfriend did.' Then, as if further explanation was needed, she added, 'I'm heterosexual.'

'Good for you. And your boyfriend, does he have two mommas or two daddies, or one of each?'

'Rupert? He has two daddies and one momma,' said Boudicca. 'But only one of his daddies is his biological daddy. They mixed their sperm together, before they put it into his momma's vagina. *I* think his daddy Paul is his biological daddy, because Rupert looks like him.'

'Well, you sure know a lot about the facts of life, for a seven-year-old.'

'I'm seven and a quarter,' Boudicca reminded her primly.

As they walked past the assembling Ocarina Choir of Santa Barbara, players came out to talk with Mavis. 'You've got us right in front of the Arizona Lesbian Brass Band,' they complained. 'How on earth do you expect us to make ourselves heard? Listen to that tuba!'

'Sorry, sorry, sorry!' said Mavis. 'How about we move up the Bankers for Human Rights? Bankers! Bankers!' she yelled. 'Move on up, please . . . to the next available teller!' A group of men and women wearing matching pinstripe suits and carrying matching black leather attaché cases squeezed in between the ocarina players and the brass band. Frinton's friend Luke was not among them. 'Arizona Lesbians, back up! Back up!' shouted Mavis.

The Arizona Lesbians were not too happy about backing up, because it brought them into a mushroom cloud of blue smoke, at the nucleus of which the members of the Homophile Cigar-Smokers' League of America was puffing away. They were a motley collection of men, most of whom looked like they would have preferred to ride motorbikes down the Boulevard. They stubbed out their regular smokes and lit up new cigars, the likes of which Mavis had never seen before. They must have been two feet long and over an inch in girth. Among the men, Miles Brougham stood out on account of the baton-twirler's uniform he was wearing and the baton he was carrying in his free hand. An ornate, jewel-encrusted mace, it would not have looked out of place at a royal coronation, lying opulently on a red velvet cushion. Miles waved over to Mavis, and pantomimed an offer for her to sample his cigar. When she signaled her regrets, he shouted over, 'Tell Marta I'll be there momentarily!' and he returned to his cigar talk.

After Mavis and Boudicca passed a few more groups, their way was blocked by the Rubber Queen float, which was trying to back into its allotted space. The Rubber Queen herself was not yet on her throne, but some of her mermaid acolytes – exceedingly well-built young men whose naked torsos blended sensuously into scaly fishtails – were already on board. They were smearing each other with baby oil or practising tossing condoms to the crowd.

'Dicca! Where on earth did you get to?' shouted one of Boudicca's mothers as she ran up to claim her daughter. 'Thank you so much, I was worried to death!' she said to Mavis, and she hustled Boudicca along the sidewalk to join the rest of the T-cells. Mavis followed them. She skirted the T-cells, who were chattering among themselves, comparing costumes, and trying to ignore their fretful parents. She went on to where the Act Out! troupe was gathering.

'Mave!' said Marta with a smile, and she gave her girlfriend a hug. 'I thought you were doing information.'

'I have to get back,' said Mavis. 'I brought a lost T-cell up here. Are you guys all set? Hi, gang! Hi Jimmy! New drum?'

'Yeah,' said the thin youth with a rueful grin. 'Not much left of the old one after that jaunt to Levitican.'

'Better luck today.' Mavis turned back to Marta. 'Need anything before I head back, hon?'

'Just our sergeant-major.'

'He said he was coming right along.'

'Sure, but I'm betting the mermaids are going to hold him up.'

'Well, you've got time still. But I'll hurry him up.'

A Rolls-Royce Silver Cloud eased its way down the street toward them. It had to pause frequently for groups of assembled marchers to move out of its way. 'Who the hell let this guy through . . . are they fast asleep up there?' said Mavis. She moved forward to wave down the car, then she noticed the license number: OBGYN 1. 'It's Frinton!' she said. 'Don't tell me *he's* going to ride in the parade. Whatever next!'

Jasper parked the car in the center of the street and came over to Marta and her group. He looked tired and disheveled. 'Marta,' he said, 'you people have got to stay out of the parade.'

'We've got to *what*?'

'Stay out . . . don't march! You're in danger.'

'What are you talking about?'

'There's a group of crazies come up from Levitican . . . military types . . . they're planning to disrupt the parade. That Albrick fellow has gone psycho.'

'How do you know this?'

'I heard it from Mary Braddock . . .'

'Crap!'

'Marta, it's not a joke. They're come up here and they're armed to the teeth.'

'Did you talk to Portillo?' Mavis broke in.

'I talked to Portillo, I talked to the whole committee . . . those I could get hold of. They won't cancel. They're bringing in some extra police, but they won't cancel.'

'Well, then, we won't cancel either,' said Marta. 'Where are those turkeys anyway?'

'Who knows? On their way, probably. But Marta,

don't you see, Act Out! will be their number one target. When they see you guys they're going to go ballistic. You must drop out.'

'No way!'

'Then go as something else. Just march as civilians . . . regular clothes, no act. Don't draw attention to yourselves.'

'No bleepin' way, Jasper.' The groups of actors had gathered round, and they all shouted, 'No way! We're marching!'

'God dammit, Marta, this is not play-acting, it is real! Mavis . . . knock some sense into her, will you? Marta, you're going to be sitting ducks! These are not some hoodlums from East LA, they're professional soldiers with guns, led by a homophobic madman!'

A voice came over the PA system: 'The parade will start in five minutes. Groups 1 though 10, you should be in position and ready to move off. Groups 11 though 20, you should be completing your assembly.' The announcement was followed by disco music.

'We are marching!' said Marta emphatically. 'We'll deal with those cretins if need be. *Venceremos!*' The group of actors yelled assent and waved clenched fists.

Mavis turned to Jasper. 'Why are you harassing them?' she said. 'If it's true what you're saying, go tell the police, have them catch these guys, have them put up roadblocks or whatever.'

'They've been alerted, but there's not a whole lot they can do. They haven't found Albrick's men and I'm not sure they believe that they're coming. But Mary is trying to get a response from the military, through her husband.'

'I'm not sure *I* believe they're coming,' said Marta.

'But if they do come, we'll whip their asses.'

'Marta, I beg you, get real . . . they are armed.'

'We're marching, that's final.'

Jasper groaned. 'Okay, I knew this was going to happen.'

'So . . . why did you even bother to come down?'

'For this reason . . . follow me.' Jasper led Marta to the back of the Rolls, opened the trunk, and pulled back a tarpaulin. Thirty AK 47 rifles and the same number of Kahr K9 pistols lay in a glistening heap. 'They're loaded,' Jasper said, 'so don't go playing any games with them.'

'Hey, hey, hey!' said Marta, grabbing one of the rifles and looking it up and down. 'I like it. Where the hell did you get these bad boys?'

'The Gun Hut on Pico. "Your twenty-four-hour Armament Supply." It's amazing what they have in their back room.'

'Did they ask any questions?'

'The guy said, "What in hell are you planning to do with these?"'

'And—?'

'I said "Murder my wife and children," and he said, "Go for it, man."'

Marta started distributing the weapons to her troupe. They put down their plywood rifles and started testing the real guns for heft and balance.

Mavis looked scared. 'This is getting too real. Marta, maybe you should think about not marching. We could—'

'No way, babe.'

Frinton got back into his car. He rolled down the window. 'Marta . . . don't use these unless it's absolutely necessary. If anything happens, I beg you, just get out of the way. And Mary told me to tell you . . . if they do show up, try to get them down to the Design Center. Her husband is trying to get a military group in place there. The Design Center, remember.'

'Okay, okay, the Design Center . . . but we could hold off an army with these things.'

Miles came hurrying up. 'Sorry, I was doing some last-minute . . . hey, what the hell have you got there?'

Jasper turned the car and started to head off. Then he leaned out once more and shouted, 'Good luck. and be careful with those things. Remember, the bullets come out the pointy end.' He drove off.

Mavis hugged Marta. 'Be careful, honey. I'm going to talk with security.' She left Marta to explain the situation to Miles, and hurried back down toward her booth.

The PA crackled again. 'And now, boys and girls, to officially start the Twenty-Seventh Annual West Hollywood Lesbian, Gay, Bisexual, Transgender, and Sexually Challenged Pride Parade, here is our very own . . . Miss Thing!'

Miss Thing sashayed her way onto the podium, adjusted her hairdo, and grabbed the microphone. She was greeted by a roar of applause and wolf-whistles. 'Ladies,' she bellowed, 'start your engines.'

Wagner's *Ride of the Valkyries* blasted out of the PA system as fifty Harley-Davidsons were given full throttle, filling the area with noise and smoke. The Dykes on Bikes eased their machines off their stands, rolled into the junction, and turned right onto Santa Monica Boulevard, where a sea of expectant faces stretched into the distance.

CHAPTER TWENTY-EIGHT

Jeff sank his head onto the console. 'I can't do it, I can't do it!' he groaned.

'What can't you do?' said Roger impatiently. 'I thought you had it figured out?'

'Figured out? I had the frequency figured out, yes. And it took me all of two hours to get that far. I'm trying to fix the pointing now . . . but it's not possible. It's just not possible. And I'm wiped out.'

'Jeff, Jeff, try and keep at it. Let me get some more coffee. Do you want some, Mary?'

'Sure, why not?' Mary gazed bleary-eyed at Roger. 'Make it a double espresso with a dash of cognac, please, and a ham croissant on the side. And how about something for this lady. What's your name, anyway?'

'Alice,' said the tied-up technician. 'You guys are on a fool's mission, let me tell you.'

'Let us be the judge of that,' said Roger. 'But if you want some coffee, I'll get it for you.'

'Why not?'

Roger went off to the kitchen and rinsed out the cups. He put a spoonful of instant coffee in each and filled them from the hot tap. He brought the cups back and put them down on a desk. 'Made with mountain spring water. Here's the creamer,' he said, passing over a jar. 'You better help her, Mary. I'll be back . . .' Roger disappeared again into the back area.

Mary helped Alice drink her coffee. In a few moments Roger returned, his arms around a TV set. 'Look what I found!' he said. 'We can watch the parade from here.' He put the TV down on a console and plugged it in.

'There's no antenna,' said Mary.

'We're sitting right under the transmitters. This set uses an attenuator . . . it has to block out most of the signal so as not to overload the amplifier.' Roger flicked through the channels. 'Hey, it's Miss Thing!' he laughed. 'The queen who took tacky prime-time.'

Jeff looked over curiously. 'Is this what I stayed gay for?' he asked with a sigh.

'That's right,' Roger said. 'By Halloween we'll have you in drag on the Boulevard, I swear it. Dammit, we should go down there. This is hopeless. You're not getting anywhere. We're not getting anywhere. Let's go and enjoy the parade, and if there's a fight, we can fight as well as anyone else.'

'For Christ's sake,' said Mary, 'there's about to be a massacre. Keep working.'

Alice had suddenly become more interested in the proceedings. 'Are you guys gay?' she asked.

'Yes, what of it?'

'So am I.'

Roger, Jeff, and Mary all stared at the technician as if she was some kind of freak. 'You are?' said Roger incredulously.

'I sure am,' she said. 'Get used to it!'

Jeff looked at Roger. 'Maybe I should let her loose?'

'No, no, don't. Who knows whether she's telling the truth.'

'Go look in that drawer,' Alice said.

Roger went over and opened the drawer. It was stuffed with well-thumbed paperbacks. Roger pulled out a few of them and scanned their titles. '*Virago* . . . *Murder at the Nightwood Bar* . . . *Desert of the Heart* . . . *Old Dyke Tales* . . . Yup, certified lesbian. Naiad Press must ship these up here by the mule train.'

'The nights are long,' Alice said. 'I was halfway through *Staying Home* when you arrived. Alix just got inseminated, and Molly's doubts are intensifying. So what the hell's going on?'

Roger and Mary took her through the events that had brought them to Mount Wilson, and explained their plan to irradiate Albrick's troops. Alice said: 'I'll help you if I can, but I don't think it's possible. You can't point the beam below the horizon, period.'

Roger untied Alice, and she got up and massaged the places on her arms and legs where the tape had bound her. 'You killed Greg?' she asked.

'He fell,' Roger said.

'I . . . I pushed him,' said Mary. 'I was desperate. I didn't mean for him to fall.'

'He was a real bastard, but he didn't deserve to die.' There was pause, then Alice went on: 'The other shift comes on at eleven. Better get done before then.'

Jeff drew Alice over to a set of screens. 'Let's work on the azimuth first,' he said. 'Maybe once we've got that we can figure out some way to do the elevation.'

'Okay, but I'm telling you, it doesn't go below the horizon.'

'Well, the required azimuth is 74 degrees to the right

of straight ahead, the way I read it from this chart. And that's minus 286 degrees in your crazy system, correct?'

'Er, yes, minus 286.'

'And that can be entered directly into the code?'

'Yes, but you have to remember that's an extreme angle. Normally, targets that far to the right would be handled by Vandenberg. You won't get more than 40 percent power.'

'Well then, we'll have to go with 40 percent power. Maybe we'll fry them for a few seconds longer. They're not going anywhere.'

'Sure, that's true. I think in terms of missiles. But you'll need to defocus the beam. Let's see, the range is what?'

'Thirty-three-point-nine kilometers.'

'Convert to miles. We haven't gone metric yet.'

'For heaven's sake! Let's see, 21 miles and . . . one furlong.'

'Say 21. Okay, at that range and azimuth the half-width of the beam at half amplitude is, let's see' – Alice hit a few keys – '47 feet. You need it wider than that, don't you?'

'If the beam's static we need it to be a good 500 yards, to be safe, I would say. Giving us a full width at half amplitude of 1000 yards. The Y axis is going to look after itself, right, at that shallow incidence?'

'We call that the Z-on-target spread. The axes are always defined with reference to the beam. But yes, you should have plenty of room there.'

'So how do we defocus?'

'Add phase noise. It does it for you . . . you just enter the desired half-width at the desired range.'

Roger and Mary were watching the TV nervously.

Like the Valkyries in the opera house, the Dykes on Bikes were doing their best to create an impression of impetuous haste, while actually moving barely at all. The first rule of the West Hollywood parade was, everyone goes at the pace of the slowest, in this case not so much the lame or the blind, but the congenital exhibitionists who had to perform their routines to completion for each and every sector of the crowd. The Dykes on Bikes gunned their motors and rode circles and made general whoopee, but after fifteen minutes or so they had hardly gotten three blocks down the parade route, and only ten contingents had even made it onto the Boulevard. The announcer was retelling the history of the Temperamental Society ('That's nothing to do with *temperance*,' she confided), in preparation for the appearance of its glorious, nonagenarian founder. The latter came into view at that very moment: he was reclining in a deck chair atop West Hollywood's Recycle-for-a-Better-Tomorrow garbage truck, surrounded by a bevy of Zuni men-women. With one hand he waved graciously to the crowd, while with the other he kept a tight grip on a flask of some rejuvenating beverage.

'Maybe Albrick's men will get bored and go home,' said Roger.

'I wish!' said Mary. 'Say, Alice, could you check the phone? When I tried earlier, I couldn't get a line. I should really try Marcus again.'

Alice tried, but came up blank. 'It's a radio-phone,' she said, 'It's nothing but static. And it looks like our data lines and our secure lines are all the same. Somebody doesn't want us to phone home.'

'Sugar,' said Mary. 'It looks like Albrick knows we're

here. How the hell d'you think he found *that* out?'

'No idea,' said Roger, 'but we better work fast. Jeff, what's happening?'

'Okay, we've got the azimuth. Now, Alice, explain about the elevation. Zero elevation is the horizon, right?'

'That's right,' said Alice.

'Plus values above the horizon?'

'Correct.'

'So negative values below?'

'There *are* no negative values. The computer doesn't know anything about negative values. Why would we be zapping Los Angeles?'

'To quell riots?' suggested Roger. 'Weld earthquake faults together? Do special effects at the Academy Awards? Seems like there could have been all kinds of useful applications.'

'We do national defense. If an ICBM makes it as far as Olympic Boulevard, we give up and go home.'

'Okay,' said Jeff, 'but still, the basic physics is there. We just need to introduce phase leads in the upper antennae.'

'Yes,' said Alice. 'So?'

'Well, let's get into the code and do it there.'

'Why, certainly, be my guest. It's machine language, by the way.'

Jeff groaned and slumped onto the console once more.

Roger patted him on the back. 'I'll get you some more coffee.'

CHAPTER TWENTY-NINE

It was an hour and a half later. At the western end of the city the Zuni men-women had completed the parade route. They hoisted their ancient guru down off the garbage truck and led him off to a local hostelry. At the eastern end, the last few contingents – the Gay and Lesbian Atheists and Humanists, Digital Queers, and the Imperial Court of the San Fernando Valley – were still waiting to start. Between them, the parade, like a Japanese scroll painting, was unrolling itself to the public's view. Seventy-five thousand spectators expressed their approval with cheers and waves.

In front of the Bird Store, on the north side of Santa Monica Boulevard at Harper Avenue, Andy McInnis stood with his arm around his boyfriend Reg. Andy was wearing a baseball cap to protect his latest crop of hair plugs from the sun. He was thinking obsessively about the Bar examination, which he was due to take for the third time the following week.

At the municipal parking structure at Santa Monica and Kings Road, Thomas Gregory was joking with a group of black and Latino friends. A tall, willowy black hairstylist with hardly a T-cell to his name, Gregory was holding a plastic cup half-full of white wine and saying: 'Don't bitch *me* . . . bitch!'

By the box office of the Wilde Playhouse, librarian Kate Oszwieski was doing a little bump-and-grind routine with her partner June Hapgood. They were keeping time to the music from the Arizona Lesbians' Brass Band. They had driven their VW bus from Barstow the previous evening and had slept uncomfortably in the parking lot of the Mayfair supermarket.

In front of the Value supermarket, just to the west of City Hall, stood Jack Blasius, MD. A laser-jock from Oklahoma, Blasius had made his fortune zapping gay men's anal warts. He knew that no one was going to bare his butt to him today, so he had closed and locked his offices for the weekend. He was checking out a number of well-built men in the vicinity and wondering whether the phrase 'monogamous relationship' allowed for any exceptions.

Making her way toward the delicatessen at the corner of Santa Monica and Sweetzer was Eva Schulman, an elderly Russian Jewish woman. She was complaining loudly to her husband Leon about the disruption the homosexuals were causing to their daily routine. Luckily, no one in the vicinity understood Russian.

In the forecourt of the Mobil service station at Santa Monica and Orlando, Jason Petrocelli, who was deaf, was admiring the mermaids on the Rubber Queen float. He had recently moved from New Jersey to attend school at California State University. No one in the whole wide world knew that he was gay, but he was hoping to change that before the day was out.

All of these people would shortly be dead.

* * *

Act Out! had made it as far as Sweetzer Avenue. They were one of the most popular groups in the parade. For a while they would strut like wooden soldiers, jointed only at the shoulders and hips. They marched with shouldered arms, their eyes straight ahead, their boots stomping the pavement in time with Jimmy's drumbeat. Then, at a sign from Marta, *Mamma Mia* blared out, and the troupe switched to their musical routine. Holding their Kalashnikovs low and horizontal in front of them, they swiveled to and fro in time to the music, revealing alternately their uniformed fronts and their bare asses to the onlookers. They saluted, cavorted, dueled with crossed rifles, and gave each other air kisses. Then at another signal they switched back to their Tinkertoy march.

In front of the group, Miles twisted and spun the sparkling baton. Immediately after they crossed Sweetzer Avenue, they came abreast of West Hollywood City Hall, on the south side of the street. A large crowd of city employees and their friends were gathered on the steps, and they gave Act Out! a rousing cheer. Others waved from the first- and second-floor windows. Miles hurled the baton skyward: the imitation rubies flashed in the sunshine as the baton looped end-over-end into the air.

A single rifle shot rang out, and the baton exploded and fell to the pavement in fragments.

'What the—' Miles had time to say, when a second shot rang out. The bullet struck the pavement and ricocheted into Jimmy's left leg just below the knee. He collapsed howling in pain; his drum rolled into the gutter and his rifle, which had been slung over his shoulder, fell by his side.

'Off the street, off the street!' yelled Marta. The actors broke formation and dove for the side of the street; the crowd lining the sidewalk buckled and yielded. Marta and Miles grabbed Jimmy by the arms and dragged him to the north side of the street, then Miles dashed out again and grabbed Jimmy's rifle. Most people in the crowd still had no idea what was happening, but that changed quickly as a fusillade of shots were heard. Miles looked up and saw men standing on the roof of the City Hall, pointing their rifles at the crowd.

'Go back, go back!' Miles yelled, and those in the crowd near him followed his instructions and started pushing their way eastward along the Boulevard. Others ran up Sweetzer or took cover under the overhanging facade of City Hall. The rate of firing increased, and people were falling down or shouting in pain. One bullet passed through Andy McInnis's baseball cap, messed up his hair plugs, and sent his brains through the glass front of the Bird Store. Two rainbow lorikeets flew through the shattered window and squawked their way toward the roof of the waterbed store across the street.

Miles took cover behind a bus stop bench. He found himself next to a crouching policeman who had fired off a couple of useless shots from his service revolver in the direction of the City Hall roof. Now he was talking urgently into his radio. Miles snuggled up next to him and drew a bead on one of the attackers, who stood right on the parapet of the roof. Although his combat training had taken second place to his baton twirling, Miles had always been a good shot. A friend of his, who had brought an AK 47 home from Vietnam as a war trophy, had let him use it a few times. He knew the magazine held thirty rounds and he was determined to make every one of them count. His first shot brought the man tumbling from the roof to the sidewalk, splintering his skull. Seeing their companion go down, the other attackers spread-eagled themselves behind the parapet, but they continued firing.

A mass of marchers and onlookers, now hopelessly intermixed, pushed back toward Crescent Heights. But at this moment another fusillade of shots rang out from the east. It came from the roof of the Laser Medical Center at Santa Monica and Harper. The crowd was now so densely packed that almost every shot hit someone, and many of the bullets passed through two or three people before being stopped by some especially dense vertebra or shinbone.

Utter panic broke out as the crowd pushed frantically in both directions, compressing itself into a dense knot between Harper and Sweetzer. The pressure forced many people to the ground. Eva Shulman was among them, and a moment after she fell a boot came down heavily on her throat, breaking her neck. Then a large group of people blistered out of the crowd and ran along the north side of the street, braving the bullets to find the safety of Sweetzer Avenue.

Very much the same scenario played itself out to the west of City Hall. The people there ran forward, charging into the marchers in front of them and propelling them down toward Kings Road and Olive Street. But just as they seemed to be out of range of the gunmen, bullets started coming at them from straight ahead: Marksmen were shooting from the roof of the Leder Rug Company, an elegant seven-story building at the corner of Olive. And shots also came from the roof of the *West Hollywood Blade* offices, at the back of the Mobil station on the marchers' left.

Jason Petrocelli did not hear the shots, but he saw a Rubber Queen mermaid take a bullet in the chest. He ran forward, climbed onto the float, and put his arms around the beautiful dying fish-man. He felt the warmth of his oil-smooth body and smelled the intoxicating odor of his maleness. The man seemed to be gazing at him peacefully, even lovingly. Not knowing what else to do, Jason kissed him full on the mouth. Then he turned his head and saw a soldier pointing a gun at him from the roof. But he didn't see the bullet.

The other mermaids struggled out of their fishtails and jumped down to the pavement in their Calvin Klein underwear. The Rubber Queen tried to do the same, but she caught one high-heeled shoe in a bucket of condoms and fell face-forward into a sea of people. The float rocked to and fro by the pressure of the panicking crowd, and the driver blew his horn and screamed at the people in front to get out of the way.

Back at Sweetzer, most of the Act Out! contingent had regrouped. They were sheltering behind some cars that stood on the forecourt of an automobile workshop, kitty-corner to City Hall. Miles tried to explain how to aim and shoot the AK 47s, but some of the actors were too shaken to pay any heed to what he was saying. The riflemen atop City Hall had identified the Act Out! group as the only source of serious counter-fire, and they were sending much of their ordnance in their direction. Bullets lightened the sides of cars that faced City Hall, and most of the windows were shot out, but so far the actors were unscathed – except for Jimmy, who was gently moaning to himself at the rear of the garage, where he had been dragged.

'We've got to get them away from here . . . got to get them down to the Design Center,' Marta shouted to her comrades.

'How in the hell do you plan to do that?' asked one of the group.

'Broken wing,' Marta said. 'You know, be provocative, make yourself look vulnerable, then retreat in that direction. We're the ones they want to get, anyway, so let's lead them a dance.'

At that moment a man sprinted across the forecourt and dove behind one of the cars. It was Jack Blasius. 'If you're not going to use that gun, then let me,' he shouted at one of the actors, and seized the rifle out of his hands. Blasius was incensed to see that the attackers were trespassing on the roof of his medical building. A crack shot on foot or on horseback, he set about dislodging them. He ran up Sweezer a few steps and turned right into the service alley. When he got to Harper he dashed across the street, reaching the back entrance of the Medical Center unscathed. He reached for his key but found that the lock had already been forced. He let himself in and started cautiously climbing the stairs.

Meanwhile, the sound of sirens announced the approach of police reinforcements. The squad cars advanced along Santa Monica Boulevard from both the Beverly Hills and Hollywood directions, but they soon became stalled by the panicking crowd and the abandoned floats and other paraphernalia that littered the street. They turned off onto the side streets to get closer to the action, but even the side streets were difficult to navigate. The police left their vehicles and made their way down to the Boulevard on foot, taking their shotguns with them. At their first view of the scene at Sweetzer and Monica they radioed for the SWAT team and helicopters. Then they began firing at the rooftops, occasionally hitting one of the attackers.

The area of the Boulevard in the immediate vicinity of Sweetzer was now nearly empty, except for a number of bodies. Most of the crowd had escaped down the side streets or were further up the Boulevard, struggling with the masses of humanity there. The marksmen on the roof of City Hall and the nearby buildings were finding less and less to shoot at. At this point, Marta and her comrades began to make little dashes into the open. They would expose their backsides at the shooters for the briefest of moments and then jump back behind cover. It was a dangerous game, but it succeeded in getting the attackers' attention. Every little dash provoked a hail of bullets, but none reached their target before he or she was safely back behind a car or a bench. The police screamed at Marta's group to get away from the scene, and they gradually retreated backward along Sweetzer, both in a southerly and in a northerly direction, scuttling between hiding places as they went. Determined to nail the actors, Albrick's troops at City Hall and the Value supermarket left their rooftop vantage points and descended to the street. Keeping the police at bay with a barrage of fire, they began chasing the actors down the side streets.

The first SWAT team moved down the Boulevard from the east. In their armored van they made better progress than the squad cars before them. They got as far as Havenhurst Drive, where they piled out of the vehicle, and, using it as a shield, began firing at the rooftops that were still occupied. With their heavier, laser-sighted guns, the SWAT team was able to hit several of Albrick's men.

Jack Blasius had now reached the rooftop of the Medical Center. Instead of stepping out onto the roof, however, he climbed a few more steps up the elevator shaft, reaching a window guarded with a set of bars. He saw that there were four marksmen on the rooftop, shooting down into the street. He took a few moments to collect himself, then he opened fire. He killed two of the men before they even had a chance to turn. The other two spun around and, having nowhere to hide, they simply opened fire at the window, but Blasius nailed them both. He ran down and out onto the roof, checked that the men were indeed dead, and then leaned over the parapet and took aim at the marksmen on the roof of the bookstore across the street. Since they were two floors below him, they offered a fairly easy target. As he was about to squeeze off the first round, however, he noticed a ruby spot sparkling on his jacket. He knew instantly what it was, and he commanded his body to dive for cover. But for once his reflexes were too slow. Blasius became the day's first victim of friendly fire, but not the last.

The four people at Mount Wilson had not seen the beginning of the fighting, because the TV station that was covering the parade had cameras only at Crescent Heights and San Vicente. But it soon became clear that there was a disturbance, as people started running back toward Crescent Heights. The announcer spoke of a traffic accident, but Roger and the others knew that the attack must have started.

While Roger and Mary clustered anxiously round the television set, Jeff, sometimes aided by Alice, tried to stay focused on the required computations. Jeff was interrogating the system concerning the phase settings for all the antennae, for a beam elevation 52 degrees above the horizon. His plan was to reverse the sequence of phase values in the vertical plane, thus deflecting the beam the desired 52 degrees *below* the horizon. But that would still leave the question of how the values could be entered into the code, which presented itself as a featureless string of ones and zeros.

After a while another station, Channel 7, interrupted its programming to report on the disturbance. Its helicopter was circling low over the intersection of Santa Monica Boulevard and Kings Road. Roger, Mary, and Alice watched aghast as the camera revealed the surging mass of people and the bodies lying on the pavement. 'There is the most terrible fighting going on here,' the reporter in the helicopter was saying. 'Actually it's more of a massacre, as the people in the street are simply being cut down by sniper fire. We're trying to get a little lower so we can see who it is that's doing the shooting. It looks very much as if they're soldiers . . . they certainly seem to be wearing military uniforms of some kind. This is absolutely frightful . . .' Roger could see Albrick's men on the rooftops, some of whom looked up at the helicopter and gesticulated. 'There's no place for these poor people to go,' the reporter went on. 'They're being attacked from . . . hey, hey, Tony, Tony! . . . My pilot's been shot, my pilot! . . . Tony! . . . How do I . . . help, we're going down, we're going down!' On the screen, the image of the street gyrated wildly as the helicopter corkscrewed downward. *'Help!* . . .' The transmission ceased, with the last frame frozen in place. It showed the marquee of the Wilde Playhouse with the words JEFFREY – THE MUSICAL, and below, the horror-struck faces of Kate Oszwieski and June Hapgood.

Over at the VA Medical Center, Albrick was growing angry, and his men were growing impatient. What was supposed to be an attack on the Gay Pride Parade was turning into a battle between his men and the police, as far as Albrick could learn from the messages he was receiving. He ordered those of his marksmen who were still on the rooftops to descend to the street and chase the marchers. Then he gave the go-ahead for his troops at the VA to join the battle. The convoy of trucks rolled out onto Wilshire Boulevard and headed east. As they reached Westwood Boulevard, the radioman called over to Albrick: 'Sir, our guys are reporting unciphered call attempts from Mount Wilson,' he said. 'Four in the last ten minutes.'

'Unciphered?'

'Yes sir. Irregular, sir.'

'Jesus! Have them lift the channel block long enough to figure out who's calling. And have the helicopter brought over. Meet us at Santa Monica and Robertson.'

'Yes, sir.'

'James, do we have fire-fighting suits?'

'Yes, we have four, I think, in Grant's vehicle.'

'The aluminum-faced ones?'

'I believe so. But there's no fire, so far as I know.'

'When we stop, have Grant unload them.'

'As you say, generalissimo!'

The trucks continued down Wilshire to Beverly Hills,

and turned left onto Santa Monica Boulevard. As they did so, Albrick and his men saw a column of smoke rising in the distance, and at the same time two fire trucks came racing by on the wrong side of the street, their klaxons blaring.

'How the hell did you know there was a fire, chief?' asked James.

'I didn't,' Albrick replied curtly.

The heat and smoke from the burning Wilde Playhouse helped drive the crowd further westward along the Boulevard. As the marksmen on the Leder Rug building and the Blade offices had left their positions, nothing hindered the people in the street from surging past those buildings. Nothing, that is, except the bodies, the capsized floats, and the abandoned musical instruments that were strewn across their route. Eventually however, the majority of the crowd had made it through to the open area at Croft Avenue where the Boulevard took a slight leftward turn. Now, many of them were able to run down Croft, Holloway, and the other side streets.

Within a minute or two, however, Albrick's gunmen had descended to the street and were chasing the stragglers, picking off whoever they could and causing renewed panic among those ahead. Among them, Tom Gregory and Mavis Trautheim were hurrying up Holloway. They were shepherding a group of children in fur-ball costumes. Tom was carrying a child on his shoulders and leading another by the hand, while Mavis was cradling an injured child in her arms and trying to chivy the remaining children along. Tom's lungs were scarred by five bouts with *Pneumocystis* pneumonia, and his breathing was not good at the best of times. Mavis was a hundred and fifty pounds overweight. They were both laboring hard up the gentle grade, and from time to time bullets came whistling by.

It seemed that they were about to be cut down when a diversion saved them. Three of the Act Out! players, who had been concealed at the sides of buildings, started shooting at the pursuers, hitting one of them. Then the actors flashed their butts and ran up Alta Loma Road toward Sunset. One of them shouted 'Go, Mave!' as he disappeared up the street. Albrick's men chased after them, but the actors were fitter and more light-footed than their heavily accoutered pursuers. Ahead of them, at the junction of Alta Loma and Sunset, two police cars were slewed across the street, and LAPD marksmen used the cars as cover and began shooting in the direction of Albrick's men. Caught in the cross-fire, the three actors darted into a service alley that ran behind a luxury condominium tower on the left side of the street. As they disappeared down the alley, they bared their behinds to their pursuers once more. Albrick's men ran after them. Meanwhile, Tom and Mavis were able to gather their breath before continuing up Holloway.

To the south of the Boulevard, Marta, Miles, and the other actors were also drawing Albrick's men toward the Design Center. Miles was slower on his feet than the others, but he made up for it by his superior marksmanship. As they gradually worked their way through the residential streets to La Cienega and then to Melrose, they fell into a routine whereby one or two of the actors lured the soldiers forward, while Miles picked them off from a side street. He had twice used up the ammunition in his AK 47, but each time he had swapped weapons with another member of the troupe.

Eventually, both of the Act Out! groups reached the Design Center. Marta and Miles's group entered the Blue Building from Melrose Avenue, while the other group, having completed a long detour around the northwest part of the city, entered the Green Building from San Vicente. Both groups were followed into the Center by their pursuers.

Meanwhile, Albrick's convoy had arrived at Roberston Boulevard, just two blocks short of the finishing point of the parade. The vehicles stopped and Albrick and the others jumped out. They could see the fire trucks, which had halted a short way ahead at San Vicente and Santa Monica. The firefighters were talking with the police; either they couldn't get through, or they didn't want to risk being fired on. When the police saw Albrick's convoy to the west of them, they ordered the drivers of the fire trucks to back their vehicles across the road. Within a couple of minutes both carriageways were effectively barricaded.

Very soon afterward the helicopter arrived. It landed on the grassy median strip and four Marines jumped out. Albrick grabbed James. 'I'm going up to Mount Wilson to take out the phased array,' he said. 'You deal with the homos down here.' He ordered Grant to give the Marines the fire-fighting suits. Then, as if doubtful of James's influence, he addressed some brief words of encouragement to the assembled troops. 'The fags have killed twenty of your comrades,' he shouted. 'Now it's your chance to get revenge. Give them everything you've got. Don't spare anything. Drive the perverts out of West Hollywood . . . out of LA . . . out of California!' The men roared their approval, and without waiting for instructions from James they began unloading their armaments. Albrick grabbed a rifle and jumped into the helicopter with the Marines; soon they were aloft and heading for the San Gabriels.

After Albrick had left, James shouted to the men to gather round. He intended to have them set up a defensive line and await Albrick's return. But the men had other ideas. Seeing the Boulevard blocked ahead of them, they ran fifty yards south down Roberston. From there they could see the Design Center fronting onto San Vicente on the other side of West Hollywood Park. The park itself had been set up with booths and stages for the festival that had been due to start once the parade was over. Many hundreds of people fleeing the fighting on the Boulevard had broken into the festival grounds from the San Vicente side and were milling about in the area. When they saw the soldiers on Roberston they took fright and stampeded eastward back toward San Vicente, but not before Albrick's men opened fire through the cyclone fencing and hit several of them. The soldiers waved for the heavy trucks to come down. Soon the lead vehicle flattened the chain-link fencing and dozens of soldiers fanned out among the booths, looking for people in hiding. Another group of soldiers maneuvered a light field gun into position. At the same time, however, a group of SWAT officers returned fire from an armored vehicle on San Vincente. They had moved down from the Sheriff's station at Santa Monica as soon as the soldiers' intentions became apparent. Albrick's men tried to conceal themselves among the booths, but the canvas offered flimsy protection: The police were able to hit several of them (as well as several of the civilians) with blind, raking fire. The remainder of Albrick's men retreated to the shelter of their vehicles.

Within a few minutes after Channel 7 lost its helicopter, four other channels had their own machines in the air over West Hollywood. The group at Mount Wilson, by switching from channel to channel, could see most of what was going on in the western half of the city, although from a higher altitude than before. The major focus of the panic and the shooting was now near the finishing point of the parade, between La Cienega and San Vicente. Thousands of people had been sitting on bleachers set up on the grassy median strip, and their rush to get down and escape had caused many casualties. The eastern half of the city was obscured by the drifting pall of smoke rising from the Wilde Playhouse. Fire engines approached the scene from the Crescent Heights end, but the playhouse burned furiously, and the fire spread to the Red Dog Cafe and the Flores liquor store.

Channel 7, no longer able to transmit views of the action, sent a truck to Fairfax and Santa Monica, where LAPD police chief Brian Jones and Los Angeles deputy mayor Juan Rubio had set up a center of operations. Strictly speaking, West Hollywood was not their turf, but the entire West Hollywood city council, most of the employees, and the city's two police units had been participating in or watching the parade, and all contact with them had been lost.

Rubio came out for a brief word to the camera. The mayor, he explained, was off-road bicycling in Topanga State Park, and could not be reached. But the situation was being brought under control, and he appealed to the populace to stay away from the area until order had been fully restored. Another functionary took the microphone and appealed for blood donations.

'Being brought under control!' Alice repeated jeeringly. 'Maybe he should watch some TV.'

Jones was more realistic. They had lost a number of police officers, he said, and the attackers, whoever they were, were too heavily armed for his officers to be able to neutralize them. He had called for assistance from the military and from other police departments. No, he didn't know when they would arrive. And in the meantime, the police were concentrating on setting up roadblocks on the streets leading to the scene of the disturbance.

'For what purpose?' asked the interviewer.

'To prevent the disturbance from spreading to the rest of the city.'

Now it was Roger's turn to jeer. 'Yeah, it's only homosexuals in there. Just keep the real people safe, for Christ's sake,' he said bitterly. 'And while you're calling the military, tell them to drop a few thousand-pounders on the Boulevard . . . that should resolve the matter to your satisfaction.'

'Roger, it's not their fault, they're doing what they can,' said Mary.

'Not their fault? That's a very heterosexual point of view, if I may say so, Mary. What you don't realize is, the LAPD and the County Sheriff's Department are the most blatant bunch of homophobic assholes in this country. Racist, yes, you heard about that, I'm sure. But homophobic, no, you don't hear about that because you don't want to hear about that. But listen to the Fuhrman

tapes. Read about the Phelps case . . . the Kierman case
. . . the Mendoza case . . . you've never even heard of
them, right?'

'I . . .'

'They have never, ever, ever done a single damn
thing to protect gays and lesbians, even though we're
the most hated, the most attacked, the . . .'

'But . . .'

'Don't "but" me! They could have provided some
serious protection for the parade. They *knew* what was
going to happen . . . Frinton told them, right? They
could have forced Portillo to cancel. But no. They
probably said, "Hey, an attack on the fags? That should
be worth watching, let me check that I've got a case of
beer in the refrigerator."'

'Roger, there are police officers giving their lives
down there, right now. I mean, I understand your
bitterness, but to blame this whole thing on the LAPD,
isn't that a bit unfair? Because really, we all of us share
a part of the blame.'

'We do? Like how?'

'Well, for my part, I guess I've never gotten much
involved, even though I knew your community was
facing a lot of discrimination, a lot of hate crimes. And
you, well, I mean, let's face the reality . . . if you hadn't
done your research on the hypothalamus, *none* of this
would be happening. Now I'm not saying—'

'That's *it!*' Roger exploded, jumping to his feet. 'I
knew this was coming. I *knew* it – this is all *my* fault,
that's what you're saying, isn't it? It's—'

'Roger, that's not—'

'It's all part of *my* personal plan to wipe gays and
lesbians off the face of the earth. And all because I'm

so tortured about being gay, I want everyone else to suffer along with me, or something like that? Yes, I'm loving it – look, see those dead bodies . . . there! . . . there! . . . I'm *loving* every minute of it, because all my self-hatred is coming up to the surface and boiling away – that's what you think, isn't it? That's—'

'No, Roger—'

'Well, let me tell you, I'm *not* tortured about being gay. I've *never* been tortured about being gay. I'm a *happy* homosexual, if you can conceive of such a thing – always have been. And I had every right to do that research! *Every right!* God, you talk. You, who've been paying for Albrick to do all of this, the last three years . . . to create those zombies . . . right there! . . . and there! – look at them, shooting us, killing us! They're *your* creation, not mine! And all part of some cozy deal you had with the Navy . . . so you could get money for the only people you cared about! And you tell me—'

'Roger! Mary! For God's sake!' shouted Jeff. He and Alice had been cringing on the other side of the room. 'We're making progress, but we can't work with you guys screaming at each other. Cool it, will you?'

'I'm sorry,' Roger said, burying his head in his hands. 'This is all getting too much for me. Mary—'

'It's okay . . .'

'I'm sorry. Look, I'm going to take a breather outside for a sec.' Roger made his way down the corridor toward the front entrance. 'I'll buzz you when I'm ready to come back in,' he shouted back to them as he headed out into the sunshine.

Mary took a deep breath. 'It's getting a bit much for me, too. How are you two getting along?'

Alice left Jeff to continue working and came over to

Mary. 'We've got the required settings for all the antennas,' she said. 'Now we're trying to figure how to enter them into the code. What Jeff's been doing is he's been changing big chunks of the code and then seeing what comes out when he dumps the phase settings. He's found the general area that sets the phases, now he's changing smaller sections to see how the individual values are coded.'

'I don't know the first thing about computers, but I get the general idea. It's like what molecular biologists call "site-directed mutagenesis."'

'Yeah? Maybe. Or like what I call "pulling fuses to see which lights go out." What time is it anyway?'

'Ten o'clock.'

'Ten? Well, we have an hour before the next shift arrives. And then we'll have some explaining to do.'

Tom and Mavis had finally made it up to Sunset Boulevard, and they stopped for another breather. The tall, thin, queeny, black Tom and the short, fat, dykey, white Mavis, with their clutch of bizarrely costumed children – they looked like the very embodiment of the Alternative Family. One of the fur-balls – it was Boudicca – tugged at Mavis and said, 'I think we should go over there . . . it's the hospital.' She pointed at the Scorpion Room, a purple-walled nightclub at the top of San Vicente. The club had been converted into a makeshift triage and first aid center. The wounded walked or were carried through the entrance on San Vicente, and ambulances shuttled the most urgent cases from the front entrance on Sunset. None of the ambulances were permitted to pass the roadblock and go down to Santa Monica Boulevard. Indeed, they would have had a hard time doing so, because there were still floods of people struggling up the hill.

Mavis handed an injured child over to the staff. 'You'll be fine, sweetie,' she had said. 'Your mom and dad will be coming to see you soon.' She wasn't sure that either of those statements were true. The child had lost a lot of blood, and her right arm was thoroughly mangled. As for her parents, who knows, she thought. The panic had been so general that not a single person, probably, was still with whoever they had started the day with.

The thought reminded her of Marta. 'Tom, I've got to go find my girlfriend. She was heading for the Design Center. Could you be a sweetie and look after these kids?'

'Don't sweetie *me*, sweetie!' Tom replied. 'I'm coming *with* you. I haven't had a chance to whip white ass in a while and, girl, I am horny as a bitch.'

So they palmed off the dancing T-cells on a group of women who had just made it up the hill. As they headed down San Vicente, they heard a prim voice behind them saying, 'My name is Boudicca Hensley-Ferraro. I was conceived by oocyte fusion.'

'That kid!' said Mavis. 'I hope she finds her mommas.'

Because of the crowds, getting down San Vicente proved almost as effortful as climbing Holloway, but eventually they reached Santa Monica Boulevard. To their right, the two fire trucks still blocked off the street. Some police were using them as cover and shooting westward toward Roberston. To their left, there were still masses of people running, but there did not seem to be any more shooting going on in that direction. They could see dead and injured men and women in the bleachers and on the pavement. Directly ahead, a hundred yards or so down San Vicente, the SWAT armored van was parked in the middle of the street, in front of the Green Building of the Design Center. Twenty or so SWAT officers were in or around it. They were keeping up a furious fire across the park, and plenty of bullets were coming back, some of them bouncing off the van.

Straight ahead did not look like a healthy option, so they turned left on Santa Monica and walked a hundred yards or so to the entrance to the Metro bus station. By jumping a low wall they found themselves in the bus storage yard, and from there they slithered down a short embankment to the parking lot of the Design Center's Green Building. In front of them was the entrance to the North Rotunda – a glass tower within which escalators zig-zagged their way to all nine floors. They dashed into the building. As they entered, Mavis looked to the right. They could see the men working around the field gun on the other side of the park. Suddenly, the gun spouted flame, and within an instant the SWAT van exploded. The noise was deafening. A large chunk of metal crashed through the plate glass just in front of her and skidded across the red-tiled floor. Outside she saw a severed head strike the asphalt, bounce once, and then roll across the parking lot until it came to a stop up against the left front wheel of a Toyota Tercel. Immediately afterward, Albrick's troops began moving across the park towards San Vicente.

Both of the Act Out! groups, after they had entered the Design Center, decided to hide as best they could. They had done their job, which was to bring Albrick's forces to the Center, and they believed that some kind of military rescue mission was on the way. They were hopelessly outgunned: Many of them had used up all the ammunition for their AK 47s and were left with their K9 handguns, which were of questionable stopping power and held only seven rounds apiece. And most of them were such poor shots that they would need more than seven rounds to hit a person ten feet away. So they decided their best tactic was keep out of sight.

Albrick's men, on the other hand, were determined to hunt them down. Ever since sighting the Act Out! contingent in the parade, they had focused on obliterating it. Yet so far, against all the odds, they had not succeeded in killing any of them, and had lost several of their own men from Miles's sharp-shooting. Now they had the actors trapped, and they set their minds to finishing them off, even if it meant postponing the final attack on the Boulevard. They started systematically searching the buildings, starting at the first floor and moving upward. It was slow work, because the atria and foyers and connecting galleries formed a confusing labyrinth that lacked all system or symmetry. The design plan did not even repeat itself from floor to floor. And the showrooms that led off the galleries, with their endless nooks and alcoves and fitting rooms and large pieces of furniture, offered a thousand hiding places. After they had reached the third floor without finding any trace of their quarry, they gathered themselves in the Green Building and called down to the soldiers in the park, who at that moment were checking the remains of the SWAT van to make sure that none of the officers had survived. Some of them ran back and maneuvered the field gun into position, while the remainder ran into the Green Building to help their comrades.

The first shell went through the long north wall of the Blue Building and exploded inside the mall-like galleria. About five acres of glass blew out of the wall and fell as a sparkling blue rain onto the plaza. Smoke started to billow out of the gaping hole. The soldiers saw figures running across the glass-enclosed bridge that connected the two buildings at the level of the sixth floor. They re-aimed the gun, and the second shell hit the bridge right where it attached to the Blue Building. Its moorings blown away, that end of the bridge hinged down and smashed into the fifth and fourth floors of the Green Building. Then its northern moorings also separated, and the bridge fell straight down, hugging the side of the Green Building as it gathered speed. It penetrated the third-floor terrace like a cruise missile heading for the interior of a bunker, continued on through the second level, and finally impacted on the red-tiled expanse of the Center's main lobby, sending a display of 214 Tiffany lamps, thirty ink drawings by David Hockney, and a twenty-foot terracotta image of Bahuchara Mata, patron goddess of the transsexual *hijras* of Ahmedabad, out through the front door in a fine dust cloud.

Marta's group had in fact succeeded in crossing safely to the Green Building, where they soon found the other members of the troupe. But the gunners on San Vicente, who had probably never been presented with a target so large, so close by, or so satisfyingly fragile, sent shell after shell into the Blue Building, and soon flames were emerging from many of the gaps in the walls. The rest of their contingent dashed into the Green Building to aid their comrades there.

Mavis and Tom, who had reached the second floor of the Green Building, heard the men entering the building below them. 'We've got to go higher,' said Mavis.

'Honey, this queen is not climbing another step,' said Tom. 'We are taking the elevator.' He led Mavis to an elevator and pressed the Up button.

'I don't know about this,' said Mavis. But the elevator quickly arrived and, when the doors opened, there was no one inside. So they stepped in and pressed the button for the ninth floor. The elevator started to ascend, but it immediately slowed again at the third floor. 'Sweetie, I think we just fucked up,' Mavis had time to say. But Tom grabbed her, bent her head back, and gave her the most passionate kiss he could muster, while at the same time grabbing a handful of her ample bottom. As the doors opened, Tom saw out of the corner of his eye a man in combat dress who was pointing a rifle directly at them. But he paused for an instant. Tom pushed the struggling Mavis into the corner of the elevator and made as if he were about to tear off her slacks, his mouth still planted firmly against hers.

'Way to go, guy!' said the soldier. The doors closed again, and they continued their ascent.

'Am I good or what, honey?' said Tom, releasing a quivering Mavis from his grip. 'One more time at the top, just in case.'

The Act Out! players meanwhile had climbed a stairwell to the ninth floor, the top floor of the Green Building. This floor was arranged as a circular balcony around a central light well. If they looked up, they could see the eight panels of the roof rising cathedral-like to a central window, the highest point of the Design Center. If they looked over the balcony's balustrades, they could see all the way down to the first-floor lobby, where one of Alexander Calder's 'stabiles' was on display, set on a plinth in the center of a reflecting pool. Around the balcony, glass doors led into a variety of showrooms. One displayed furniture, another kitchens, a third had wall hangings and carpets, and yet another contained home organs and pianos.

'Find places where we can cover each other, if necessary,' Marta whispered. Aside from the intermittent sound of explosions coming from the neighboring building, it was very quiet, and Marta felt as if the slightest sound could be heard down below. Miles chose to hide amongst a rack of carpet samples. Another member of the troupe hid herself in a carved oaken wardrobe. Yet another chose a shower stall in the bathroom showroom.

Marta remained on the balcony until the other members of the troupe had hidden themselves. She was about to find her own hiding place when she saw the lights indicating the approach of an elevator. She lifted her pistol and, holding it in both hands, aimed for the crack between the doors. When the door opened, she recognized with amazement her own girlfriend in the process of being raped by a tall black man. She pulled the trigger. The shot echoed through the building as the bullet drilled a hole through Tom's left ear and buried itself in the rear wall of the elevator.

'*Don't shoot!*' screamed Mavis, a half-second too late. '*He's gay!*'

'That fucking *hurt*!' Tom yelled. He was wincing and looking at his wound in the mirrored side wall of the elevator. 'Next time I want my fucking ear pierced I'll fucking ask . . . *bitch*!'

There was a tumult of voices below. 'Get in hiding, quick!' said Marta.

Roger sat outside the Weather Bureau, perched on a boulder. The early morning fog had burned away and the warm sunshine helped settle his nerves. The whole area was very quiet. Generators were humming behind him, but aside from that, the loudest sound was being made by a woodpecker knocking at the trunk of a ponderosa pine, over to the left. Perhaps people were staying at home, watching Los Angeles' latest cataclysm unfold on television. Far away to the right, a column of smoke was visible behind Griffith Park. But Roger did not look in that direction. Instead, he watched a lone cyclist, two thousand feet below him, struggling up the rocky trail from Altadena. His scarlet jersey appeared and disappeared behind granite crags or clumps of weather-beaten pine trees. Sometimes he had to carry his bike over rock slides or negotiate around fallen tree trunks, but he continued upward with what seemed like unconscious, antlike persistence.

Unconscious, Roger thought, *the highest joy*. Not conscious, not constantly agonizing over reasons and motives and the right course of action. Not remembering or regretting or planning or plotting. Just being oneself and doing whatever flowed from that. Acting natural. It was easier said than done. Some tracks were worn too deep.

A sense of guilt overwhelmed him. Not for the

science . . . that quest was still noble and unsullied, in his own conscience at least, whatever anyone might say. That was something he had been able to hold to, when all else seemed to slip through his fingers. But for Jeff. For someone he had, maybe out of pure selfishness, diverted from his chosen life path. Someone whose faith and upbringing and his own free choice called him to be straight, and who had striven mightily to become so. And he, Roger, had been so confident, so self-righteous. So sure that the river of Jeff's life was flowing out of its course. So sure that Jeff needed only to break through the floodgates that held back his own true nature. So sure, that he had willfully undone what Jeff was on the brink of achieving. Roger thought of the bumper sticker: *If you love something, let it go. If it doesn't come back, hunt it down and kill it.* Maybe that was what he had done.

For being gay was, above all, a choice . . . that much Roger realized. A choice between self-denial and self-acceptance, perhaps, but a choice nonetheless. And who could make that choice for another human being? Not Albrick, no . . . but not himself either. And was it so unreasonable . . . to choose not to join so fatally marked a tribe?

A tribe that endured nothing but disease and death and unbridled, unmitigated hatred? A tribe that had pitched their tents on unclaimed land by Hollywood's western borders, only to be cut to pieces by people who begrudged them even that last refuge? Had he selflessly chosen this on Jeff's behalf, for Jeff's benefit? Or had he been thinking only of himself?

Roger gazed beyond the tireless cyclist, following the ever-winding trail down and down the steep flank of the mountain toward the city. He saw a moving mote that drifted across the dry mouth of Eaton Canyon, turned, and rose slowly toward the campsite at Henninger Flats. It was a helicopter. Roger watched with increasing unease as the machine passed the campsite and steadily gained altitude. He jumped off his perch and buzzed the door. Mary let him in. 'There's a helicopter coming our way,' he said. 'Could be some of Albrick's men.' They went back to the others. 'Do you have any weapons?' Roger asked Alice.

'Just Greg's handgun,' she said.

Roger picked up the gun. 'I'm going to try and hold them off,' he said. 'Keep working.'

'We're nearly there,' said Jeff. Then he added: 'Take care . . . I love you.'

Miles was trying not to breathe. He was standing between two hanging brocade window curtains, and he was afraid that the slightest exhalation would set the fabric into treacherous motion. He knew that there was a man with a gun searching the showroom. He heard closet doors being opened and closed. Then he saw a shadow moving down the aisle next to his, and he heard the sound of the fabrics being pushed roughly aside.

He waited till the steps had moved to the end of the aisle and then slipped out from his hiding place. Keeping the long rank of display cabinets between himself and the soldier, he moved carefully along the carpeted floor, his finger on the trigger of his pistol. There was another soldier at the entryway to the showroom. Miles slipped down another aisle, and moved through a connecting doorway into the adjacent showroom, which contained pianos. The lights were off, but enough light filtered in from the central foyer to allow him to steer clear of the bulky instruments. He knew that Marta was somewhere in the room. He moved cautiously from piano to piano, looking for a hiding place. But the grand pianos offered little concealment, and the uprights were set flush against the walls. Miles laid his hand against the side of a Story & Clark grand, touching what seemed to be a keypad.

To his horror, the piano of its own accord began playing Beethoven's opus 27, no. 2, the Moonlight Sonata – and not the languid opening movement but the hammer strokes of the stormy finale. Invisible hands crashed down in ear-splitting chords, or flew in tumultuous runs up and down the keyboard. Miles dove for the side wall as the front doors opened and a soldier fired a burst of shots across the darkened showroom. Miles got a clear view of the man silhouetted against the light and put a bullet through his chest, but three other soldiers were right behind him. They sent a hail of bullets into the room. The piano continued playing, even though all the notes of the third octave above middle C were reduced to toneless thuddings.

Miles ran into an office and from there into a curving service corridor that ran behind the showrooms. He started to circumnavigate the entire set of showrooms, but a gunman appeared ahead of him and he jumped into the nearest doorway, just escaping a barrage of bullets. It was a brilliantly lit store full of chandeliers, gilt mirrors, and statuary. He ran to the center of the room. The gunman appeared at the rear doorway and started firing toward him, shattering a tower of ten bronze elephants and sending fragments of metal and glass flying around the room. But Tom Gregory had been hiding behind the door, holding a blue and white porcelain vase that was painted with thirty-two storks perched in the contorted branches of a pine tree. He brought the vase down on the gunman's head, smashing both.

Tom and Miles ran to the center balcony, where a hand-to-hand struggle was going on. Marta had jumped from her hiding place under the lid of a grand piano and had made a grab for the gun of the dead man by the entryway, but two soldiers had seized her and were attempting to throw her over the balustrade. Another actor appeared out of nowhere and joined the scrimmage. Miles picked up the dead soldier's rifle but was afraid to fire into the dense tangle of friend and foe. Marta was struggling desperately, but the soldiers had got her to the rim of the balustrade. Yet another actor, however, ran up, wielding an ornate Japanese sword, its brass handle shaped into the form of a rampant lion. He plunged the blade into the back of one of the soldiers, who let go of Marta with a bellow of pain. Then a human cannonball in the shape of Mavis Trautheim came hurtling at the group. She crashed into the other soldier, catching him against the balustrade. The glass cracked and gave way. The soldier fell spinning downward, screaming as he went, until the giant vertical fin of the Calder stabile sliced him in two. Both halves of his body fell into the reflecting pool, quickly staining it blood-red.

Most of the Act Out! contingent had emerged from their hiding places. But their respite was brief. The main cohort of Albrick's men had seen what was going on from the floor below and hurried up the stairs. 'This way!' said Marta, and she led them back through the piano showroom and into the service corridor. She tried an unmarked door on the outer wall of the corridor. It opened to a narrow passageway. As they headed along it and up a short stairway, the music of Beethoven faded and was replaced by the noise of fans and motors. The corridor ended blindly, but there was an open door on the right. Two huge generators were running, and large pipes of all colors ran across the ceiling and connected to the machines. The pipes were stenciled with arrows and labels like Chilled Water Return.

There was nowhere to hide, but there was a window that looked out toward the Blue Building – now engulfed in flames. Marta ran to the window and looked down. It was a giddy two-hundred-foot drop to the plaza. But there was a kind of up-curled lip sticking maybe ten inches out of the face of the building, which led from underneath the window to a metal stairway about five feet away. It was the attachment point for the window washers' cradles. The stairway itself led up onto the roof of the building. They could see, at the peaked center of the roof, the window that provided light for the inner atrium.

'We've got to get onto the roof,' said Marta. 'From there, we can shoot anyone who tries to follow us.'

'No way!' said several of the group, as soon as they saw the lip they would have to crawl along.

'You've got to!' shouted Marta. 'Hey, I'll show you.' Suiting her action to words, she climbed out onto the ledge, inched her way along to the stairway, and ran up to the roof. Then she came all the way back. 'I did it,' she said breathlessly. 'So can you. Candy, go! Don't look down!'

One by one the members of the group summoned up the courage to follow her example. The actors may have been scared, but they had the requisite sense of balance to make the crossing without too much danger. Tom was so thin, he was able to stay glued to the wall the whole way, although his pulse was racing and he felt an ever-increasing discomfort in his chest. Mavis proved herself a trooper. She inched her bulk along the creaking strip of metal, assisted by helpers at both ends. Only Miles steadfastly refused. 'Go, Marta,' he said. 'I'm too old for these tricks. I'll hold them off from here.' Marta could not dissuade him, so she hugged him and climbed out the window once more. 'And honey,' Miles added as she was disappearing from view, 'if they ever get to hand out awards this year, we'll get one . . . I just have a feeling.' Marta smiled and leaped across the roof.

Miles put down his rifle. He knew he would be able to hear the door opening at the end of the corridor. He looked down at his uniform, which had started the day so sparkling and clean, and now was a mass of dirt and tatters. He sighed and reached into some inner recess of his jacket. He brought out a not-impossibly damaged *presidente* and performed his ever-faithful lighting-up routine. The cigar did not draw well, but the flavor was good.

By the time Roger got back outside of the Weather Bureau, the helicopter was circling overhead. Because of the pylons, it could not land on Video Drive. Instead it settled down on Mount Wilson Circle, right below where Roger was standing. The four Marines and Albrick got out. Roger immediately fired off a warning shot. He had never fired a gun in his life, and the recoil caught him by surprise. All five of the men below took cover behind the helicopter.

'Put on the suits!' Roger heard Albrick say. 'You'll need them if they fire the beam.'

The four marines struggled into their aluminum-coated suits. 'What about you, sir?' one of them asked.

'I don't need one,' Albrick replied curtly.

'No, you don't need one!' Roger shouted down. 'Cause you're the genuine article, the true native-born bigot and murderer! You need no brain grafts, no gold, right? You got all you needed with your mother's milk!' He fired off another shot.

'Get him!' snarled Albrick. The marines grabbed their guns and started firing in Roger's direction, but he only needed to step back a few paces on the asphalt to be hidden from their view. The marines crossed to the uphill side of Mount Wilson Circle to begin the difficult ascent to Video Drive. They immediately came on the body of Greg, still lying where Roger and Jeff had dumped it behind the bloodstained yucca. Hordes of flies were now swarming around his mutilated face. Even Albrick was revolted by the sight.

'Murderer? Who's the murderer?' he yelled upward. 'Get up there!' he shouted at his men, and they began laboring up the rocky slope, hampered by their weapons and their bulky suits.

'Why are you doing this?' Roger shouted. 'You're crazy! Do you think you can get away with it? You can destroy West Hollywood, you can kill all of us, but you'll be caught, you'll be brought to justice, and you'll hang!' He craned over the edge of the slope to take a shot at the marines, but they were covering each other skillfully as they climbed, and a stream of bullets whizzed past his head and spent themselves in the sky. He ducked back.

'Let me worry about that,' Albrick shouted back. 'I have begun the cleansing, and I will see it through.'

'The cleansing? Lunatic! You're a scientist! Go back to your lab, before you get yourself killed!'

'Science is to use, to—'

'To use? For what? To kill innocent—'

'To serve humanity—'

'*What?*'

'The humanity of the future! We will give them the gift . . . the gift of their own perfection! Made so by human thought! . . . By human will! Cleansed of disease and vice and selfish lust – all that cruel Nature burdened us with. Rational! . . . Noble! . . . Powerful beyond dreams! . . . I *will* achieve it!'

'Fool! Why then do humans resist you? Because we see a better future than you can ever imagine . . . a future of love . . . of fellowship . . .'

'*Love? Fellowship?* Ha! Those words mean *nothing*! Shadows! Specters! Why do you resist? I'll tell you why! Because to face this truth is to face your own imperfections . . . the terrible birthmark that disfigures you . . . more foully than anything men see on me . . . a birthmark that men shrink back from in horror . . . or having it, they tear wildly at with their own hands . . .'

At that moment a loud rumbling began behind them. Roger turned. The fiberglass siding that covered the upper part of the front of the building was moving slowly upward and backward as if on giant hinges. As the immense screen lifted, Roger began to see the antennas; row after row of shining titanium domes, each highlighted by a burning image of the sun, each reflecting images of its neighbors and its neighbors' neighbors, so that the eye tracking across them lost its hold in the array and fell away in confusion.

'Roger, get inside!' came a voice from the control room.

Roger ducked inside the doorway but kept gazing outward. 'I'm okay!' he shouted.

'Draw power!' shouted Jeff.

'Power on!' came Alice's voice. 'Hold for the capacitors . . . five . . . four . . . three . . .'

Roger saw a hand grab a rock at the side of the road, and the first marine hauled himself high enough to aim his gun at the doorway.

'. . . two . . . one . . . let her rip!'

There was a quiet, high-pitched hum, and an intense blue light played over the metal of the marine's suit. He fell backward. Roger waited. Alice was counting the seconds: 'Five . . . ten . . . fifteen . . . twenty . . . twenty-five . . . off!' Roger raced to the edge of the road. The marines lay in a charred heap at the bottom of the slope, and the helicopter was smoking, its rotor blades melted down onto the fuselage. Thirty yards away, Albrick was stumbling off down the hill. Roger fired off a couple of shots, but Albrick was soon lost to sight among the pine trees.

Miles was able to smoke only about one quarter the length of his cigar before the door at the end of the corridor opened. He grabbed his gun, and a moment later a soldier appeared in the doorway. They both let off a fusillade of bullets, cutting each other to pieces. Several bullets hit the water pipes, and one of the pipes ruptured completely. A gush of icy water hit the floor and quickly flooded the room and the passageway. The soldiers who had been following the lead man fell back in the face of the bloodstained torrent.

'The roof! They're on the roof!' shouted the soldiers to their comrades. They raced back to the central balcony: Marta had climbed to the very top of the roof, keeping to the north side to protect herself from the searing heat radiating from the Blue Building seventy feet away. She peered down through the central window, a vantage point that offered an unusual perspective on the Calder stabile nine floors below. But art appreciation was not on her mind, and as soon as she saw the soldiers, she ducked back. They started firing randomly at the roof, sweeping their weapons to and fro to cover the area. The bullets easily pierced the green aluminum panels and it could not have been more than a few seconds before one of the people on the roof was hit. But then the lights went out, the mechanical pianist interrupted his recital, and the motors for the air-conditioning units coasted to a halt. In surprise, the soldiers ceased firing for a moment. And then they held their heads in pain, and their weapons clattered to the floor.

At that very moment a colony of *Mycobacter endocarditidis*, who had spent the previous seven months chewing through a weak spot in the wall of Tom Gregory's ascending aorta, finally completed their work.

CHAPTER THIRTY

'I . . . um . . . well . . .' Jeff paused and blushed.

'How?' Roger pressed him, 'I mean you don't just naturally know how to do that stuff. Somebody must have shown you.' Roger was not talking about computers.

'I . . . I read about it in *Badboy* Magazine.'

Roger burst into laughter. 'All right! Good student!' he said. Jeff's face creased into a smile, and then they laughed and laughed. Somber-faced people at nearby tables looked around for the source of amusement.

They were sitting in the Cafe Albertine on Melrose Avenue. Across the street, workers were boarding up the perimeter of the Pacific Design Center. Although it was twenty-four hours since the fire had been put out, a slight veil of smoke and dust still rose from the burned-out ruins. It drifted eastward on the afternoon sea breeze, blurring the skyline of the Hollywood Hills and the San Gabriels beyond. The sound of jackhammers, like urban woodpeckers, could be heard off to the left.

'It's terrible to be laughing, I guess,' Jeff said. 'When I think of all the people this morning . . .' They had been volunteering at Cedars-Sinai Hospital, where the injured had filled the wards to overflowing.

'Sometimes that's all you can do,' said Roger. 'Laugh, and pick up the pieces. We should be getting back.'

The two men rose and walked out onto Melrose. From where the Design Center had stood, running diagonally across the street and turning down San Vicente, was a broad, frozen river of blue glass. Curious onlookers stood along the edges of the ice blue flow, or ventured cautiously out onto it, like tourists at the Pasterze glacier. Workers were drilling at the river's margins, and some teenage entrepreneurs were collecting the fragments to sell as souvenirs. But it would take a long time before the street was clear.

Roger and Jeff followed the banks of the blue stream toward the hospital. As they came to Beverly Boulevard, Jeff said, 'Hey, that's Dr Leblanc!' He waved to the pathologist, who came over to greet them.

'Jean-Michel, what are you doing here?' asked Roger. 'Oh, I can guess . . .'

'Yes,' said Leblanc. 'The counties have exchange arrangements, for these contingencies. There is a lot of work, I am sure that you are able to imagine. And my counterpart here, unfortunate to say, was himself a victim.'

'Really? That's terrible.'

'Yes, indeed. A fine man. Tone deaf . . . but an artist with the scalpel. I had the sad duty to examine his body this morning. He was, curiously enough, dressed as a woman. So I have the honor to be the acting Medical Examiner for Los Angeles County, as of this morning.'

'And perhaps the next permanent one?'

'I do not think so. There would be certain problems. And it would be hard to leave the quartet. After all these years, we have developed a certain understanding, a certain *ensemble*. The recital was well received, I think I may permit myself to say.'

'I hope I get a chance to hear you sometime.'

'Well, there will be a professorship opening up at Levitican, I expect.'

'Ha! Albrick's lab? Heir to the Devil? Thanks, but no thanks. I'd rather work as a *diener* in your morgue.'

'Well, that I could arrange, very easily, but—'

Jeff broke in. 'If Mary gets her promotion, maybe you could get her job. You're a sex researcher, after all. And I could transfer to Georgetown.'

'At the National Institute of Reproductive Health? A non-reproducer?'

Jeff grinned at Roger. 'You mean, we're not going to have a baby?'

Roger groaned. 'Domesticity, here we come.'

Don't miss James Cobb's next exciting thriller

Stormdragon

Commander Amanda Lee Garrett, captain of the stealth missile destroyer the USS *Cunningham*, faces two urgent challenges: coming to terms with her new-found status as a naval heroine following the bitterly fought Antarctic campaign, and getting the newly repaired *Cunningham* through its sea trials and back into active service. But events halfway across the world are about to present her with an infinitely more dangerous test.

In China the simmering conflict between the communist regime and rebel forces has boiled over into a full-scale civil war – and the Nationalists in Taiwan have taken advantage of the situation to launch a lightning strike on the mainland.

In Washington Intelligence analysts fear that with their backs to the wall the communists may try one last desperate throw of the dice – launching a missile against Taiwan from one of their nuclear submarines. The results could be catastrophic.

The only option is to send the *Cunningham* into the East China Sea, using its unique stealth capabilities to track down the submarine and destroy it before it can release its deadly payload. But hunting her prey in the midst of a high-tech shooting war and with the risk of triggering a global conflict ever-present, Amanda Garrett may just find out she's stretching the capabilities of her ship and its crew beyond their limits . . .

ISBN 0 7472 1750 5 (Hardcover)

ISBN 0 7472 7710 9 (Trade paperback)

HEADLINE
FEATURE

Inheritance

Keith Baker

When retired RUC officer Bob McCallan is killed in a gas explosion in a caravan in Donegal, his son Jack inherits an unexpected fortune. He also inherits a key to the past.

The violence in Northern Ireland has been over for two decades, but there are still secrets that could shatter the foundations of peace. Secrets that Bob McCallan's untimely death threatens to bring to the surface. Secrets that some people would do anything to keep buried.

'A gripping read' Michael Dobbs

'Breathtaking . . . if you buy no other thriller this year, buy this one' *Irish Times*

'Gripping' *Belfast Telegraph*

0 7472 5235 1

HEADLINE
FEATURE

If you enjoyed this book here is a selection of other bestselling Thriller titles from Headline

STRAIT	Kit Craig	£5.99	☐
DON'T TALK TO STRANGERS	Bethany Campbell	£5.99	☐
HARVEST	Tess Gerritsen	£5.99	☐
SORTED	Jeff Gulvin	£5.99	☐
INHERITANCE	Keith Baker	£5.99	☐
PRAYERS FOR THE DEAD	Faye Kellerman	£5.99	☐
UNDONE	Michael Kimball	£5.99	☐
THE VIG	John Lescroart	£5.99	☐
ACQUIRED MOTIVE	Sarah Lovett	£5.99	☐
THE JUDGE	Steve Martini	£5.99	☐
BODY BLOW	Dianne Pugh	£5.99	☐
BLOOD RELATIONS	Barbara Parker	£5.99	☐

Headline books are available at your local bookshop or newsagent. Alternatively, books can be ordered direct from the publisher. Just tick the titles you want and fill in the form below. Prices and availability subject to change without notice.

Buy four books from the selection above and get free postage and packaging and delivery within 48 hours. Just send a cheque or postal order made payable to Bookpoint Ltd to the value of the total cover price of the four books. Alternatively, if you wish to buy fewer than four books the following postage and packaging applies:

UK and BFPO £4.30 for one book; £6.30 for two books; £8.30 for three books.

Overseas and Eire: £4.80 for one book; £7.10 for 2 or 3 books (surface mail)

Please enclose a cheque or postal order made payable to *Bookpoint Limited*, and send to: Headline Publishing Ltd, 39 Milton Park, Abingdon, OXON OX14 4TD, UK.
Email Address: orders@bookpoint.co.uk

If you would prefer to pay by credit card, our call team would be delighted to take your order by telephone. Our direct line 01235 400 414 (lines open 9.00 am–6.00 pm Monday to Saturday 24 hour message answering service). Alternatively you can send a fax on 01235 400 454.

Name   ....

Address ....

....

....

If you would prefer to pay by credit card, please complete:
Please debit my Visa/Access/Diner's Card/American Express (delete as applicable) card number:

Signature .... Expiry Date ....